RISE
OF THE
ALPHA
GOD

ALSO BY ABIGAIL BARNETTE

Bad Boy, Good Man

Surrender

Where We Land

THE ALPHA SERIES

Taken by the Alpha King

THE BY-THE-NUMBERS SERIES

First Time (Penny's Story)

First Time (Ian's Story)

Second Chance (Penny's Story)

Second Chance (Ian's Story)

Baby Makes Three (Penny's Story)

Baby Makes Three (Ian's Story)

THE CANIS CLAN SERIES:

Bride Of The Wolf

Wolf's Honor

FABLEMERE

The Ogre's Fairytale Bride

THE SOPHIE SCAIFE SERIES

The Stranger

The Boss

The Girlfriend

The Bride

The Ex

The Baby

The Sister

The Boyfriend

Sophie

THE NORTHERN CIRCLE SERIES

Awakening Delilah

Writing as Jenny Trout

Choosing You

Say Goodbye To Hollywood

THE NIGHTMARE BORN SERIES

Nightmare Born

RISE OF THE ALPHA GOD

ABIGAIL BARNETTE

CHAPTER 1

Running away to the wilderness to hide sounded great to the primal, wolfish side of me.

Once Xiao starts guiding the pontoon plane down toward an inky black pool dotted with algae, I consider changing my mind.

"Hold on," she warns mildly, and from her tone I can tell it's not her first time flying a plane. Well, from her tone *and* from the number of times I made her swear it wasn't her first time flying a plane.

Nathan takes my hand and gives me a reassuring smile. I've been shaking like a leaf with fear of certain death ever since we got to the airstrip. Now, as the twilight quickly fades in the vast Manitoba sky, I might be shaking from exhaustion.

As we splash onto the surface of the lake, I spy a short dock jutting from the reeds. Xiao kills the engine, and our momentum drifts us the rest of the way. Once we're close enough, she deplanes and tethers the craft to the dock, but she won't let us get out.

"Wait here," she advises before jogging off into the tall,

dead grass at the shore. There's a shack some way off, a narrow square against the green-black wall of trees around the clearing. A flashlight beam bounces over the outside of the structure, then disappears momentarily and reappears through a murky window.

"Where's the cabin?" I ask, squinting at the shack.

"That *is* the cabin," Nathan says and chuckles at my expression of shock and disgust.

"Go ahead and laugh. You have to stay here, too," I remind him. "We're *both* hooped."

The beam darkens and a dimmer, golden light warms the windows, illuminating the outline of Xiao as she returns to us.

Though we personally didn't bring much with us the plane was loaded to near capacity with supplies packed before we arrived at the airstrip. The thralls made sure we've got plenty of food and fresh water, as well as blankets, extra warm clothes, first aid kits, everything we need to stay in hiding. I lift one side of a plastic tote with my hand and awkwardly slide my non-handed arm under the other side, awkwardly balancing it against my body and I shuffled off toward our horrifying new home.

Not that the property is without its amenities. Xiao points them out as we lug our totes across the marshy clearing.

"Pump is over there." She gestures with her head toward one side of the clearing. "you'll want to boil the water before you drink it." With a nod in the opposite direction, she says, "Privy's over there."

"Privy?" Is she saying what I think she's saying?

"No indoor plumbing," she confirms. "No electricity."

I have a misplaced stab of fear at the thought of not being able to charge my phone before I remember that we left our phones in Toronto. No electronics. Nothing traceable.

What the hell am I going to do to pass the time? Talk to my mate?

Nathan reaches the porch and drops his tote, returning to take mine. "You shouldn't be lifting these."

"Why?"

"Because you're pregnant," Xiao says before he can, totally unaware that she's just saved his sexist life. "I agree with him."

"We have no idea what the effects of this spell might be on the baby. Or if the thralls have done something else to it. It's not worth taking any risks," Nathan says.

"Risks like deserting civilization entirely?" I blink at him.

Xiao heads back to the plane and Nathan jerks his head toward the cabin door. "Come on. Let's have a look around."

I step into the cabin, turn in a circle, and say, "I've had a look around."

Nathan's mouth is a grim line. "As have I."

An oil lamp hangs on a metal bracket by the door. Nathan takes it down and ventures a few steps inside. The space is about as big as my walk-in closet at Aconitum Hall. Possibly smaller. One end is dominated by a fieldstone fireplace. There's a narrow table and two benches by the only window, and a plain metal bedframe that's sagging beneath the weight of what appears to be the world's lumpiest mattress.

"If you're not going to let me help outside, then find me the sheets and pillows." The less time I have to look at the state of the ancient mattress, the more likely I'll be able to sleep on it.

Although, I could probably sleep soundly on a bed of hot coals tonight.

Nathan places the lamp on the table and goes out to find what I need before heading off for another load from the plane.

I paw through a tote full of useful items and find some bedding. There are two sets of sheets, which will be handy when one of them is drying. *Oh no. I'm going to have to do laundry in a lake.* I wrestle the fitted bottom sheet onto the mattress, and by the time I'm finished making the bed, Nathan returns with a suspicious-looking case slung over his shoulder.

"That's a guitar, right?" I ask, knowing it's not.

Xiao enters behind him with a similar bag. "For protection and hunting." She reaches into a pocket on her tactical vest and produces a small baggie, which she puts on the table. "Also, for protection and hunting."

Nathan leans the guns against the wall by the door and looks down at the contents of the bag. Round, polished stones glint and glitter inside. "Black moonstone bracelets?"

"Like I said," Xiao repeats, "for protection and hunting."

A chill goes up my back.

"I don't know how to shoot," I remind her and gesture with my stump. "And definitely not one-handed."

"I can shoot," Nathan says. "I'm sure we can find a way to modify things for you."

Xiao nods in agreement, but adds, "You have fresh food for now. I would recommend using it up first. I can sink the cooler into the mud at the shoreline. That should provide some refrigeration. There's still plenty of ice hanging on in the reeds."

"What about bears?" That's been one of my major worries the whole way here.

"The bears in this area aren't used to relying on humans for sustenance. Chances are, more of the wildlife isn't going to be interested in coming anywhere near. To most of them, werewolves aren't something they'll want to mess with. But I'm talking about black bears. If you run into a polar bear, use the guns. Not the bracelets."

That did *not* make me feel safer.

Xiao unclips something from her belt. "Satellite phone. For emergencies only. Once you use it, we have to get you out of here."

"Because it can be traced?" Nathan asks, taking the phone.

"Exactly." Xiao looks between the two of us, then settles on me. "Are you going to be okay out here?"

She's not asking *us*. She's asking *me*.

Does she think there's a reason I won't be safe with Nathan? I won't let myself even begin to consider that possibility. Nathan is the only protection I have.

"We're going to be fine," I assure her. "But what about you? Will you be safe now that you've helped us?"

"From the pack? Not if they find out about any of this. From my fellow thralls? For now." But she doesn't sound sure of that. "I'll be back in two weeks with fresh supplies."

"And news from our allies," Nathan adds pointedly.

"As much as I can carry," she vows.

It's hard to watch Xiao—our only lifeline—get back in the plane and disappear into the darkness. I stand outside the cabin and watch the plane's lights until I can't see her anymore. Even when she's gone, I stare, transfixed, at the sky.

"I've never seen anything like this,' I whisper to Nathan when he exits the cabin to stand beside me.

He lifts his gaze to the impossible quantity of stars above us. "It's incredible."

We watch the universe in silence until he takes my hand and squeezes it. The peace is broken when he exclaims, "For fuck's sake, Bailey, you're freezing!"

"ever the romantic," I snort. But he's right. The temperature is falling fast and the big, fluffy plumes of my breath on the air have reduced to lukewarm ghosts.

Spring means something different this close to the Arctic Circle.

"We need to get the fire going," he says, lifting a few logs from the pile near the door. "There's wood inside, we can start with that and let this dry."

"You seem pretty confident about this whole situation,' I say, somewhat nervously. I've never been in a situation like this. I'm used to surviving because someone else turned the thermostat up or cooked me some food. I've never even been camping.

Nathan shrugs and takes the fire starter and some twigs and dead leaves from a cardboard box near the hearth. "I've spent time outdoors."

"Really?" That's hard for me to believe, considering the wealth he came from.

"Why do you find that so unlikely?"

"You were in line for the throne of Greater London. Sounds a little aristocratic for roughing it," I muse.

"Even the human royals 'rough it.'" He leans into the fireplace and swiftly arranges the firewood and twigs. The fire starter clicks, and he carefully coaxes an ember to life with his breath, adding bits of the dry tinder a little at a time until a flame grows beneath the larger logs.

"Remember, I spent five years away. I'm sure you learned some things in your time off from the pack, as well."

"Nothing as useful as that," I say, awed as I watch the flames quickly flicker and grow. "But if we need to use Microsoft Excel for any reason, I've got our back."

"Don't worry. We may have plenty of time out here for you to learn." His expression falls. "I should have taught you right then."

"We'll have another chance." Besides, there's no reason to worry about it when I've got Nathan here.

"Bailey,' he begins patiently. "We can't guarantee that. We might feel safe now, but we don't know who'll be looking for us. There have already been attacks on our lives. Plus, this is the wilderness. Anything can happen. We can't guarantee that we'll make it through the night."

I know it's true. I just don't want it to be.

CHAPTER 2

Once the fire is burning and it finally feels slightly less cold in the cabin, I take my coat and shoes off. There are thick wool socks in the supplies Xiao brought, and I eagerly slide my feet into them.

"This is pretty cozy," I remark, injecting as much toxic positivity into my voice as I can.

"It is," Nathan agrees, the springs on the bed screeching like a chorus of demons as he *just* barely shifts his position. He's been happily reclined with a book for the past hour, but I'm restless and pacing.

"I wish I brought something to do," I say, to nobody in particular since he's absorbed in reading.

"I wish you did, too,' he says with a wry lift of his eyebrows.

"Ha ha." I go to the bed and flop down next to him. For a moment, it seems the entire thing will collapse. "How did people survive this back in olden times?"

"I find it quite peaceful,' Nathan muses. He adds, "With one caveat."

I can take a hint, but not boredom. "You don't understand. My attention span is that of an infant."

"That's been apparent for the past hour," he quips.

Speaking of infants... I rub my hand over my stomach. "I wonder how long it will be until I can feel it moving in there."

"You should have brought a baby book," he observes with a sidelong glance.

"I have some pamphlets the doctor gave me. But do I actually trust the thralls?" I brought the materials with me, but I don't even want to see them, now.

He puts his open book page-down on his chest. "At the very least, I think we can trust them with the child's life. And, while the child is still inside of you, with your life, as well."

I wait for him to explain.

"Why go to the trouble of maintaining a spell for centuries if you end up harming the result?"

"You have me there," I admit, but something still rankles. "Maybe when the time comes, I can just run off into the woods somewhere and have the baby."

"Possibly," he says, and I'm concerned that he might not realize it was a joke. After a silent second, he closes his book and pushes himself up. "There *is* something we could do to pass the time."

The connection between us surges.

I roll my eyes, but the stupid bond is going to make me give in, anyway. There's not much point in fighting it. *Maybe if you did, you could make yourself fall out of love with him,* my rational brain suggests. Because that's still a huge problem. I don't need to gobble up crumbs of physical intimacy to satiate my emotional hunger. It won't work.

But it'll feel *really* good.

He grabs me around my waist and lifts me up before I track his movements, and I find myself breathlessly straddling his lap.

"You're very strong. I'm so impressed." I tap the end of his nose with my fingertip. "But I mean, can you even do it? You don't have any of your little tricks here. No toys or ropes or magic werewolf cum…"

"You know I don't need the toys and ropes." He covers my mouth with his, sweeps his tongue in tantalizing flicks along my lower lip. Drawing back, he whispers, "But as for the latter…"

I can't help my giggle. "Don't be gross."

"Who can I be gross with, if not my mate?" He kisses me again and all I can do is melt.

"The oil lamp," I remind him, nodding toward where he's moved it beside the bed.

He sets me aside and rises while I'm still vocalizing my admittedly exaggerated outrage at being so unceremoniously displaced. He blows out the wick of the lamp and carries it back to the hook by the door. "There. I shouldn't think we'll collide with it this far away."

"I can never tell with you, though." I pull my shirt over my head. Gooseflesh raises across the tops of my breasts.

"Did you get that on the first try?" Nathan asks, gesturing to where my shirt landed.

I beam at him. "You're married to an adult who can dress herself. Congratulations."

He blows out the lamp, plunging us into the dim orange light from the fireplace. "Undress herself,' he corrects me, climbing onto the end of the bed and prowling toward me. "But let me do the rest."

I lay back obediently and let him unbutton my jeans

and pull the fly down. I help him work them down my legs with a little wiggle. He leaves my panties in place, rubbing his thumb along my slit over the satin.

"It's been a long time," he murmurs, almost to himself.

"No, it hasn't." I think back. There hasn't even *been* a lot of time since London. Since the night of...

I cover my face. "Oh my god. Nathan."

He looks up at me, cocking his head in question.

"I think the last time we did it was when we destroyed Jonah's...office? Apartment? Whatever that was."

Heat flares in Nathan's eyes at the memory, but the recollection of that night makes me shiver. The desperation. The feral hunger that drove us while the potion denied us.

"There's no magic aphrodisiac tonight," Nathan says, pushing the crotch of my panties aside. Two fingers part me, brush over my opening, which is already wet with anticipation.

"Thank every god," I breathe, stopping myself from lifting my hips and driving those fingers in further. "I don't know if I ever want to experience that again."

"The end result was enjoyable," he reminds me.

So "enjoyable," I can't believe the intensity of it didn't kill me. "It was," I agree. "But there's something to be said for a nice, gentle orgasm."

"So, you want me to be nice and gentle tonight?" He chuckles softly.

"Maybe," I tease him. "But it's not going to happen, is it?"

He pushes himself down the bed, dragging my panties along with him, and brings my legs over his shoulders. My chest hitches. The cold of the cabin makes me hyper-aware of the heat of his body, the touch of his mouth against my inner thigh as he works his way toward his goal.

Well, my goal, to be honest. His goal is usually to tease me, to torment me, to *win*. All I want at this moment is his mouth on me, his tongue inside me, lapping up every drop of my arousal.

I sink my hand into his hair and give a little tug. "Don't make me wait tonight. Don't make me beg. Just make me come until I can't move anymore."

"Ever?" He laughs against my skin; the puff of breath is enough to make me squirm.

"Please."

"You're already begging," he points out, but he mercifully lowers his head and parts me with his thumbs, exposing the stiff, wanting bud there. He licks me, slow at first, with the flat of his tongue, then faster, more pointed. He sucks me into his mouth, still flicking his tongue, and pushes two fingers inside. His knowledge of my body and my responses is unnerving, considering how short a time we've been together. In no time at all, he has me panting and gripping the sheets in my fist as I move against his mouth.

"That's it," I urge him on. "You're going to make me—"

The slow, rhythmic plunge of his fingers into me, his tongue curling over my clit, bring me to the brink. His deep groan of pure satisfaction at the first flutters of my cunt takes me the rest of the way over.

Even if he doesn't love me, he wants me. This isn't about making an heir. I'm already pregnant. He wants me. And if his desire is all I can have, maybe it will be enough.

He didn't want just *you, though.*

I won't let myself ruin this with those thoughts. It doesn't matter who he wants. He's with me.

He's *my* mate.

And though he said he wasn't sure he could love me, he did say he felt more for me than he's ever felt for anyone. That might not be the same as love, but if it's all he can offer, I'll take it. Gladly.

He sits up, gasping for air, and pulls his sweater over his head, but that's all the delay he allows. He moves over me, opening the fly of his jeans. The bedsprings scream and I open my legs so he can settle between them. I lift my hips at the first touch of his cock against me and he slides deep.

The bed groans along with him.

We lie there, joined together, reveling in the feel of each other.

"I really don't like you," I whisper, and he catches my bottom lip in his teeth. When he releases me, I finish my thought. "So, why can't I get enough of this?"

"It could be the binding." He grinds deep and I tip my head back on the pillow, a gasp catching at the back of my throat. "But I think we both know it's because we're so very good at this."

I laugh a little, but I'm gazing into his eyes and it's suddenly difficult to breathe. I take a deep, shuddering inhale as he slowly withdraws. Binding or no binding, Nathan is my mate. And whether I like him or not, I crave him, always will. He's a jerk and I can't stand him, but I love him. We're perfectly terrible for each other in all the right ways.

He looks away first, before I can glimpse anything beyond the Nathan he wants me to know.

In fairness, I haven't exactly given him anything other than the Bailey I want *him* to know. And suddenly, that's not enough. I wrap my legs around his back and roll my hips in time with his, as if I can pull him into my soul. I want to reveal everything to him. I want to—

The bed springs pick up our rhythm, pulling me from my thoughts and back into the moment. It's both a welcome *and* silly interruption.

"Oh my gosh," I giggle, covering my mouth with my hand.

"This isn't exactly...conducive..." Nathan rasps.

Slowing his thrusts does nothing to make the cacophony of rusty scraping any less funny. In fact, I just laugh harder.

"This isn't going to work." With a growl of frustration, he rolls off me and orders, "Get up."

I have to, because he takes my hand and pulls me to my feet. In a flash, the mattress is on the floor, and we're tumbling onto it. I don't even get a breath before he's inside me again, pinning me on my stomach as he drives harder and deeper.

He sinks a hand into my hair and tugs. "Much better."

I writhe back on him.

"Oh, did you want more?" he asks, jerking my hips up. I gasp and he retreats, releasing my hair. "Did I hurt you?"

"What?" I don't understand where the sudden concern has come from. We're always rough with each other. "No. I like it."

He pulls out and I turn onto my back. I see his hand move in the darkness, indicating my stomach. "The baby. I don't know if I'm going to jostle something or—"

I laugh. It's not fair, because it *is* sweet of him to be concerned. So sweet, it makes my heart ache. "I don't think you're going to. I don't feel fragile."

"Oh, I'm aware." His chuckle makes me weak.

And impatient.

I open my legs wider, knees apart. "Fuck me."

"I love—"

My heart jumps.

"—the way that sounds."

And it plummets again. I push down the lump in my throat and repeat, "Fuck me."

He slides his hands under my calves and jerks me to him as he covers me. I hug his waist with my knees and hold on, pleading over and over, "fuck me," even as he obliges. His mouth finds mine and he kisses me, harder and harder, as his thrusts speed up and he growls, "You're going to have to take care of yourself."

I can't help the laugh that explodes from me. It's sort of a triumph, knowing that I feel so good to him, he can't hold back. I reach between us and rub my clit—artlessly, as I'm not used to masturbating with the only hand I have left—and I'm almost there when he stiffens, mutters, "Fuck!" and shoves as deep as he can. The burst of warmth and silky wet inside me raises my arousal to its peak and beyond. I grip him hard with my knees at his waist, riding out my pleasure to the last possible moment as he twitches and throbs. He buries his head against my shoulder, grunting with every slide of his cock in me, until he pulls out with a strangled, "Enough."

"You say it's enough," I tease with a grin. "I could keep doing that."

"Knowing how much it tortures me?" He pretends to be offended. "That's sick."

I say nothing, but give a little wiggle against him, reveling in his hiss of oversensitivity.

He falls on the mattress beside me and says, "Come here." But he comes to me, rolling over and nestling his head against my breasts. He doesn't hold me; I hold him. I hold him tight, hoping he can feel how much I love him, even if he can't love me back.

CHAPTER 3

As it turns out, moving the mattress to the floor was a wise decision. Even with the fire, it's freezing; the cabin is too drafty and damp, even for werewolves and our heightened defense against cold. When my chattering teeth wake him, Nathan scoots the lumpy mattress as close to the hearth as he deems safe and puts me on the side nearest the fire.

It hits me then that we're really in a survival situation. The fear makes it almost impossible to sleep.

After a few hours of fitful dozing, I blink awake and find myself alone. Wrapping one of the thick quilts around myself, I stagger to the only window and peer out.

Nathan has built a fire in the pit outside, and the smell of sizzling ham threatens to draw my soul from my body. I'll regret it, I'm sure, but I don't wait to get dressed. I pad out across the frost-encrusted grass huddled in my blanket.

"Good morning," I say as I get closer.

He turns and glances at me, then goes back to tending the ham in a big iron pan over the fire. "You're finally up."

"Finally?" I blink at the sky. "The sun is barely risen. Besides, you could have woken me."

"No, I couldn't have. In fact, if you hadn't been snoring so hard, I would have worried you were dead." He gestures to the ring of stumps and logs serving as makeshift seating around the fire pit.

"So, you decided to turn the whole camp into one big, ham-scented air freshener to attract predators?" I tease him. "I didn't die of hypothermia, so you're going to see if the polar bears can finish me off?"

"I thought I would make breakfast for my eternally complaining mate." He turns away from the fire to give me a wink.

I don't know why, but I go to his side and rise up on my toes to kiss his cheek. I can't even blame the bond for that; there's nothing sexual behind the act. I just want to kiss him because I...

Ugh.

"You didn't have to make breakfast without help," I say. "Although, I'm not sure I would have been much."

"I'm just using the fresh food while we have it," he says cheerfully. "There are biscuits in that pot."

"Wow, you're really domestic.' I never expected that out of him.

"There was a campfire cookbook in the manuals they left us," he admits. He puts a slab of ham on a plate and passes it to me. "We don't have much in the way of housewares, though, so no four course meals, I'm afraid. You'll have to eat with your hands." He winces. "Sorry."

"I'll get by." I don't comment on his error. I forget all the time. My dreams even get it wrong. I sit on one of the logs and try to hold the blanket to my chest with my forearm while I pick up the ham with my hand.

Bailey, are you naked under there?" Nathan shakes his head. "You're going to freeze to death out here."

"I was too hungry to wait and get dressed." I tear a big strip of meat off with my teeth.

"Bailey—"

"Please, don't order me around.' I'm more tired than pissed off. "I just can't take any more of people telling me what to do. Even you."

Especially you.

He blows out a long breath. "That's...a difficult request."

"I'm sure it is," I say around a mouthful of ham. "For you."

He smiles and turns away to take the Dutch oven from the coals. "I so enjoy criticizing you and telling you what to do."

"I've noticed."

He lifts the lid on the pot. "You can eat these and criticize me."

"I can't wait." I hold out my plate so he can deposit one of the biscuits on it. "Although, I can't really criticize, either. I can't cook."

"What?" He gasps in mock outrage. "I've married a woman who can't cook?"

"Yeah, it was really going to be a concern, I'm sure." I roll my eyes. "I can't cook, I can't make a fire. I don't have anything helpful to contribute."

"I wouldn't say that." He sits on a stump with his own plate. "You seem to know your mythology."

"Not as well as Tara." My sister is a veritable encyclopedia of our pack's spiritual beliefs. "But I know some stuff."

"You must. You found out about the Right of Accord," he points out.

"I sure did." I nod slowly. "And look at where it

got me."

"It got you a mate who could fuck you into the mattress and out the other side."

If I wasn't so hungry and afraid of bears tracking the scent later, I would throw my biscuit at him.

"I'm serious, though," he goes on. "I've never been a particularly spiritual person. I don't know anything about the gods or mythology in general except for where those things pertain to pack law. I usually slept through the religious classes."

"Well... what do you want to know?" I ask uneasily, certain he's going to have a question I can't answer.

Nathan thinks while he chews. He swallows and says, "Tell me about these survivors of Ragnarök your sister compared us to."

"Lif and Lifthrasir?" I suppose it's a fitting story for our situation. "During Ragnarök they hide in Hoddmìmis Holt —that's a forest—and survive Surtr's fire. They're the only two people left alive. Their progeny repopulates the world."

Nathan's dark brows pull together. "You would think that would only work if there were four people left. Or six."

"Because of inbreeding." I nod vigorously. "That's what I've always thought."

"We're in a forest. We're procreating." Nathan gestures to my stomach. "But something tells me we can't be Tyr and Fenrìr and Lif and Lifthrasir at the same time."

"No, we cannot," I agree. "I mean, maybe if it's all allegorical symbolism, not meant to be taken literally?"

We eat without talking for a few minutes, listening to the crackle of the embers. It's so peaceful here, so still and deserted, and somehow the vast emptiness of the land around us shifts from untamed horror to a feeling of safety.

"What starts Ragnarök?" Nathan asks, taking another biscuit from the pot. "What causes it?"

I make a sustained "um" as I consider. "A really, really long winter. At least, that's how it starts for mankind. There's a brutal ice age, food becomes scarce, and everything falls apart exactly the way we see humankind fall apart over and over again in times of famine. The sun and the moon and all the stars go out, and all the trees will fall."

"Even Yggdrasil?" Nathan asks, adding sheepishly, "I do know *some* of it."

"It's okay. I don't think you're a dork." I shake my head fondly. "I asked Tara about that. She says there's no mention of what happens to Yggdrasil. There's mention of it shaking, but it's apparently not clear if it's included as one of the trees that falls down."

"It sounds like your sister should have been teaching the class."

A sad smile touches the corners of my mouth. For all that Tara and I have been through, I still love her as much now as I did then. "She would have been a great teacher. I don't think her mate approved."

"Where are the gods while this is happening?" Nathan asks. "We know where one is. Fenrir is all chained up."

"No, that's the thing." The pitch of my voice rises with excitement I never realized I felt for these stories. Mythology has always been Tara's thing and now I'm parroting her breathless, endless narration to someone else. "When all of this stuff is happening to the earth, Fenrir gets free. So does the serpent, Jormungand. Oh, and Loki rides in on a ship made from dead people's fingernails."

"That, I do remember." Nathan shudders. "You don't forget something like a ship made of corpse parts."

"A ship made of corpse parts crewed by giants," I

correct him. "I get a little muddled on the stuff that happens after that. But I know that like, *so many* people battle with wolves."

"Relatable," Nathan quips. "Maybe if your sister had been my teacher, I would have learned more."

A bird calls from the tree line and I sigh. "Our parents had much higher expectations for us. Teacher? Please. She would have been better off announcing her plan to be an independently employed street mime."

He chuckles.

"I've always liked the Norse myths better. The women had some agency. That must be why the Hierophant and his acolytes focus so intently on the Roman ones." That, or they knew that if they ignored the Norse myths, only served us a small sampling of them, no one would ever put together the binding with the lore. Of course, they never intended for anyone to know about the binding, at all. "You must have had the same experience, growing up. Always being told you should be what other people want you to be."

"In a sense," he admits. "But it sounds like your life was different to mine."

"I'm sure it was. You're a male after all." The word "male" drips with disgust I didn't mean to apply.

Before I can scramble to take it back, Nathan agrees with me. "Yes, I'm sure that made the pressure much easier to bear. I was in my late twenties before anyone started hinting that I should find a mate. I assume you were—"

"Much, much younger." My face flames at the memory of that first conversation with my mother, when she handed me a pamphlet from the doctor's office and a package of sanitary napkins. "My parents were expecting to see me transform one full moon, have my mating ceremony the next."

"Not our daughter," Nathan says firmly. "I won't be signing her off to another child just so they can go and produce more children."

A lump rises in my throat. "I didn't..."

Nathan glances up at my face and his eyes widen. "Are you choking?"

I shake my head. I am choking, but not on food. On all these stupid tears and anxieties. "I didn't think about the fact that the baby..."

I can't even say it.

Nathan sets his food aside. He gets up and takes mine, too, so I don't spill it when I fall into his arms, weeping.

"Bailey, what is it?" he asks, petting my hair while he kneels beside me on the wet grass. "Whatever it is, we can fix it."

He would say that. He's always so infuriatingly sure of his power and control. But even if he can promise me a totally different world, he can't fix the wounds in my heart. Not where this is concerned.

I suck in a deep breath. "I never considered that the baby might be a girl."

It seems to occur to him right then, too, despite his earlier proclamation about our potential daughter. I see the fear in his eyes at the thought of our child being treated the way I was treated by my parents, by the pack...

By himself.

"Imagine someone telling our daughter that he's decided to pursue her.' My words make Nathan look away. He remembers, then, that arrogant statement that he made to me. Good. Because he needs to know that he's complicit in the whole, shitty system. "What she wants, that doesn't matter. You're going to forcibly remove her from her family, anyway. She'll be your faithful, obedient mate. You won't be faithful to her, but you don't have to worry that she'll stray because you can lock her up in a tower."

His jaw is tight. I've hurt his feelings.

Maybe I'll hurt them enough that he'll remember the changes we need to make to the pack when we return to power.

If we return to power.

"If you teach us to ignore the women in the pack, we will," he says grimly. "I think I understand."

"you don't understand, though. And that's why, when we're back in Toronto, when we're leading the pack again? There are just some things you won't have a say in." I'm aware of the frustration creeping into my voice but I'm not afraid of starting an argument. He won't argue with me over this. "When we go back, things are going to change."

He stares into the coals for a long moment. Then he looks at me, his expression too serious for just a second before he gives me a smile that makes the chains of sadness and regret around my heart loosen. "And that is exactly why I wanted you for my queen."

CHAPTER 4

TARA

Aconitum Hall is empty.

It's always *felt* empty, even when Clare was here with me.

With *us.*

For weeks now, I wondered whether or not I wanted to see Bailey, to speak to her. After what she did to Clare...

I push the memories of that night away for the hundredth, thousandth, millionth time. Every day is an endless loop.

Sometimes, I change the story. Sometimes, I'm brave enough to scream for the executioner to stop. Or to scream it at Bailey.

Or to sink a knife into the king's neck.

I wasn't brave enough to do those things, then. I hate myself more for that with every breath I take.

But at least now, I have other things to focus on. Like trying to stop my entire species from being exterminated. I didn't help Clare. Maybe I can help everyone else.

But the house is so disturbingly empty, it's hard to focus. Working out of Bailey's office is eerie. Just a few weeks ago, Clare, Bailey and I sat on the newly-installed, plush carpet in the repurposed room, talking about the realities of being someone's mate.

Our three experiences differed vastly.

Her office is the one place in Aconitum Hall that I can't escape the ghosts of my sister; Clare, now dead and buried in our sacred woods, Bailey alive but very much not the Bailey I knew.

It's better than working out of the king's office, though. I hate every reminder of him stamped on this place. I hate how he treats my sister, hate how much his influence has changed her.

And I'll hate him forever for what he did to Clare.

The only bright spot in my dreary days waits for me at her usual post in Bailey's office, beside the door. Xiao can't exactly be described as "sunny" or "cheerful," but she's also not sullen and chopping my family members' heads off, and she's *present*. I prefer her to the few staff members still working here.

"You should sleep in the royal residence," she says, instead of a "good morning."

"Unless you can guarantee that he didn't bone my sister on every horizontal surface in the room—" and some vertical ones, probably— "I'm not going anywhere near there."

"I could better protect you," Xiao protests. "There are secure areas that can't be left unguarded. I can't leave my post in the residence to hang around outside your door at night."

"I never asked you to hang around outside my door at night," I remind her. "Besides, you have to sleep sometime."

"It's surprisingly difficult to sleep when the fate of the pack is hanging by a thread, you're tasked with guarding that thread, and that thread is hundreds of miles away," she says mildly, but I detect a hint of humor there. Maybe I'm just imagining it out of desperation and loneliness.

"And when everyone has freshly sharpened scissors," I add to her metaphor. I've no sooner sat down at my sister's desk when a light on the multi-line phone blinks. "Ah, speaking of."

"It'll be the head of security," Xiao says, before I even lift the receiver. "The Hierophant has arrived."

I glance at the phone again. I'm supposed to be in charge of the pack while my sister and her mate are in hiding. I'm also not supposed to *know* that they're in hiding. The Hierophant needs me to believe that he has no idea that the king and queen are missing. . . so, he'll pretend to be here for the king. I head straight to the king's office.

Xiao follows me to the study and opens the door for me. Inside, the Hierophant stands up from his chair, visibly startled.

"Sorry to keep you waiting." I hope that indicates that I know he's been here for some time. "Thank you for meeting with me."

He sits again before I gesture for him to have a seat, an obvious power move. Is this what Bailey means when she complains about speaking carefully and picking up subtle cues? No wonder she's a natural at it. We did it through our entire childhoods.

"I thought I was meeting with the king." The Hierophant's dark eyes narrow. "Is there some reason I'm meeting with you, instead?"

I thought this part through very carefully this morning. "Because my brother-in-law the king and my dear sister, the queen, are missing. And have been for some time. I fear the worst."

I find it's easier to obfuscate than outright lie. A little truth, some things left unspoken, and I could navigate most obstacles. I learned that when I was younger. Mother always caught us in our lies; there was no point in trying. Only Clare persisted in attempting to deceive her.

Apparently, she developed a talent for deception.

Now, I have to hope that talent lies dormant somewhere in me. The thralls believe they control the king and queen. I can't let on that I know anything about their absence, or about their plans.

"Missing?" The Hierophant is a good actor. He seems concerned but not overly alarmed. "Since when?"

"I saw them both three nights ago." I have to modulate myself, so I don't sound like I'm reading from a script.

Even though that's what I'm doing. I went over and over the details in my head last night. Nothing can differ from what Xiao, Hannah, or Ryan might tell someone. We all have to be meticulously on the same page, like we committed a murder.

I go on, "I assumed they went away on some kind of business. But then Xiao—"

"Yes, why is Xiao here, if the queen isn't?" the Hierophant interrupted. He thinks she's on his side. He thinks *he's* the one playing a role.

"I didn't know they intended to leave," Xiao replies. "I go where the king commands, and he didn't command me."

"Hmm." The Hierophant pretends to consider. "Lady Tara, did you speak to the head of security about this before coming to me?"

"Of course."

"And what did he tell you?"

Exactly what you told him to tell me. "He said the

movement of the king and queen is privileged information."

He spreads his hands. "Then it's privileged information."

"If the king and queen are missing, then I have the privilege. But I have to know that the king and queen *are* missing before I assert the privilege." I wait for signs of understanding to dawn on the Hierophant's expression. While Nathan and Bailey are gone, I'm as good as queen. The fact that I don't know that they're gone, and that the Hierophant didn't tell me immediately, is a clear indication that the thralls don't want me to know that I'm in charge now.

"I'm not sure what you're suggesting here, but it's possible that the king and queen didn't inform you of their plans because they don't trust you." The Hierophant props his ankle on his opposite knee and leans back in his chair. "Your mate is banished for treason. Your other sister was executed as a traitor."

Anger surges up in me. Joke's on anger; I can suppress it easier than I can express it. "But this sister is loyal enough that the king entrusted her with the regency."

The Hierophant squints, his gaze darting to Xiao. "I know of no such proclamation."

"Perhaps the king did not trust you with this information," I say. It feels triumphant and bitchy, but the moment it fully leaves my mouth, I realize how badly the remark can be interpreted. I need him to believe that we trust his leadership unquestioningly.

I stand without further comment and move to the bookcase behind the king's desk. I push on one of the fake books and a shelf springs out to reveal the safe behind it. I punch the code Nathan left me into the keypad and retrieve the envelope inside, marked with an unbroken royal seal.

"The king drew this up after my sister was attacked," I lie smoothly; we hastily signed it on the morning that Nathan and Bailey fled. I drop the document onto the desk, daring the Hierophant to pick it up. "He worried about further assassination attempts."

The Hierophant's eyes flick to the envelope. Finally, he sits forward and scoops it up. He slides a finger under the seal and makes a small, surprised noise. At its integrity, I assume. He slides the paper out and takes his time reading every word.

I'm not sure what he'll do. Rip it up? Declare it void? The only witness to this meeting is Xiao, and she's completely under the Hierophant's purview. Even though she's on our side, he could reassign her, outside of the royal household. He could cut off our direct line of communication with Bailey and Nathan.

Or he could do something worse to her.

But I can't let my worry show. A person who knows empirically that they have the right to a kingdom wouldn't be worried about the opinion of their lesser. At least, that's how Nathan acts all the time.

Bailey is beginning to take on some of that attitude, herself. I don't like it.

Finally, the Hierophant places the paper back in its envelope. "Do you have a pen?"

Wary, I pick up the fountain pen on the desk and pass it to him.

"The seal is broken now," he explains as he scrawls his signature across the envelope's flap. "Should anyone else require proof of your regency— Do you have any tape?"

Pretending I know exactly what he's doing, I open a few

drawers until I find some and hand it to him. He applies the tape in a strip across his fresh signature, and I understand.

"This should serve as good as my seal. Provided no one opens it without a witness." The last part is a warning. But it sounds like he won't continue to challenge my rule. At least, not openly. "I'll take a delegation to the Ottawa pack and find out what I can from the thralls there. With your permission, of course, Your Majesty."

The title sounds so weird to me that for a moment, I think he's using it sarcastically. I force myself not to react either way. "It's of the utmost urgency that we find my sister."

The Hierophant arches a brow. "And the king, as well."

"Of course." I know he thinks I stumbled there. I didn't. I'm fine with him believing that I don't care about Nathan because I *don't* care about Nathan. "Report what you find to me. And let's keep this quiet, for now. Until we have answers, there's no point in raising questions."

With a nod, the Hierophant rises, bows, and leaves. The door closes and Xiao casts me a look I can't discern.

"What?" I ask, sharper than strictly necessary.

"Nothing." My tone seems to amuse her, because the corner of her mouth twitches like the precursor to a smile. "Your Majesty."

CHAPTER 5

TARA

After my meeting with the Hierophant, the rest of the day is just as empty as every other day since I arrived.

"This place is so boring," I complain, pacing the length of my sitting room.

"You might find something more exciting in the royal residence," Xiao suggests.

"No." We already fought about this once, today. "It might be easier to guard me in the residence, but it's not going to be easier for me to sleep in a bed my sister and her dumbass mate have boned down in."

"You never had to stand outside and listen to your sister and her dumbass mate bone down," Xiao blurts, and we're both so startled, we just stare at each other. She's waiting for a reprimand, I think, and for me to demand an apology, but I can't help myself. It's too funny and I have to laugh.

Xiao laughs cautiously along with me, more out of embarrassment, it seems. "I'm sorry. That was... not appropriate, Your Majesty."

"Don't call me that." It's better to nip that kind of thing in the bud. "I'm not interested in being queen. I'm not interested in any of this so. Just call me Tara." She opens her mouth to respond, but I cut her off. "And not 'Lady Tara.' We both know I'm not a Lady-in-Waiting or whatever archaic bullshit my sister tried to pull. I'm just furniture."

"With respect, Your— Tara," Xiao stumbles over my name. "At the moment, you're the hub in a wheel of conspiracy that will, frankly, collapse without you."

"I... what?" That makes the entire thing sound a lot less like covering for my sister while she breaks the rules and more like something that could potentially get my head chopped off.

I know they're willing to do it. I just don't know which *they*.

"If you're not here, the pack leadership isn't secure. The king and queen have no heirs. They left you in charge to hold the throne. Without you, everything falls apart." Xiao softens her tone. "You're important, Tara. I just don't think you've ever felt that way."

Her statement strikes me hard in the chest. She's completely right; I've never felt important. Not to my family, certainly not to my mate.

Which means my lack of importance is visible. I'm mortified.

"How do you know that?" I demand. "You don't know anything about me."

She shrugs. "I watch."

"You watch."

"It's my job to stand by silently and observe things while the royal family lives their lives in front of me, as if I'm not there. You learn to read people quickly. It's not like I have time to read books."

"Was that a joke?" I'm stunned.

"Not all of it." She smiles and shakes her head. "We shouldn't be talking like this."

"Because it interferes with your watching?" I mean it in a playful way, but something in me freezes when I hear the words aloud. Am I accusing her of being dishonest? Implying that she's surveilling us for nefarious purposes?

"Why are you so worried about talking to us? It's not like you're risking getting to know us. You just said you observe us for that. So, why no chit-chat?" I ask.

"I'm an outside observer," she says. "I get to know your habits and your personalities, and I use those to gauge what kind of danger you might put yourselves in. But if I grew to like you, became friendly with you? What if we're 'chit-chatting,' as you say, and I'm distracted enough to miss an attack?"

"I'm not going to get attacked in here," I argue. I argue, against someone trying to do her job correctly. "Sorry. I'm being super pushy. Like, be my friend, be my friend, be my friend."

She laughs and shakes her head. "I understand. I really do. This is a lonely place. If you're not used to being alone, that's a kind of torture."

"Well, now it is. Before I came here, not so much," I say, but that's more conversation. And while I want to ask what she means by not being used to being alone—is she used to it? why? —I can't keep undermining her. "I'll leave you alone. You know best."

"I'll stand outside the door," she tells me. She pauses at the threshold then turns back. "The full moon is coming."

I nod. "I know. I wanted to get all of this wrapped up before then."

"Because you'll be vulnerable," she finishes my thought.

"We can't transform." I tap my lips with my index

finger. "I don't suppose we could put a warning out on the network?"

"The network is compromised. Thralls have access," she reminds me. "And you can't address them, yourself. The pack doesn't know His Majesty and Her Majesty are missing."

Just say 'Nathan and Bailey' I think, but I know that even if I requested it, she wouldn't do it. Xiao seems to live and breathe protocol.

"There has to be a way we can spread the word and stop the ceremony. And there has to be a way we can do it without arousing suspicion."

"Asking the pack to skip another full moon will arouse suspicion, regardless," she points out. "It was one thing to cancel the ceremony soon after the attack on your sister, but a second time? They'll know something is wrong. And even if you cancel the ceremony officially, some of the pack will still gather and turn. They did the last time."

"Then I need to think of some other way." *There is no other way,* the worst, most destructive part of my brain taunts me. It's wrong. There's always another way, I know this.

There was no way to save your sister.

I see the blade fall, again and again. Not on the necks of the betrayers. Just my sister.

"Tara?" Xiao asks softly.

I jerk myself back to reality. "Sorry. I have this weird thing... never mind."

I don't want to distract her with personal trauma. She's set a boundary and explained why, and I need to respect that.

"It's okay, tell me." Her brow crinkles. "Do you have

seizures or narcolepsy or something? I didn't see anything about it in the dossier."

"There's a file on me?" Of course, there's a file on me. It's probably so thorough, the king knows my cycle. I don't wait for Xiao to answer. "No, I don't have those. I just have weird moments. You know, the way that when something really bad happens, you're suddenly back in that moment and you feel like you're reliving it and reliving it for hours, but it's really only been a few seconds?"

She blinks at me.

"Is that not..." I take a breath and hold it. "That's not a universal thing, is it?"

She shakes her head slowly.

I exhale loudly and brush the whole thing off. "It's just my brain's way of dealing with it. You know, the sister getting beheaded thing."

My palms are sweaty. I wipe them on the thighs of my jeans.

"I'm sorry for your loss," Xiao says stiffly. To my astonishment, she comes to sit at my side, even puts an awkward hand on my shoulder.

She wants to comfort me. It's stiff and weird and the opposite of comforting, but I'll take it. She's the only contact I have anymore.

"That thing you're describing?" Xiao says carefully. "It's not something that everyone just does. And it's not a coping strategy. It's an injury."

I scoff.

She is undeterred. "A lot of the thralls who were in the castle the day of the coronation attack are going through the same thing. They're having to take time off, get therapy... you should, too."

"Werewolves don't go to therapy," I joke. Kind of. I

heard my mother say those exact words all my life. "We're too strong for that."

"You didn't look very strong a minute ago," Xiao points out.

"Maybe I'm just tired from staying up all night, reading about mythology until my eyes cross." I don't look forward to going into my bedroom and being confronted with all my piles of research.

"That could be." Her tone makes it obvious that she doesn't believe me.

A part of me rebels at the casual way she just addressed my mental health. She's a thrall. If my mother were here, she'd be outraged that a thrall didn't know her place. But I'm not my mother, and a few minutes ago, I wanted Xiao to stay.

"I need to stop thinking like my mother," I blurt out. When Xiao says nothing, I go on. "She was really not into the idea of anyone in the family being less than absolutely perfect. Therapy wasn't an option. And my marriage..."

Couples therapy was right out. When I suggested it to my mate—former mate? I'm not sure where that stands, legally—he went through the roof and then straight to my parents.

"You're acting queen," Xiao reminds me. "You can do whatever you want. And if what you want to do is therapy, I say go for it."

"Thanks. Are there even werewolf therapists?" I ask.

She shrugs. "There are thrall therapists. You'd have to watch what you say, of course. Knowing what we know."

"I'm fine talking to thralls. I'm talking to one right now." The only one I trust, but that doesn't mean I couldn't possibly trust another. "As long as they don't work for the Hierophant."

Xiao stands. "Right now, I think you should forgo the research in favor of sleep. When Hannah and Ryan arrive tonight, you can go back into work mode."

"Are you sure *you're* not a therapist?" I joke.

She doesn't find it funny. "I'm not, and you can't treat me like I'm yours. I'm here to protect you, not fix you."

"You're right." I get up, too, a yawn surprising me. "Wake me when they get here?"

"I'll wake you before then. You need to have dinner tonight. You haven't been eating." She stops herself. "I notice things. I shouldn't comment on them."

"Comment on them all you want," I tell her. "You're the only person who seems to care about my wellbeing anymore."

It's sad to me how true that statement is.

CHAPTER 6

TARA

My dinner arrives, delivered by palace thralls, and the scent of the food wakes me before anyone else has to. The chefs at Aconitum Hall cook every meal like it's a state dinner; my stomach roars and snarls at the smell of rare roast beef wafting from the dining room.

I'm not expecting to see three places set when I enter the room, nor my sister's friends seated at the table.

"Surprise!" Hannah exclaims. "We're early."

"We were told you might need some company outside of research mode," Ryan, her mate-in-name-only adds.

I'm not sure how to *be* when I'm around them. They're my sister's friends, not mine, and Bailey and I are as different as night and day.

"Oh no. Are we intruding?" Hannah asks, and I realize my face must be a mask of horror.

"No, not at all!" Now that there are people here, I don't want them to leave. "I just have to adjust my brain. I was expecting to spend dinner alone."

"It has to be tough, living in this house by yourself," Ryan sympathizes.

I nod and take my seat at the head of the table. Where a queen sits. I motion to their bare plates and the platters of food in front of us. "Eat up. You don't have to wait for me. I'm not really queen."

As we fill our plates, Ryan asks, "How did the meeting go today?"

My stomach clenches and for a moment, I'm not as hungry as I was before. "Tense. The Hierophant pretended not to know where Bailey and Nathan are, like we expected him to. He accepted my claim to rule in the interim, though."

"Word around the council is that Nathan and Bailey left due to a plot by the St. Laurent pack." Hannah raises her eyebrows, gaze fixed on the giant clump of mashed potatoes she's excavating from the serving bowl.

"It's not entirely untrue." The St. Laurent pack *did* attack the king and queen. "And we do still have them to worry about."

"Especially with what we know about the thralls' plans," Ryan adds. "We're not sure yet if this is isolated just to the Toronto and London packs."

"If it's happening in London, it's happening everywhere." There's no doubt in my mind, judging from what we know about the weird behavior of Nathan's uncle, that this is a world-wide effort on behalf of the thralls.

"I'll do my best to keep the council focused on our developing war with St. Laurent. There's no reason everyone needs to suspect their thralls." Ryan lowers his voice. "I shouldn't have said that here."

I shake my head. "Xiao is keeping everyone at a distance. She's been using the disappearance of the king and queen to up security. There's no way anyone is lurking around or listening in. She'll have done a headcount on everyone who came in here."

Hannah and Ryan exchange a look, but they say nothing.

I know it's because they don't fully trust Xiao. They don't know her like I do, and like my sister does. And Nathan, bastard that he is, wouldn't trust anyone who would put his mate in danger.

Must be nice.

"Our newest problem, though," I begin, cutting into my meat, "is the full moon. It's coming up."

"And we wanted to have this entire problem solved by then," Hannah says with a sigh.

"I think we were a tad optimistic," Ryan observes.

"When it comes to the ceremony, we'll all be vulnerable." I'm sure they've thought of this already, but I have to know we're all on the same page. "Any magic from the thralls could be dangerous to us. We don't know their rituals beyond what they've told us."

"If they wanted to hurt the pack, they could do something as simple as poisoning the hearts," Hannah suggests, her eyes going wide. "But why would they do that?"

"Because they want to get rid of us all, and Bailey is already their prisoner," Ryan answers. "They've got her isolated from the rest of the pack, she's carrying the baby they're invested in... none of the rest of us matter."

I shake my head, a sudden clarity coming to me. "They're not safe until the baby is born. If something happened to Bailey or the pup, and they already killed the rest of us..."

"Good point." Hannah chews thoughtfully. "Would canceling the ceremony now raise suspicion?"

"What if we announce the disappearance of the king and queen? And we blame it on St. Laurent?" Ryan says.

I shake my head firmly. "That will throw the council into chaos."

"Chaos we can use to our advantage," Ryan counters. "If the council is busy waging war against St. Laurent, they won't have time to look at you too closely, Tara."

"With the only downside being that we'll be *at war*." Hannah emphasizes those words with a tone that clearly conveys just how unacceptable the idea is.

But Ryan is right, and I have to back him up. "We're going to war with St. Laurent, anyway. A lie would just give the council the kick in the pants it needs to go forward with it."

"They've already attacked the queen. They took her hand." Ryan holds his up and wiggles his fingers. "Even if the pack didn't want to go to war, the king will still make it happen. He cares about Bailey too much to let an attack against her go unpunished."

That takes me aback. "An attack on his property, maybe. From what I've seen and heard around here, the king doesn't care about my sister as a person, at all."

"He's her mate," Ryan says simply.

"Her mate who's been cheating on her and treating her like an incubator, not a wife," Hannah grumbles, pushing her food around her plate.

I hated Nathan already, but after learning about his mistress, the way his actions took a toll on my sister, that hatred grew large enough to crush the whole city. But I do have to give him some credit, where it's due. "He's a cheating dickhead who treats Bailey like a means to an end, but Ryan is right. Nathan *is* protective of her. He wouldn't let anyone into her room while she recuperated from her surgery, and the medical staff had to be completely cleared by security."

Of course, he wouldn't let me or Clare in to see our sister because he was convinced we had something to do with the attack. And Clare did.

My heart aches, and I push the image of Clare climbing those scaffold steps from my mind. Now is not the time for a blank-out.

Ryan nods. "And not to pull rank here, but I *am* on the council. I'm telling you; we're going to war. The difference is going to be whether it happens now or in a few months."

"Fine." Hannah drops her fork and sighs deeply. Her shoulders rise with tension and she leans back in her chair, arms folding over her chest. "Fine, we go to war. St. Laurent did break the peace when they chose to harbor traitors after the coronation attack. And they did try to assassinate Bailey. What do we do about the thralls, in the meantime? Just let them work magic on us, not knowing what's going to happen?"

The gears in my head begin to turn. "We don't have magic but... some humans do."

None of us say a word. The clock on the mantle ticks like cannon fire.

"You know how the thralls feel about human magicians," Ryan says slowly, as if just speaking will make a bomb explode at the table.

"The thralls don't have to know." Except for one. As a thrall, Xiao is more connected to the outside world than any of us are.

"The king and queen should," Hannah says.

"And obviously they should know before I declare war on St. Laurent," I add.

"You're acting monarch," Ryan reminds me.

No matter how many times I'm reminded, it doesn't feel right. "I'm acting monarch because we're trying to navigate a conspiracy here. I'm not acting monarch to start wars and make big decisions by myself."

"How do we get a message to them, when they're way out in the wilds of Mani-*fucking*-toba?" Hannah huffs. "The pack up there couldn't even survive."

That's true. The harsh climate was fine for our ancestors and for the indigenous people who'd been our allies centuries ahead of the murderer Columbus's bogus claim to "discovery," but eventually, wolves had settled further south, where their thralls could survive.

"The pack could survive. The thralls couldn't," I muse aloud.

"Maybe we should all move back up there," Ryan says with a snort of laughter. "Return to the wild, let the weather sort the thralls out."

"No thanks," Hannah says grumpily. "I ask again, how do we get them a message?"

"Xiao planned a supply run for after the full moon. We can bump it up." I chew my bottom lip. "That doesn't give us much time to find a human magician, though."

Hannah lifts one hand slowly, like she's guilty of something. "Nathan and Bailey know a magician."

None of us want to acknowledge what that magician *did*. *They* didn't even want to acknowledge it to us, but full disclosure was necessary for research purposes. I wish I could manually scrub the mental images from my brain.

"They trusted him with... a lot," Hannah continues. "What's the harm in running it past them?"

"No harm, as long as the thralls don't find out," I say.

Which means I have to convince Xiao to take me with her.

CHAPTER 7
TARA

"With all respect due to your current position as reigning ruler of the Toronto and Greater London packs," Xiao begins, "absolutely not."

I expected this response. That doesn't mean I'll accept it. I stay planted on my sitting room sofa, though I want to jump to my feet and pace the way she's doing. "There's no way I'm involving human magicians without speaking to my sister first."

"Send a note. On paper, so it can be destroyed." Xiao states it as if it's the final word, chiseled into stone. She ceases her pacing at a window, moves the curtain aside to give a quick scan of the grounds outside.

Her word might be stone, but I will be a wrecking ball. "There's no reason to prevent me from being involved in this."

"You'll be involved when we go to London," she argues. "And the reason is, I'm supposed to be going on this supply run. You're not. They *will* miss you here. How do you plan to explain your absence from the palace?"

Damn. I didn't think of that. I should have. It's just more proof that I'm not cut out for court intrigue.

In fairness to myself, it's not like I was important or even noticed around the palace before a few days ago. I certainly never planned to be involved in royal business. My sister becoming queen was an event none of us saw coming. She was supposed to be mated to Ashton. *Then you would have had two headless sisters.* Maybe becoming queen saved Bailey's life. I just wish it didn't complicate mine so much.

"How long does a supply run take?" I ask, because to me, Manitoba is some far off place from our far-off history. Werewolves don't learn the same geography in school that humans are concerned with. We recognize territorial borders as old as our medieval ancestors who made contact with the First Peoples here. And while we've adopted the names given to the land by humans to describe ourselves, our territories often overlap the lines drawn by human governments. For us, there is no Manitoba pack; therefore, Manitoba might as well not exist.

The fact that Xiao hesitates to give me the information indicates that it must not be terribly far. At least, not so far that my absence couldn't be explained. Finally, she admits, "A day. I plan to fly out early and return late."

"Is it unusual for a queen to be gone all day?" I ask. "And if it is, how are we going to manage a trip to London?"

"You're currently ruling their pack as Queen Regent. It wouldn't be unusual for you to go there to see how things are running," Xiao points out. "Getting into a small prop plane with your sister's bodyguard and going to some secret location looks a lot different. Especially to the thralls. They're going to be watching."

"Then we have to be sneaky." But how to sneak myself onto a plane? "What if we put me in a duffle bag?"

"A duffle bag." Xiao lifts an eyebrow, silently imploring me to rethink the suggestion.

"Yeah, a duffle bag," I go on. "I could get in, you could zip me up and carry me out. Then you could put me in the trunk and—"

"Suffocate you to death before we reached the airfield," she says with a quirk of her lips.

"Then don't zip it all the way up!" I run a hand through my hair in frustration. "Look, I'm willing to brainstorm solutions here and you're shooting them all down."

"Because if I get caught smuggling you out, there will be consequences for me." Xiao says it quietly, as if she's embarrassed to be afraid of whatever those consequences might be.

But if they're anything like the sentences the king has been passing out lately...

"I'm not a coward," she goes on. "But I'm the only person on the inside who's on your side. And believe me, if we're discovered, you're going to lose me."

I know she means that we'll lose her as a valuable resource in keeping my sister safe, but Xiao's words strike me in an intensely personal place. She's the only person at Aconitum Hall who talks to me. The only person who seems to give a damn about what I'm going through.

A lump rises in my throat as I realize that losing Xiao wouldn't just be losing an important resource. I would be losing a friend, even if she resists the title.

"What's our option, then?" I throw my hands up and let them fall with a gentle thud beside my thighs. "I write a letter and you get caught with it?"

"You'll write a letter explaining why the involvement of human magicians is necessary. Hannah and Ryan should both write one, as well, or at least, sign yours. That should be enough to convince the king." Xiao moves from the window to stand beside the arm of the couch. "Frankly, if you go in person... I'm not sure he'll trust you."

I know that. "I don't really care. I fucking hate him."

"I know you do." Xiao delivers the sentiment gently. "If I were in your place..."

I give her a weak smile. "I know you're trying not to commit treason. I get your meaning. But can I be treasonous, just for a minute?"

"I..."

"I never wanted Bailey to marry him." No matter how often I think it or say it, it will never relieve the sick feeling that rises from my stomach to my chest, an invisible, burning sickness up my throat. "I don't trust him. And I don't believe he has Bailey's interests at heart. If he did, he wouldn't have hurt her so badly with his mistress and by murdering our sister."

It takes a long moment for Xiao to speak again. "I'm your sister's bodyguard, so it's not treason to say that protecting her is my main goal. May I be blunt?"

"I wish you would."

"If anyone threatened your sister's safety, I would do what needs to be done." She makes hard, intense eye contact. "*Anyone.*"

It's the most outrageous thing I've ever heard her say. "I will never tell anyone what you just said," I promise.

"I know you won't. That's why I said it to you and not to anyone else." The corner of her mouth lifts, like she might give me one of her rare smiles. But this isn't a moment for humor, no matter how it might strike us.

She sits beside me. It's a gesture I've noted her becoming more comfortable with. "I know you're not planning to hurt your sister. The king doesn't. Put yourself in his position; so far, every member of your family, except you, has tried to get him or his wife killed."

"I don't believe Clare really wanted Bailey dead," I argue. I have to. Because even now, with all the evidence I've seen to prove it, I don't believe it.

"I believe she wanted the queen dead," Xiao says softly. "And I think she probably regretted that the queen happened to be your sister. But that didn't deter her from her goal."

"Maybe. Most of us thought Amber would be queen again," I say, the words bitter on my tongue. It wasn't enough that the former queen had been a grasping, power-hungry bitch during her rule. She had to become a grasping, power-hungry side-chick and hurt my sister.

"Why does Bailey love him so much?" I ask, and Xiao's face lights up with surprise.

She blinks at me, her mouth open, before stammering, "I-I didn't realize that she did."

"I know her. I know how she responds to people. If she didn't love him, she wouldn't be out in the woods with him in the middle of nowhere." My sister can be loyal to a fault, but she would never have shown such devotion to Ashton. "Do you think it's the spell?"

"It has to be," Xiao states firmly.

"So, is that part of how it works?" As a thrall, she knows more about their magic than I do. She was the first person to tell us that a binding was placed on my sister and her mate; we would never have known, otherwise.

Xiao shrugs. "Maybe? I'm just assuming, based on the circumstances."

I raise an eyebrow in question.

With a nervous laugh, she adds, "You know the king. Could you imagine anyone truly falling in love with him?"

We both laugh and the air is suddenly easier to breathe. The room doesn't feel as grim and oppressive.

"I can't take you with me," she says again. "It's a dangerous trip, already. I wasn't supposed to go until after the full moon. Moving up the date without arousing suspicion is going to take some work on my part. But it means I'm going to be watched, every step of the way."

"I understand." I hate it, but I understand. "What excuse are you going to use to go out there again?"

"I don't know. She forgot her prenatal vitamins?" Xiao snorts. "I'll figure something out. You write your letter. Discuss it with Ryan and Hannah. And I promise, Tara, your sister, and this pack, are safe in my care."

I don't understand why a thrall would work against her own kind. But I don't have to understand it to trust her. It's the way she says my name, the tender look in her brown eyes that implores me that we're all safe, that she can fix everything.

I can't help but believe her.

CHAPTER 8
BAILEY

It only takes a few days for us to fall into a surprisingly efficient routine. Nathan chops firewood every day and brings it into the cabin to dry by the hearth. I run shrieking from the huge spiders that somehow always hitchhike on the split logs and find their way into our house. Sometimes I cook, sometimes Nathan does, but we both fish from the dock and I turn out to be pretty good at it. I have a feeling that by the time we leave, I'll never want to eat walleye again, though.

Despite the bitter cold at night—which continues to challenge our usually chill-resistant werewolf biology—the days aren't bad, at all. Early spring might as well be winter, but the small stream behind the cabin is starting to thaw, and we've taken to getting our drinking and washing water from there, rather than the rusty old pump. We heat water in the cabin to bathe ourselves.

Usually.

Today, my mate has decided that a brief break in cloud cover has raised the temperature enough to wash up in the lake. I watch with amusement concealed behind disdain as he strips off his clothes at the edge of the shore.

"If you're trying to prove how tough you are, don't worry. I don't care," I tell him with a snort of derision.

"If you're trying to prove how much you don't care, you're failing," he teases, hopping on one foot to kick his jeans aside.

I shiver, but not from the cold. The pull between us makes the air hot as summer, and that heat radiates through me, twisting into hunger as I watch the muscles bunch and ripple under his naked skin.

He feels it, too, and turns to me with a crooked grin. "You could come in with me."

"I'll wait out here." I squeeze my thighs against the ache there that never seems to be soothed. Being alone together constantly, without any other distractions, has only made the mystical attraction more powerful.

With a harrumph of disappointment, he turns back to the lake and wades in up to his ankles. Thinking better of it, I guess, he turns around and heads back to the shore.

"See, I told you it was—" I begin, but he breaks into a run down the dock and cannonballs in.

"Nathan!" I jolt to my feet. I have no idea how deep the water is there. He could have broken his back, for all I know. I race to the end of the dock myself and almost topple in just as he surfaces, hair falling flat and unattractive over his stupid, beautiful head.

"You scared the shit out of me!"

"Why?" He wipes water from his eyes and smooths his hair back with both hands. His breath is visible in little puffs on the air. "I'm not so sheltered that I've never jumped in a lake before. I know how to do it."

"Well, you still scared me." I tromp back to land, my

boots echoing like explosions through the otherwise silent woods. I stop at Nathan's pile of discarded clothes and pick up the bar of soap he forgot. I carry it back to him and drop it into his cupped hands. "You're going to need this. You smell terrible."

"You love the way I smell."

I do. It's weird as hell and I can't fathom what it is about his b.o. that makes me feel so content and comforted. I blame the binding.

I've been blaming the binding for a lot, lately. Mostly, the relentless amount of sex we've been having. Watching him lather up his chest makes me twist the ball of my foot against the dock restlessly. To stop from jumping into the water with him, I go back to the fireside and set about tidying up from our breakfast. It's a serious job, and one we can't leave undone for too long; the dangers from bears and other scavengers are real. In the city, Nathan and I are the most fearsome predators. Out here, we're not as helpless as humans, but the odds aren't quite as firmly in our favor.

I'm not exactly a camper, though, so my solution thus far has been to scrape our leftovers directly into the fire and stoke it up super big in the hopes anything we didn't eat will get burned away. I've never had to really clean anything and having just the one hand makes things extra challenging. By the time I've sealed up everything we're keeping and returned the cold goods back to the cooler, Nathan is done with his bath and headed back toward the fire.

Despite the frigid temp, Nathan strides back from the lake naked, with his clothes over one arm and his other hand rubbing his towel over his hair.

I turn away and sit on one of the stumps ringing the fire pit. "Okay, we get it. All of nature gets it. You're hot."

"No, I'm cold," he corrects me, coming to stand beside me. "I'm very cold, in fact."

I toss a glance at his crotch, which is level with my face at the moment. "Yup, looks like."

"That's not very nice," he mock scolds me.

I want to say something snarky, but he's too close and too naked and I'm too ridiculously attracted to him. I turn and grab his butt, pulling him a step closer, and he barks a surprised laugh.

Leaning my face against his hip, I trace the path of the long scar across his abdomen with my tongue. He hisses; I know the scar and the area around it are bizarrely ticklish now that they've healed. It must not be an entirely bad sensation, because his cock stirs, probably due to the proximity of my mouth. I blow a teasing stream of my warm breath across the head of him, and he makes a noise low in his throat.

Everything about Nathan has intimidated me from the moment we first met. He's powerful even when he's not transformed, physically strong even after the attack that nearly claimed his life, and he has a ruthlessly calculating mind. But the binding between us renders him helpless to me, as helpless as I am to him.

I run my fingers down his abs, my touch growing lighter as I approach his cock. He's fully hard now, and I trace down the center of his shaft with one fingertip. He makes a sound low in his throat; I take him into mine.

He's hot and unyielding as I encircle his shaft with my hand. I can't close my fist all the way around him. My jaw opens wider as I take him down as far as I can, until I choke and pull back. His hand falls to the back of my head, but he doesn't push me. Instead, he fumbles with the hairband holding together my messy bun. He gives it a tug, then winds it around his finger and snaps it.

My gasp of outrage is obscured by his dick in my mouth. I raise my head, a little out of breath. "Hey! I have a finite number of those, and they *do* get lost."

"I'm sorry," he says, but the way he combs his fingers through my fallen hair suggests he's not sorry, at all. He tilts my face up with two fingers crooked under my chin and brushes his thumb across my bottom lip. "I just wanted to see you like this. And like this."

He reaches down and pops the buttons on my flannel shirt, pushing it open to reveal my bare breasts beneath.

"You're adjusting a view that was lacking?" I quip.

"Enhancing an already gorgeous view. And I can think of better things you could do with that mouth than talk back to your mate." To illustrate, he taps his cock against my mouth, brushing the head back and forth in a gesture that mimics the path of his tongue along his bottom lip. "Go on. Finish what you started."

Finish. As if him finishing would actually be the end. I know exactly how the encounter will proceed; once I've swallowed down mouthfuls of his cum, he'll lay me out on the frost-kissed grass and feast on me until I'm shaking and screaming. He'll fuck me for hours, a nonstop mating that won't end until we're too exhausted to move. And we'll still want each other, still ache to be joined, a need that can never be satiated.

Maybe I'll miss the binding when it's gone.

I suck him into my mouth again, slide my head and tongue down him in a slow, steady rhythm matched by the glide of my hand along the length of his shaft that I can't take in. I wrap my other arm around his thighs, pulling him in closer, never picking up my pace even when his hips pump ever so slightly. I rock in time to those movements, my cunt growing slick and desperate, begging to be touched. Torturing myself with patience—and with the seam of my jeans— I continue until Nathan's throaty vocalizations indicate it won't be long now.

"Stop!"

It's not an entirely unusual command, but the way he tenses and urgently steps back is.

"Do you hear that?" He tilts his head and holds up a finger.

Dazed with horniness, I don't understand what he's asking.

"There." He narrows his gaze at the cloud-covered sky.

That's when I hear it. The far-off throb of a distant engine high on the air.

"Xiao isn't supposed to be back yet," I say, the hairs on the back of my neck standing up.

"No, she's not." Nathan scans the sky all around us, but if he can tell which direction the plane is coming from, he's got a better idea of it than I do.

"It could be just like... air traffic?" I say hopefully, but I know it's not. There hasn't been a plane overhead since Xiao left us. "Search and rescue?"

Nathan grips my hand and jerks me to my feet. "Get your coat, a compass, and a canteen. I want you to run into the woods. Go south until you can't see the cabin anymore and wait for me."

"Do you think it's—" I begin.

"Go," he orders, and the fear in his tone forces me to obey, to run to the cabin like whoever is pursuing us is right at our backs.

My hand shakes as I screw the lid onto my full canteen. I can barely get the zipper up on my puffy coat. By the time

I have the compass, I can barely get the strength in my fingers to open the lid, and I yelp in despair.

The sound overhead is louder now, and the only thoughts in my head are, *the pack found out about us, about the binding, about all of it, they're looking for us, they're going to find us.*

They want us dead.

Our own pack might want us dead. Our own kind. And if they've found us, there's no way we can escape them. I can't run far enough, fast enough, through dangerous terrain. I don't even know how I'm going to make it over the stream as I charge toward it. I want to look back to get a glimpse of Nathan, but that's always what trips people up when they're running from danger. I reach the edge of the stream and launch myself over it, landing hard and shocking my ankles, but clearing the water with dry boots.

The tree line is so close, I feel like I can reach my hand out and grab it, but it's still another twelve or so steps before I actually make it. My lungs burn. I grit my teeth and dash into the shadow of the trees.

I am alone, in a strange forest, and I'm running for my life.

CHAPTER 9
BAILEY

Low limbs slash at my face as I run headlong into the forest with no plan whatsoever. I'm not sure Nathan had much of one, either, when he sent me into the woods. I understand his immediate course of action: hide Bailey from the plane. I don't understand what he thinks will happen to me if whoever gets off that plane kills him.

The thought sticks in my throat as I run. I can't go very fast; there are too many obstacles to avoid, and the ground is dangerously uneven. I clutch the compass to my chest and check it often, to make sure I'm going south, to make sure Nathan will be able to find me.

If Nathan is the one who ends up finding me.

I can't think about that right now. Thoughts of my mate in danger awaken a primal force in me that demands I run back to him. I know he's right in sending me alone, though. Even if someone has come from the pack to kill us, I'm their main target. I'm the one carrying the baby they would want to destroy.

I step into a mushy hole and my ankle twists. This would be so much easier if I were in werewolf form.

The moonstone! *Why didn't I think to grab the black moonstone?*

I hook my arm around a leaning trunk for support and fight my way forward. Nothing on the ground seems particularly stable, and as I continue on, the woods thin and the trees seem shorter. Stunted, maybe, or just sinking into the muddy ground. Suddenly, I'm standing beneath open sky again, and I look up, certain I'll see the dread airplane. I can still hear it. I know it's close now, but I can't see it.

A small meadow with dead, yellow grass stretches in a bleak line between the cover I've just come from and another line of trees farther off. I hold deathly still as I consider my next move. If I keep going south, directly south like Nathan instructed, I'll have to cross all that open ground. Someone very well could see me from the air. I could try to stay in the woods I've just come from, but it seems like a small area to search, should someone try to track me down. Maybe more distance is better?

I start out across the meadow, checking my surroundings in a pattern of feet-compass-sky-feet-compass-sky to avoid stumbling, veering too far off course, or being spotted by the plane. If they do fly overhead, I'll drop to the ground on my belly and hope my puffy black coat makes me look like a bear or a bag of garbage.

The meadow is squishy, and more than once it tries to claim a boot from my foot. My thighs burn with every step and I'm only halfway across.

Something white flickers at the edge of the tree line and I freeze.

My first thought is *polar bear*, but I know those are larger than what I'm seeing in front of me. This is smaller, lower to the ground.

Canine.

"Wolf," I whisper to myself. I'm looking across the dead meadow, directly into the eyes of a snow-white wolf.

The ground under me disappears. I don't even have time to cry out before I plunge into bone-chillingly cold water. It's dark below the surface, and mucky; foul sludge invades my mouth and nose as I fight my coat to get to the surface. My head breaks through and I manage to take a sputtering breath, but I know it's more water than air coming into my lungs. My sodden coat might as well be made of lead. The nylon outer covering inflates, but not helpfully. It does nothing for buoyancy and everything for obscuring my vision. I flail helplessly beneath the water, but once I'm above it again, my ability to move deserts me. All I can do is hold my arms pathetically up until I'm too tired and I sink into the fight beneath the water again.

I know I can't keep doing it forever. I know this is how I die.

Just as I slip under again, something grabs my wrist where my hand is missing, and I'm pulled up with impossible force. *Nathan! Nathan found me!* But whatever holds me lets go. I reach desperately for Nathan's hand, and something catches the hood of my coat, propelling me backward, out of the water, trampling the dead, yellow grass beneath my body as it drags me.

The polar bear has me! is my next, terrified thought. I choke up mouthfuls of slimy, black water and bits of things I don't want to think about as I roll onto my hand and knees, vomiting, wondering the whole time if a massive bear paw is going to knock my head right off of my shoulders.

When my head clears, I realize that no polar bear would patiently wait for me to stop puking before killing me, and it wasn't a bear I saw. I saw...

I sit back on my heels, casting my bleary gaze all around

the meadow. About six feet away, the white wolf stands still, watching me.

"Did you..." I begin, before another wave of swampy water discharges from my stomach, doubling me over. I don't hear the plane, but I don't care about it anymore, either. I was just rescued by a wolf. The animal kind. Maybe now, it will eat me. If the alternative is to keep puking like this, death doesn't sound so bad.

The wolf just watches, like he's making sure I'm okay. Maybe he knows what I am. Animals often do. But I have no idea what he plans to do with that information, or with me, for that matter.

I collapse in a heap, rolling away from my sick splashed all over the ground, and breathe heavily. The ground ripples beneath my back and I panic, scrabbling on my elbows to get further from the hole I'd plunged into.

The wolf gives a low, warning growl, and I hold very still, my terrified eyes locked with its gaze. It doesn't move. It remains motionless.

It's telling *me* to remain motionless.

The waves beneath the ground calm. I give myself a tentative push back and note that the motion under me isn't as pronounced. The wolf stands and takes two very slow steps backward. There's no tremor beneath me, now. Emboldened, I push myself back again, further from the hole. I watch with repulsed terror as the mouth that had opened in the earth to swallow me slowly closes back up, clumps of muddy grass floating placidly on the disappearing water.

"Thank you," I whisper to the wolf, who continues to put as much slow, careful space between us as possible. He doesn't want to mess with me, I don't want to mess with him. I'm glad we're in agreement.

"Bailey!" A far-off voice shouts. A familiar voice, but not Nathan's. The wolf's ears prick up, and faster than I can track him, he's gone, disappearing through the tall, stiff grass.

"Xiao?" I call back, my throat so raw I barely make a sound. "Xiao!"

"Bailey!" Nathan's voice joins hers. I flip onto my belly and army crawl across the wriggling ground. None of it is stable. It's only sheer luck that I got as far out into it as I did.

The bad kind of luck.

"I'm here!" I try to shout, and I see Xiao break through the trees. "Stay where you are! It's not safe!"

"It's not safe" is like a special Xiao call, though. The second the woman hears that something might be dangerous, she wants to be all up in the middle of it. If that means she's coming to my rescue, though, I'll take it. My limbs are stiff with the cold, my wet coat weighs about fifty pounds on my back, and I'm terrified that at any moment, I'll plunge through the surface again.

"Don't move!" Xiao calls out, and I push up on my hand to spot Nathan beside her. It's him she's warning, not me.

Slowly, a few inches at a time, I pull myself along, still not trusting myself to stand. I've always heard that if you fall through ice into water, you should stay on your belly when you pull yourself out, so the ice doesn't crumble under your feet. I'm not on ice—it would be more stable than this shit—but the advice seems to apply. My teeth chatter so hard, I'm sure they'll break, and all my muscles cramp from the intense shivering. The only thought in my head is that I have to make it out. I have to make it to Xiao, to Nathan. I have to make it out of here for my baby.

When it feels like the ground isn't made of liquid earthquake, I rest. More accurately, I fall, sprawling onto solid safety. Xiao is there in an instant gripping my under my arms and hauling me to my feet.

"She's soaked!" Xiao shouts back. "And she's frozen!"

Then she lifts me up, dripping coat and all, and carries me like I'm a baby. Not even a particularly heavy baby.

"You're so strong," I manage, despite my chattering jaw.

"I know," she replies grimly.

"Give her here!" Nathan is at our side in an instant, and I keenly feel the difference in temperature between his body and Xiao's. He's so much warmer, and I nuzzle my face against his neck, desperate for heat.

"Go," Xiao tells him, and he takes off at a run no human could manage, cradling me to his chest with one arm as he knocks branches out of his path.

"There was a wolf," I rasp, the warm peace of sleep beckoning me. "There was a wolf."

CHAPTER 10
BAILEY

Even wrapped in a blanket, naked and skin-to-skin with Nathan in front of the fire, my teeth still chatter while Xiao explains what's going on back at Aconitum Hall.

"You see why I made the trip early, then," she finishes, fixing Nathan with a hard glare.

He deserves it, at least, a little. He's been giving her the worst time about showing up unannounced, scaring us, and endangering my life. At first, I tried to defend her, but Nathan's protective instincts will not be appeased.

He seems chastened now that he knows the reason for her early visit. "You were right to bring this to us, Xiao. I'm sorry for how I reacted."

"You were keeping your mate safe," she says. Though she's motionless, her tone is the equivalent of a shrug. "But you have to be careful. There are muskegs all over this area that will swallow you up, especially now that the spring thaws are in progress."

"How do you know so much about this place?" I never heard of a muskeg, deceptive bogs disguised by moss and swamp vegetation, until I nearly died in one.

"I researched before I brought you." She blinks as if the answer is obvious. Maybe it should be obvious; I've taken her skills and dedication as a royal bodyguard for granted.

Nathan pulls me tighter against him and adjusts the blanket, maintaining our modesty. He's sitting cross-legged, holding me in his lap on the lumpy mattress we never moved back to the bedframe. Somehow, he still sounds regal despite how ridiculous we must look. "I am concerned about potential involvement with the human magician. Jonah is... gray. From a moral standpoint. He'll never be dedicated to our cause."

I shake my head. "If the thralls become super powerful, they'll go after the human magicians next."

Xiao lifts an eyebrow in question.

I shrug, and the blanket slips from my shoulder. Nathan fixes it for me while I explain. "I don't have any insider knowledge. But if thralls are power hungry enough to wipe out werewolves entirely, they won't stop there. I mean, I wouldn't."

Yikes, that was a scary thing to admit, especially considering my position.

"I mean, I'm not going to try to wipe out anybody," I quickly add. "But from the perspective of someone willing to go that far—"

Nathan tenses up behind me; he wants me to stop talking about what I will and won't do with our power. That becomes crystal clear when he interrupts me. "How do we explain the reason for Tara's trip? The Hierophant knows that we're not running the pack right now, but nobody else does. What reason would the queen's sister have to visit London, if not on business with the Greater London pack?"

"And how does it look to have the queen's remaining

sister visiting the Greater London pack when the Toronto pack is already touchy about them?" I hope Nathan recognizes the subtle scolding in my tone. People are touchy because *he* joined the two packs. And because he did it without clearing it with the council.

"A sightseeing trip?" Xiao suggests. "It's all I've been able to think up. It's easy enough to explain to the Hierophant that she's going to check on the status of things with the London pack on Your Majesties' behalf, and I don't believe the pack is all that concerned with Lady Tara's day-to-day."

"It would make sense that she might need time away, after..." Nathan clears his throat and avoids mentioning Clare's death and my family's banishment. "But it's too dangerous for her to stay at Wyrding House."

"It's too dangerous for her to *not* stay at Wyrding House," I argue. "If the Hierophant thinks she's running the pack right now, he's going to wonder why she went to London if it's not on official business."

"But the thralls—" Xiao began.

"You're a thrall," I remind her. "And there's no reason they should think you're disloyal to them. Not that you're disloyal to the thralls here, I didn't mean—"

"No, I understand." She waves a hand. "My loyalties are supposed to be to my people, not to the werewolves I've sworn an oath to. They should have told us that our dedication to the thralls should supersede that oath, if they wanted us to behave that way."

"Your service is deeply appreciated," Nathan says, and there's more to it than the trite sentiment of a boss thanking his employee. He understands as well as I do the toll duty takes.

But I can only imagine how this must all affect Xiao,

who believed in the thralls' mission enough to swear that protection oath only to learn that the thralls want to destroy us. That she still abides by that vow she made suggests she deeply honors loyalty. What must she think of her people now? Her oath?

Her entire life has been a lie.

"The King and Queen have granted permission for Lady Tara to visit London, purely for tourism. That's what we'll tell the pack," Nathan says firmly. "The Hierophant can believe it's about normal pack operations."

"There isn't much time for her to make the trip." The full moon is bearing down on us, and it'll take her a day to travel there, another to travel back. "Who goes to London for just a couple of days?"

He considers. "Say it's a shopping trip, then. Not a sightseeing excursion. That will take less time. We'll say it's a gift from her sister, the queen."

"It's not unheard of for a queen to spend recklessly," I say with a snort of contempt. I don't like to bring up Nathan's former mistress but I'm still bitter enough that I can't resist the occasional opening to snipe about her.

He says nothing.

"Just remember to actually bring stuff back," I tell Xiao. "If it's a shopping trip, she needs to be seen returning with purchases."

"I'll see to it," Xiao promises.

"What excuse did you give for coming here early?" I ask, because I know the thralls are watching her—and us—like hawks.

"Prenatal vitamins. And literature from your physician." She goes to the bag by the door and unzips it, pulling out the items and tossing them onto the small table.

"I convinced them it's dangerous for you to be uneducated and unmedicated."

I laugh, though I probably do need to take my vitamins. Even werewolves need a little extra help getting through pregnancy.

"I also brought..." Xiao's voice trails off as she pulls something from the bag. It's a soft-sided, lunch sack style cooler. "These."

Since Nathan and I are bundled up, she reaches in and removes a plastic bag. Bubbles of clear show through the blood inside wherever the plastic touches itself above the raw human hearts.

"For the full moon," she says.

"Ah." Nathan sounds sheepishly embarrassed. "We appreciate them, but without the thralls' magic, they're really unnecessary."

"You have the black moonstone," Xiao says.

I turn a little in Nathan's arms to see his face and judge his expression. I know that mine is hopeful. "We do have those. There's no reason we shouldn't turn at the full moon."

"No reason, except that our pack won't be turning," he says grimly.

"Your pack isn't here," Xiao says flatly.

"And our pack may have been trying to kill us ever since you took the throne," I add. "You don't owe them anything."

"I'm their king, whether they like me or not. And I vowed to lead them." His jaw tightens.

Oh, so you give a shit about vows all of a sudden? I want to snap, but I've already permitted the ghost of his betrayal into the cabin with us. I can't banish it again if I won't stop invoking it.

"At the very least, they're rich in iron," Xiao says, slipping the bag back inside the cooler. "Don't waste them. It was a risk for me to even bring them."

This might be the first time Xiao has given us a direct order or even asked us to consider her feelings. At least, the first that I can remember.

"I promise, they won't go to waste," I say solemnly.

But Nathan and I aren't finished with the subject of turning at the full moon.

"There's one more thing," Xiao begins cautiously. "It's not my place to ask, so please forgive me. But if you could send your sister a message, it would ease her mind considerably."

My sister wants to hear from me? We were barely speaking before Nathan and I left Aconitum Hall. I'm not sure what I'll say in the message. *Sorry I murdered our sister?* "Yeah, no problem. Um. Do you have a pen?"

Xiao reaches into the backpack and produces a pen and a small notepad. My teeth chattering, I extricate my naked self from the blanket—Xiao has already seen everything, anyway—and go to the table. It's difficult enough to communicate my feelings through writing; having an audience patiently waiting for me to finish doesn't make it easier. Then, there's the issue of the mechanics. I pin the notebook to the table with my truncated forearm and once again regret thrusting my dominant hand into a werewolf's mouth.

"Do you want me to write it for you?" Nathan asks in an uncharacteristically quiet voice, like he's afraid of embarrassing me.

I shake my head and give him a smile. "I need to learn to do things on my own."

And Tara wouldn't trust anything that came from him, probably not even if Xiao swore she saw me dictate it.

I keep the message short: *We're all right. Focus on what's happening in Toronto. I'll be fine. I love you.* Because there's really nothing else to report.

As I finish writing, I hear Nathan chuckle. I look up and realize that my tongue has been determinedly poking out of the side out of my mouth as I concentrate. I quickly pull it back, and that just makes him laugh again.

"What?" I demand, folding the paper so Xiao won't see my childish handwriting.

He shakes his head. "You're cute."

Warmth spreads through my chest. He's called me beautiful; I know he desires me sexually, but "cute" seems more personal, somehow. "Cute" feels like he likes me.

Ugh, how gross is it to have a crush on my mate and feel weird about it? Why should I feel weird?

Because he's made it clear that he doesn't believe he can love someone. All I'm doing is hanging on to the hope that one day, we'll have something real. Something that has nothing to do with the binding or our political arrangement.

"Here," I say, handing Xiao the message. It feels like I'm saying goodbye to my sister all over again.

She takes it and tucks it into the pocket of her uniform. "I'll be back as soon as we return from London. It should be time enough for a real supply run by then."

I rush back to the warmth of the blanket and Nathan. I don't think I'm ever going to be warm again.

"Bring bacon," Nathan tells Xiao, a little too eagerly. Probably because he's eaten through most of our supply already. He eyes the bag of hearts. "And thank you for thinking of... that."

With a wordless nod, she turns and heads for the door. It takes everything in me not to grab onto her and beg her to take me back to Toronto.

"Maybe bring me something to do, too?" I ask in a small, embarrassed voice. "It gets a little boring here."

"There's a chess set in my study," Nathan suggests. I guess he's been pretty bored, too, if he wants to play chess with someone who doesn't know how.

"I'll see what I can do," she promises, and then she's gone. A few minutes later, we hear the plane's engine and its take-off from the water.

We're all alone again. In a wilderness that just tried to kill me.

CHAPTER 11
BAILEY

"It isn't that I don't believe you," Nathan tells me patiently. "It just seems unlikely, from what little I know about wolves."

"I know, but I know what I saw," I protest, still wrapped in the blanket beside the fire. After Xiao left, Nathan got up and dressed to bring in more firewood. I'm still recovering; the cabin swings from way too hot to bone-chillingly cold again and again, despite the roaring hearth.

"And I know I couldn't have pulled myself out. I was drowning, Nathan. The wolf saved me." Whether it's scientifically possible or not, I know what happened to me.

"A solitary wolf rescuing a human... it just doesn't seem possible." He stops himself and reconsiders. "Although, I suppose it's not that unheard of. It is one of the three pillars of our religion."

I rise to my knees, swaying a little. "Exactly! Lupa saved Romulus and Remus. She rescued them and created the foundation of a new society and—"

My voice sticks in my throat.

Nathan is similarly shocked at the meaning of the

words, but he recovers faster. "Your hand. Tyr. The thralls trying to recreate Ragnarök…"

"Trying to destroy us and create a new order," I finish for him. "Now, a wolf rescues me *and* our baby. What if… what if our mythology is more than tradition and religion? What if it's a roadmap out of this?"

"Lycaon fed his son to Zeus," Nathan reminds me. "I'm not willing to do the same, should that time come."

"No but… we've already condemned members of the pack to Lycaon's banquet." My stomach churns. Had that been what started this whole thing? Our reenactment of Lycaon's sins?

My head fills with images of the stone circle, the site of our pack's most sacred rituals. Lycaon. Fenrir. Lupa. The circle spins, slowly at first, then faster and faster, until I'm dizzy. No matter how hard I close my eyes, I can't get rid of the whirling feeling, even after I stop thinking about those stones.

"Bailey!" Nathan is suddenly kneeling at my side, steadying me. I blink and find that I've slumped over.

"I'm fine," I reassure him, though my vision still isn't quite clear. The cabin keeps shifting to the right, then snapping back and shifting again. I close my eyes and lean against him. "I'm just tired."

He lays me back on the mattress and pets my hair soothingly. "Just rest. That's all you need to do right now. You've had a hell of a day."

"I have," I agree sleepily, and drift off.

The next thing I know, it's night, and I'm outside. The deceptive, deadly meadow stretches out before me.

"I don't remember how I got here." Though I whisper, it echoes across the space and up into the boundless night sky. It's cold; I'm naked and I see my breath on the air, but I don't feel the temperature.

A swirling, ghostly light winds its way through the tall grass between me and the other side of the forest. Spectral wolves, translucent blue and shimmering, prowl toward me, streaks of glittering illumination falling on the ground. When the spirits are near enough to touch, they vanish, but their trail remains.

Excited heat rises in me, from my very core. Primal longing draws me onto the path. I know the land is dangerous, but the ache low in my belly demands I move forward, follow the twinkling lights that disappear behind me with every footstep.

There's no going back now.

Has there been? My own voice echoes in my head, twined with another, one I don't recognize. *Have you been able to turn back ever since the moment you became a wolf?*

"A werewolf," I answer aloud, in that same, dual voice.

Only the other voice, a deep one that wraps my brain in sinuous silver threads, answers me: *A wolf.*

They emerge from the tree line ahead. White wolves, their coats shining in the light of the moon that shouldn't yet be full, waiting for me with eyes that flash an unearthly silver. I don't have any reason to be afraid of them. They won't hurt me.

I find myself standing before them much sooner than I anticipated. Did I run? My bare feet didn't feel the ground. They don't feel the prick of pine needles under my soles as I fall into the line of wolves that leads me deeper into the forest. The blue light surrounds us, darting around us, circling me and covering my body in a sheer coating of ethereal glow that winks like millions of tiny diamonds.

There's a life behind me, a cabin by a lake, a kingdom in a human city, but none of that matters now. The only thing that exists for me is this forest, the incongruously full moon through the branches overhead, the pack that leads me deeper into the dark woods. With each step I take, the aching anticipation grows. My thighs are slick, my nerves aflame. I want. So deeply. I want as I've never wanted before.

The trees thin at a small, rocky clearing. I wind between standing stones more ancient than those in my previous life, the ones I can only vaguely remember now. In the center, a larger, flat boulder serves as a kind of altar. I know that's why it's there. For worship of ancient spirits long forgotten.

To worship our queen, that sensuous voice whispers.

The wolves encircle the space and sit back on their haunches, watching. Waiting for me to do something.

Then he emerges.

I know him from his voice in my head, without him speaking. I know him. I've always known him.

He's not in human form, not fully werewolf. Towering, with broad shoulders, he strides into the circle. His face is human, he walks on two legs, but snow-white wolf's ears rise from his head. His silky white hair falls in a shimmering curtain down his back, and downy fur covers the pale skin of his human hands and arms, his werewolf's legs and paws. A human's chest and abs give him the look of an alabaster statue; his tail destroys that illusion of civilization. He is my kind, my werewolf kin, and yet nothing like us at all.

Without making a conscious decision to do so, I find that I've climbed onto the stone altar. I push up on my hands—my *hands!* — my heart beating so fast and so loud it fills the circle with the sound of drums. He prowls toward me, eyes a blank silver that should frighten me. Instead, my thighs fall open and I reach for him.

He hesitates at the end of the altar, staring down at me as if in disbelief. I'm here. I'm finally here, I'm finally ready for him. He's been waiting all this time.

His cock stands out, impossibly huge, glistening with pre-cum, and I take in a shuddering breath. I want all of him, hard, rough, desperate. I lock eyes with him, press my thighs tight together in a helpless, soundless plea.

Take me. You've waited so long.

I've waited, too, without knowing. Maybe I've been waiting for this, for him, since the moment I *could* want this. His hand trembles as he reaches out to touch me. There's no movement at all before he's on top of me, his cock prodding at my sopping opening. I grip his arms, nails sinking into his thick, soft fur, and he spears into me, stealing my breath on a wave of pleasure more intense than anything I've ever felt. He withdraws, growls, bites down on my shoulder, his teeth and cock penetrating not just my skin and my cunt, but every cell of my body, every memory I've ever made, every moment in my life that has been a journey to this.

To him.

The urgency between us is unleashed and runs through our veins, flows through me into him and back. I squeeze him with my knees and my pussy, arch into him, try to fill myself more. He hammers into me, howls above me, and I feel him erupt deep inside, bathing my cunt with the liquid aphrodisiac that sets my body alight.

I go up in flames. I *am* flame. The fire deep in my core bursts to consume me, ravages the landscape of my nervous system, sweeps away every pleasure I've ever known and replaces it with his touch, his seed inside me. I explode from the heat of my release.

"Bailey!"

I hear a voice from somewhere far off. I know who it is, but it takes me a moment to find the name, the face.

The heat is gone, replaced by cold that makes my teeth chatter. I open my eyes, dimly aware of the sky above me and the ground beneath me. I focus on the blades of grass beside my face, the frost that tints them silver in the light of the no longer full moon.

"Bailey!"

Nathan gathers me up in his arms, and every running step he takes jostles my bones.

"Come on." He slaps my cheek lightly. "Open your eyes. Come on, Bailey."

Then, softer, "Please. Please."

And a small, strangled, "No."

It breaks my heart. I have to respond to him, though ice is in my every cell. I stir a little against him, against the burning bare skin beneath my cheek.

"Wake up, Bailey. Please. Come on. Come on, baby, not like this. Not like this." He kisses my forehead, and another small, helpless sound escapes him.

"Are you crying?" I mumble, and his body jolts with shock.

"Bailey?" His voice is full of disbelief.

"Who else would I be?" My teeth chatter through the sentence, but with every word, things become clearer. "What—"

"You got up. I didn't hear you. And when I woke, you were missing." He kisses my head again. "I thought I lost you."

"I was dreaming." It was so vivid. So real. I can still feel the wolf over me, inside of me, and I shiver.

"If you're going to start sleepwalking, I'm going to have

to tie you down," Nathan half-heartedly jokes, his voice thick.

I tilt my face up to look at him, and through my hazy vision, I see tears on his face.

"You can't keep almost freezing to death. This is twice in one day," he scolds me with a nervous, relieved laugh.

"I promise," I tell him, and instantly regret it. Because the more I regain my senses, the more I doubt that any of it was a dream.

CHAPTER 12
TARA

There was a time in my life when the thought of a no-holds-barred shopping excursion to London would have been a dream come true. Though we were comfortable enough, my mate always kept a tight leash on the bank cards, demanding that I justify every purchase, right down to the last tampon. A limitless splurge on designer clothing—from human designers, no less—would never have happened. He probably would have smacked me for even daydreaming.

I don't miss that.

I'm not as psyched for the London trip as I would be if it weren't for subterfuge. And if I didn't have to stay in Wyrding House.

"It's not so bad," Xiao tries to assure me as she pulls our loaned car over beside a building with a facade that could be right out of *Sweeney Todd*. "It looks so much better on the park side."

"And the inside, I hope." I hate being here, after what happened to my sister. But, as Xiao pointed out numerous times on our flight, *I'm* not the one carrying the magic, world-ending baby. It's unlikely anyone will try to murder me.

I glance over at Xiao as she turns off the engine. Her expression is her normal calm, neutral mode. As long as she's with me, I'm sure of my safety. She would die for my sister, and I have no doubt she would die for me, too.

I just hope it doesn't come to that.

"We'll go in and drop off our things," Xiao says casually. "Then we'll take a walk in the park."

"I don't know, I'm pretty tired." Isn't she? We've both been on a plane—okay, a private jet—for what felt like an eternity. I get that she's tough, but doesn't she need a rest, too?

But then she gives me a pointed look and touches a finger to her ear for just a fraction of a second. "We'll take a walk in the park."

"I could stretch my legs," I agree, remembering the warnings she gave me while we stood on the noisy airfield. Wyrding House is full of ways to eavesdrop. She doesn't trust the car or the plane, either.

The door to Wyrding House is shockingly close to the sidewalk. It feels like just anyone in the city could step right in. The entryway from the street isn't impressive; the tile floor is badly in need of repair and the narrow hallway beyond the musty foyer is dark. But we emerge into a sprawling, high-ceilinged room that just screams Pemberly.

"This is incredible!" I follow a swirling line of black marble that twines with another graceful, looping vein of pink. It's a design of ribbons that radiates out in fanciful spokes from a central medallion, each tail leading off to one of the sets of double doors around the room. Early morning sunlight streams in through tall French doors with more windowpanes than I care to count, each set topped with cheerful half-circles of matching glass. I glance up at a ceiling that would give the Sistine Chapel a run for its money.

"This belongs to Nathan and Bailey?" I haven't envied my sister's position until right this second. "I can see why Nathan wanted to be king of London."

Xiao is busy directing the thrall who carries our bags up the curved staircase. "Put them in the royal suite, please."

"The royal suite is... unsuitable for visitors," a voice says behind her, and I take a step back as a male thrall in old-fashioned livery emerges from the shadows we entered through. His tall, thin face makes me think of haunted houses and his voice the ghosts that lurk in them. "Due to the... incident."

An uncharacteristic flicker of disgust crosses Xiao's face. "I understand."

I don't, but I'll make her fill me in when we're outside. All I know is that there was some kind of attack. It sounds like details are necessary.

"We have other rooms that will suit," the butler says. He clears his throat and I expect cobwebs to come out.

I stand up a little straighter, though I'm not sure why I care if a thrall judges my posture. "Of course, you do. But they need to be adjoining. Due to the unfortunate circumstances of my sister's last visit. I'm sure you understand."

"Certainly, my lady." The butler nods to the thrall waiting on the landing, then turns his attention back to us. "I'm afraid we're also without a housekeeper, at present. I currently oversee all of her former duties. After you've had some time to settle in, we can discuss the menu for your visit. In the meantime, would a light breakfast be acceptable?"

"I think we'll go out for breakfast, thank you..." I say cheerfully, ending my sentence on a long pause to indicate that he hasn't given us his name.

His gray eyebrows lift. "Jameson, my lady."

"Thank you, Jameson," I say with a nod, then turn to Xiao. "Shall we freshen up and hit the town?"

I can tell from his even stiffer demeanor that Jameson is surprised at the informality.

"If that's your wish, my lady," Xiao replies, and the butler seems to relax a little.

"Show us to our rooms." I don't add please; back in Toronto, the thralls look at me like I'm being sarcastic if I show even the slightest hint of gratitude.

Which is weird, considering they're technically Canadian.

I hope Xiao is paying attention on our walk through Wyrding House because I'm not. I'm too distracted by the antique furnishings and giant oil-on-canvas portraits. But it's dark and gloomy upstairs, like the haunted mansion I imagine Jameson was born and raised and probably died in, because I'm not certain he isn't a specter, himself.

"My lady," he says, stopping beside a set of double doors. One of them stands open, and he holds out his arm to invite us inside.

The room isn't as modern as the ones back in Aconitum Hall, and not as big as the suite Clare and I shared. The high ceiling has lost a touch of plaster here and there, but the furnishings look comfortable and clean. Pink satin in alternating vertical stripes of lighter and darker hues cover the walls and clash with the horrible burgundy canopy over the bed. I have a feeling no decorators have seen this interior in a *while*.

Xiao enters and I watch as she assesses the situation

from top to bottom with her eyes. She follows it up by moving to check behind the door, drapes, in the soot-stained fireplace and the massive mahogany wardrobe.

Jameson, clearly unnerved by her open inspection, motions to a door that stands ajar to another bedroom. "Your quarters are this way, thrall."

The derision in his voice stuns me. They're both thralls; what's his problem with her?

If his dismissal bothers her, Xiao doesn't show it. "Who has the keys to these rooms?"

"I do," he informs her curtly.

"Anyone else?" she counters, and when he doesn't immediately answer, she adds, "Were they open before we arrived? How did our bags get brought up?"

"*Your* bags did not," Jameson clarifies. "Her ladyship's were brought here by the thrall you saw on the stairs. There was no need for a key because we don't treat Wyrding House like a fortress."

"If you did, maybe there wouldn't have been an attack on the king and queen the last time they were here." The silence that follows her statement is more cutting than the words themselves.

After a tense moment, Jameson produces a ring of keys from inside his jacket. They look like a prop from a wild west sheriff costume. He unclips the ring and slides two from it, handing both to Xiao.

"Are these the only copies?" she asks as she takes them. She doesn't look at him at all.

"Yes, so don't lose them." Jameson's chest puffs up. "It will make housekeeping matters inconvenient, of course, if staff is denied access."

"I can pick up my own room," I tell him, because I can't think of a badass way to put him off the way Xiao did. "I was used to doing it before my sister became queen."

"If that will be all, then?" Jameson asks with a stiff bow. I nod and he leaves us, closing the door behind him.

Xiao immediately slides the key in the ancient lock and turns it.

"What's up with you?" I ask, following her as she goes into the second, smaller bedroom to lock us in here, too.

"This place freaks me out," she says as the lock thunks. Then, she sets off on an investigation of her own quarters.

"It's kind of spooky, but wasn't it a werewolf that attacked Bailey here last time?" My low-level sense of dread increases as I note Xiao's agitation. I know I'm in a dangerous position, but I didn't realize this level of paranoia was necessary.

"We don't know how she carried the plan out. Which members of the household were involved. And—" Xiao pauses to check the window latches and narrow her gaze on the vines outside. "—the new guy in charge doesn't seem to care for thralls."

"Despite being one?" I hope I would have noticed the difference between a thrall and a werewolf.

But Xiao doesn't respond to that question. Instead, she heads straight for my bedroom and lifts the end of a small, fragile-looking settee, dragging it to the end of my bed.

"What are you—"

"Fixing our sleeping arrangements," she cuts me off. "I'm not going to be all the way over there. I can sleep at the foot of your bed. That way, I'll know if someone gets near you during the night."

"That's not really necessary," I say. "If anything, it's going to make me more nervous."

She drops the end of the sofa and straightens, fixing me

with her usual blank expression. "Nervous is better than dead."

I can't argue with that. I help her move the sofa.

———

Wyrding House really does look better from the park. In fact, it looks nicer and nicer the further we get from it. If we never go back, it will look even better, though I know that's not an option.

Greater London already knows we've arrived; the council sent me a gift basket and suggestions for a bunch of local, werewolf-owned businesses. I know I'll have to be spotted at one, at the very least. I keep an eye on my phone as Xiao and I stroll through historic Hyde Park, to make sure we stay in the right direction.

"So, the plan is, breakfast at Loup L'Anglais, then some shopping at all the right places to be seen, and tonight..." I trail off so Xiao can fill me in.

"I know the location of the magician's club, but I wish we could meet him on neutral ground," she muses, eyes straight ahead. "If you make a dinner reservation somewhere that isn't owned by the pack, it will be easier to sneak away."

"I don't think we should sneak, at all." I've given some thought to how our arrival must have looked to everyone in Wyrding House. We showed up like we were anticipating trouble. "We just say I want to go clubbing, then we go to clubs."

"We could be followed," Xiao argues.

"We could be followed, anyway. But we're kind of acting like we *should* be followed."

Xiao tilts her head and gives me a look from the corner of her eye.

"I'm not saying you're doing something wrong," I add. "I'm just saying, maybe Greater London would buy that I'm just the queen's younger sister, out living her best life in the wake of her mate's banishment if you didn't make our suspicion so conspicuous. And frankly, I could use some of that."

"Some of..."

"Some of living my best life," I say with a shrug. "I've never been out like this, in a major city, all on my own."

"You live in Toronto," Xiao reminds me wryly.

"I know. But something as simple as choosing where I got to eat breakfast? Walking around on my own? That stuff didn't happen for me. Not with my parents in charge, and definitely not when Josh was in charge of me." Maybe he's still in charge. I don't know what happens when one mate is banished and the other one isn't.

Xiao is quiet, thoughtful.

That just makes me talk more. "Look, what I mean is, why don't I just run around like the brakes are totally off? They kind of are, right? As long as I'm behaving like spoiled, erratic nobility, people can't think I'm up to subterfuge."

"But if you're reckless, that makes my job much more difficult," Xiao says. "I'm not averse to difficulty. I like a challenge. But if I fail at keeping you safe—"

"You won't. I know you won't." Why do I feel like I'm begging to be allowed to go to a sleepover?

"I suppose it would soften my request for the keys and my insistence on being so near you," she thinks aloud. "If I'm watching over you because you're reckless and irresponsible."

"Exactly." I like the idea of being the wild, uncontrollable member of the royal family. "This might be fun, Xiao. You know, fun? The thing people have when their faces aren't like yours all the time?"

To my shock, she laughs. It's so rare to see her break form. And after the laugh, she keeps smiling, a dazzling smile that I wish I could take a photo of, so I could look at it later and feel the same warmth that spreads through me right now.

"I have fun," she argues with a shake of her head.

Emboldened by her response, I needle her a little more. "Like when? You're always working. What could you possibly do for fun?"

She hesitates.

"Let me guess," I go on. "Your idea of fun is going to the gun range to practice being an amazing shot. Or no, working out in your home gym so you can be in peak physical condition all the time."

She arches an eyebrow. "You think I'm in peak physical condition."

My cheeks flush and I look away. I don't know why.

"You're wrong on both counts," she says.

"Then answer my question."

"I don't mix my private life with my work life," she says, becoming all-business once again. "Plus, it's more fun to know that you're trying to figure me out. And that you'll probably be unsuccessful."

"Oh, so that's what you do for fun," I say with a laugh. "You torment your employers."

"You're not my employer," she reminds me. As if I need reminding. I know that everything I have now, from the bodyguard at my side, to the pillow I'll put my head on tonight, is owned by someone else. The money I'm about to spend is someone else's, the clothes I'm wearing right now belong to the crown. Everything I am, have, or do is somehow connected to my sister.

I want something of my own.

"Tonight, let's really go out," I say suddenly. "Not just as cover to visit this magician. Let's go out and dance and drink and have a good time. Like friends."

Xiao opens her mouth to object.

I don't give her the chance. "I'm serious. Also, a little desperate. I know you're not my friend and you're just getting paid to be here to protect me, but tonight can you at least pretend?"

With a long sigh, Xiao asks, "Will it stop you from actually making my job more difficult?"

"You never know." It's not exactly a promise to behave myself, but I'm not sure I actually have it in me to go wild on my own.

Xiao stops walking and looks back toward the house. Finally, with the grimace of someone who thinks they're making a huge mistake, she relents. "Fine."

I don't assure her that she won't regret it. I just hope nothing happens to us to *make* her regret it.

CHAPTER 13

TARA

If pretending to go clubbing is anything like actually going clubbing, I've been missing out. The music, the lights, the very expensive drinks, it all feels so reckless and human. We've been to two clubs already and my feet are killing me, but Xiao thinks we'll be less conspicuous hopping from location to location, rather than starting the night at the human magician's club. So, we've been dancing and drinking—or, in Xiao's case, pretending to drink—for hours.

Xiao's a surprisingly good dancer. Or maybe not surprisingly; from what I've heard, she's like some kind of fighting genius with superhuman moves. I'm sure that translates to other movement.

"We should go," she says over the noise of the throbbing music. "I haven't seen anyone following us."

"Oh. Right." For a moment, I forgot this wasn't a fun night out. Knowing that we're about to go into a den of human magicians throws a cold bucket of nerves over me. I follow Xiao as she winds us through the crowd, though if she made a direct shot toward the door, people would have gotten out of the way. She's not easily overlooked. I've never seen her out of her form-fitting-but-unisex security uniform with its padding and pockets. Tonight, she's wearing the outfit we bought specifically for this job, and she's turning so many heads, she might as well be a chiropractor. I was shocked when she picked out a fluorescent pink fishnet body stocking and a skintight, black pleather dress with the sides split entirely open except for the thin cord holding it barely together. Her usually braided hair is up in a silky sleek high ponytail that showcases her sharp cheekbones and devastating eye makeup.

"Did I tell you how hot you look?" I ask, stumbling on my higher than usual heels.

"Yes," she says as we exit the club and walk past the appreciative gazes of people in the line. "But you have imbibed several cocktails since the last time."

"Oh." That might explain the wobbly shoes.

"I told you to go easy."

"Werewolves don't get drunk as easily as humans do." I'm sure I don't need to tell her that. Judging from her raised eyebrow, she knows, and she also knows that I drank plenty to make a werewolf tipsy.

We make it to the car, and I go for the driver's side, until Xiao clears her throat loudly.

"Okay, that's not because I'm drunk," I argue, rounding the front of the car. "I'm not used to right-hand drive vehicles."

She just smirks and gets in. "You don't look bad, yourself, you know," she says as we pull onto the street.

I'm not sure if she means that or she's just saying it. I've felt a little conservative the whole time we've been out, in my black-lace-overlaying-nude-satin corset dress. "I think it looks like Victorian bondage. But for the record, I wasn't fishing for compliments. You don't have to give me one."

"Do I seem like the kind of person who gives compliments when none are warranted?"

She has a point.

We drive for a long time in silence, Xiao growing more and more tense with every kilometer.

"I guess we were in the wrong part of town," I quip. London is less of a town, more of a region, according to maps, many smaller cities folded and clumping and overlapping.

"The club is in the wrong part of town." There's no humor in Xiao's voice as we drive into an admittedly seedier area than we were in before. "Watch yourself in there. There won't be just one magician. Where there's one, there's an infestation. They'll recognize that you're a werewolf."

"And what will happen to me then?" Will they shoot me? Do a spell on me? The danger of the situation I've chosen to put myself in strikes me suddenly. It was all fun and games when the subterfuge and espionage was about dancing and drinking. Now, it's all very real.

That sense of harsh reality intensifies when we pull up in front of The Underground, a club marked out from its otherwise industrial surroundings by a sickly yellow-green sign that mimics the public transportation logos I've seen around the city. There's no line at the door. It's not as exclusive or desirable as the clubs we've just been to, and frankly, it makes sense that it's not. The place looks dirty, rundown, the kind of grimy that suggests one could get a nasty infection whether or not one gets stabbed by a fellow patron.

"My sister came here?" I peer at the building through the windshield and resist the urge to swipe my palm over the glass. It's not going to make the place look any cleaner. "*Nathan* came here?"

"Apparently," Xiao confirms. "Now, you're going in there. You're just as brave as both of them."

I didn't realize that was a concern until she said it, but wow, I really needed that pep talk. Because I don't feel brave.

"Come on." Xiao claps her hand against my back, jarring my whole body with the force of her emotional support. "Let's get in there and find the magician."

As we cross the street, a previously unseen bouncer emerges from the shadow of the doorway. He's built just like the building, all square and plain. He holds out a beefy hand and tilts his bald, brown head. "Members only."

Xiao scoffs. "That's a new rule. We're off to see the wizard, if you don't mind."

The guy looks both of us over, then settles his gaze on Xiao. "Your kind isn't welcome."

"Hey!" I step in front of her, though I'm not sure what I think I'm doing. "That's racist!"

Then again, if a human is racist, do they even care? It seems like they would already know that about themselves.

"It's not her ethnicity at issue, lobo." He leans on the last word. "It's what she is. Thralls aren't allowed, even if they know the password."

I turn to Xiao. "Why didn't you tell me the password?"

"Because I wasn't planning to let you go into this shit heap without some protection." She says it to the bouncer, not to me.

"This is ridiculous." I press my fingertips to my now-aching temples. The problem with having a werewolf's ability to metabolize alcohol is that it wears off faster. We don't usually get hangovers, but I'm also not usually jet-lagged and exhausted and stressed out when I'm drinking. "I'm off to see the wizard. If anyone on this sidewalk has a problem with that, fight each other."

I march past both of them and up the cracked cement steps into the loud, dark club.

But I really hope Xiao doesn't fight the bouncer. I don't know how that would look to this mysterious magician guy.

The club is less a "club" and more of a warehouse with obnoxious black-light paint on the walls and cheap diner chairs leaking stuffing from wounds in their vinyl seats. The tables are visibly wobbly, leaning all sorts of directions, and any more substantial furniture is pushed to the perimeter of the room to maximize dance space. There's a bar, and a pretty bartender with a giant afro, but she doesn't seem all that eager to interact. She leans boredly on the bar top, the dark skin on her arms embellished with lime-yellow swirls of black light paint and surveys the crowd through eyes made up with the same color shadow. Her lips are painted with fluorescent blue and all I can think of is those women who got poisoned by radium at the turn of the twentieth century.

I make my way over and she greets me with a sharp, "What do you want?"

"I'm off to see the wizard?" I don't know if the password will work twice.

She flicks her long nails, blue-white in the club's glow, and a ball of flame materializes in her hand for just a second before transforming into a cigarette. She lifts it to her lips, and it lights automatically as she takes a puff. Exhaling directly into my face, she says, "You're going to have to be more specific, lobo."

"Okay, first of all? I know what that means." And I'm

tired of being called a wolf like it's some kind of insult. "Second, I'm here on business from King Nathan and Queen Bailey of the Toronto Pack. This guy knows them. He helped them out before."

A grin splits her face. It's not a comforting expression. "Oh, I heard all about how he helped. Stay here. Don't stink up the place, dog."

I roll my eyes. "Thanks. That's so much better."

When she leaves through a swinging service door, I turn back to the room. The bartender just performed magic openly in a club full of humans, and nobody seemed to notice or care. Which leads me to believe that Xiao is right; the place is infested with human magicians. I keep my senses sharp and survey the room for other signs of magic. It doesn't take me long to find them. The patrons dancing, covered in glow-paint? They're wearing designs of primal whorls and even our sacred runes. The light effects displayed on the wall behind the DJ are glowing musical notes that rise from his hands as he motions them over the equipment he never actually touches. But I didn't *see* any of this when I first entered. Maybe a non-magical human mind would only see what I first saw.

It's camouflage right out in the open.

A hand falls on my shoulder, and I jump, nearly knocking over the bar stools in my immediate vicinity. I scramble to right them before I look up.

If someone asked me to describe what a human magician looked like, I would not have described this man. He's much younger than I expected, probably in his thirties, shirtless and ripped from the waistband of his low-slung jeans to his broad shoulders. Contrary to the password, there's not a wizard's beard in sight.

"You're the third werewolf to walk in here this year," he

says, the words dripping with hostility. "What makes your kind think you're welcome here?"

I draw myself up straight. "I'm not worried about being welcome. I'm worried about the fate of my pack."

He holds my gaze and I hold his right back, and it becomes an interminably long staring contest. Finally, his mouth bends in a reluctant smile. "That was dramatic of you."

I almost snap at him but remember that I'm here to ask *him* a favor. So, I say nothing.

He puffs out a long exhale, then jerks his thumb over his shoulder. "Come on back, I guess. But that's not a contract. I'm going to hear you out. That's it."

If that's all I can get, I'll take it.

CHAPTER 14

TARA

If I thought the club was grimy, it's got nothing on the disgusting room the magician leads me to. It's a combination alchemical workshop and drug den, from the looks of it, with arcane symbols painted on the floor and bongs displayed alongside potion bottles on shelves of dubious stability. The black light motif is still present, as are two women who stumble out of the bathroom in a daze.

"Sorry," the magician says, giving me a lecherous grin. "I was entertaining."

I doubt it. He strikes me as a much, much cooler version of my mate, all cocky swagger and self-assurance. I know for a fact that confidence leads to some pretty lackluster sex.

"Bye, Jonah," one of the women says, wiggling her fingers at him. They both leave, laughing—at him, I assume —and the shade over the window in the door clatters.

"Jonah," I say, confirming that's his name.

He nods. "And you are?"

"Tara. *Lady* Tara." The noble title doesn't feel as silly when I'm wielding it over someone I don't respect. Maybe that's why Nathan is so comfortable with "His Majesty." I know Jonah won't be impressed by my standing in the pack, but I want him to know that I *have* that standing. "I'm the sister of the queen."

"The sister who still has a head." He scrutinizes me for a reaction that I don't give. "Can I get you something to drink?"

I *am* thirsty, and turning down hospitality goes against everything I was raised to believe, so I say, "Sure."

"All I've got is Red Bull. But you look like you could use one." He takes a can from what's probably a pre-war refrigerator and hands it to me. Gesturing to a ratty sofa, he says, "Have a seat."

I do, reluctantly. My feet ache and he's right, some caffeine won't hurt me. I take a long drink and put the can on the TV tray beside the arm of the couch. I have to push aside several other half-drunk cans to set mine down.

Jonah drops onto the other end of the couch and the creaky springs threaten to launch me like I'm on a trampoline. He kicks his sandal-clad feet up centimeters from me, and I resist the urge to shrink away. "So. What can I do for you?"

"I'm here on the behest of the King and Queen. You helped them discover the binding mark put on them by the thralls," I say.

"I remember." He reaches for a pack of cigarettes lying on the back of the couch and slides one out. "I assume they still haven't figured out what it's all about?"

"We're working on it. But we need your help." There, I said it. I put it right out in the open. He can either choose to help us, or not.

"Help doing what, exactly?" he mumbles as he lights up.

"Well, first, we need help preventing the pack from

turning at the full moon." I wave away the smoke he exhales in my direction.

His brow furrows and he shrugs. "Just don't change. Don't take part in the ceremony. Come on, even I know that. Give me one that's believable."

"It is believable. We can't just *not* change. The thralls will know that we're suspicious of them. But we can't change because—"

"Because you'll be vulnerable to them. I get it." He pauses. "You know what I've always wondered?"

"I couldn't even begin to imagine." *Careful*, I warn myself. *You're asking him to help you.*

The snark only seems to amuse him. "Why don't you guys just kill the thralls? They're subservient to you, right? If they're a danger, why not just cull them?"

"Because that would be an awful thing to do!"

"You've done it before. In the past." He's not wrong. "I think you all just enjoy having your built-in servants."

"I think you're right," I admit. "But we put an end to thrall culling a long time ago. It's medieval, it belongs in the middle ages."

He shrugs. "Agree to disagree. My world would be a lot simpler if there were no thralls. Think about it."

Think about it? I do. I think about Xiao waiting outside for me.

"The thralls protect us," I argue. "My bodyguard—who was not allowed in your exclusive and very posh little night club—is waiting outside for me right now. She wouldn't hesitate to put her life before mine."

"Ever wonder why that is?" He arches a brow and takes another drag. "Look, I'm not going to get paid to change your mind, but the thralls use you to gain their magic powers, their extended life spans. Their entire way of being depends on werewolves tolerating them. Do you want to know why the culls stopped?"

"Because they were barbaric."

"Because *they* stopped them. They learned their place and put you in yours, without any of you being the wiser. You're just lucky that your sister and her husband were smart enough to figure out that you're all being played. And the binding? The baby? That's the next step."

"A thrall figured it out," I snap, and wish I hadn't.

He takes another inhale off the cigarette and doesn't bother to direct the smoke away from me. "Then you're lucky that the thrall in question was too dumb to keep secrets."

"Or too noble." I hate that he's talking about Xiao this way. It's irrational, I guess; he doesn't know her personally and doesn't even know that she's the thrall he's talking about. But I don't like the implication that by doing the right thing, she's some kind of sucker or a fuck-up.

"So, what do you want from me?" He gestures around the room with the cigarette. "You want me to stop the thralls from changing you all into werewolves. How do you suggest I do that?"

"With your magic?" I scoff. "You're the one who's this all-powerful wizard, right?"

"Aww. That's cute." He snorts a laugh. "I'm not all powerful, sweetheart. I don't have a whole race of mythic beasts I can siphon magic from. There's no way I'm going to be able to out-magic a bunch of thralls."

An idea occurs to me. A terrible one. "What if you did have a mythic beast you could siphon power from?"

His eyebrows raise. "You got a gryphon in your pocket?"

"I'm a werewolf. Nathan and Bailey—the King and the

Queen, I mean—are. And there are at least two other werewolves who are working on this with us." I shouldn't be offering them up to him, but I can deal with that fallout later. "I might even be able to get a few others."

He shakes his head. "We're talking about millennia of stored up magic here. Dating all the way back to Ancient Rome. You think I can stick a straw in your magic field like you're a Capri Sun and match that?"

"Then get your friends to help. Look, we're offering to pay—"

"And I don't pay for things with my life." He sits up and leans forward, directly into my personal space. For a moment, I'm terrified he's going to try to kiss me or grope me or something, but he crushes out the half-burned cigarette on the TV tray and sits back. "I can't help you."

I wave the wisps of smoke away from my face, coughing. "Fine. Don't help us. But at least point us in the right direction."

"There isn't a magician alive who would take this job," he warns.

I'm still coughing, but I manage to wheeze out, "I don't care. Just tell us where to look. Do something. Unless you want the thralls to become even more powerful than they already are."

That strikes a nerve with him. I can tell, even though I'm practically dying from the smoke. I reach for the can of Red Bull and gulp it down, hoping to quench the fire in my throat.

"No, wait!" He dives for the can, and I jerk it back, recognizing too late the imprint of black lipstick on the rim.

"Oh, gross!" I drop the can and it spills across the floor. It doesn't look quite right; I don't remember ever having a drink that looked so... shimmery.

"Fuck." He dives both hands into his hair and casts a panicked look around the room. "We have to get you out of here."

"What? Why?" I press a hand to my chest. I'm not choking anymore, but warmth is spreading down my esophagus, into my stomach. Weird warmth.

"Trust me, you don't want to be here when what's going to happen to you happens to you." He grips my arm and propels me toward the door.

His touch is like being electrocuted and tickled and having my back scratched all at the same time. My knees buckle.

"What the fuck is going on?" I've felt this way before. One time.

During the mating ceremony.

"I told you; I was entertaining." He hurries me down the stairs that lead into a warehouse-type room. "It's an aphrodisiac. Made from... you know..."

I do know, and I want to throw up. "Did I just drink werewolf cum?"

"Where's your bodyguard?" Jonah asks, hitting a big red button that causes a huge door to roll up. The second it clears waist height he ducks me under.

My pulse pounds in my ears and between my thighs and I can't help myself. I slam him against the brick wall of his club and start tearing at his fly.

"Stop, stop," he orders, somehow managing to overcome my superior strength to force my hands to my sides. "I'm not going to do that."

"Please," I whine, sinking my teeth into his throat. I have never needed to get fucked as much as I need it now. Even if it's with this disgusting human. Need rages through every cell and pounds directly into my clit. I ache, and I'll do anything to stop it.

"Hey!" Xiao races toward us, her hand on her hip, searching for a weapon she hasn't brought with her. "Get the fuck off of her!"

"Get *her* the fuck off of *me!*" Jonah shouts back.

She throws an arm around my shoulders, and I practically climb her. In frustration, I rip the front of my skirt up so I can grind my wet panties against her thigh. I don't care what's happening, who might see, where we are. I just need to come.

"What did you do to her?" Xiao tries to hold me at arm's length. I plunge my hand between my thighs, crying out in desperation. Why won't they help me? Don't they see I'm in agony?

"It was an accident. She drank out of the wrong— Look, she accidentally dosed herself. I didn't do it." He holds his hands up and backs away.

"Fucking werewolf cum," Xiao curses to herself. "Help me get her into the car."

I don't want to get into the car. I want to get under both of them.

Together, they manage to steer me down the alley to the waiting vehicle, while I paw at them both and beg them to fuck me.

"Look, I'm sorry this happened," Jonah says as Xiao tries to force me into the passenger seat. "I owe you."

"You think?" Xiao snaps.

"Let me find out what I can, and I'll bring you whatever info I can get," he promises.

"Hyde Park. Nine o'clock tomorrow morning, or I'll find you," she warns.

My fingers slide over my clit and I groan with relief,

trying to get my mouth on Xiao's neck as she straps me into the seatbelt.

"Nine o'clock," Jonah repeats. "Good luck."

My body is on fire and just touching myself should get me off instantly, but it doesn't. I almost get there, hold my breath, braced for what I know will be a shattering release, but it doesn't happen. I'm stuck right at the edge, unable to go over.

Xiao gets into the driver's seat and swats my hand away as I grope for her. She pulls the car onto the street, eyes straight ahead as we speed off, and asks herself more than me, "What are we going to do about this?"

CHAPTER 15

TARA

From some far-off point in the back of my mind, I'm aware of what's happening to me. I was accidentally dosed with werewolf cum. It won't last forever. Nobody has ever died from horniness.

But it *feels* like I'm going to die.

I cling to Xiao as she wrestles me into Wyrding House. We don't run into any servants, though all the lights in the main rooms are blazing. I lean heavily on her as we negotiate the stairs; every step I take is agony on my throbbing clit. I'm still so close, and somehow, getting closer. Whenever I think I'm about to explode with release, it moves further away.

It's like those scenes in horror movies where hallways get longer. Not that I've seen many horror movies. Or movies in general.

"Please," I gasp, my lips pressed to Xiao's neck. "Please."

I don't know what I expect her to do. As long as someone keeps touching me, as long as I can feel a body next to mine, as long as I can get *fucked*, I'll be fine.

I'll be fine, anyway. But I'm miserable and desperate and I just know that everything will be solved by sex.

Xiao pushes me away as we enter the bedroom, ordering tersely, "Sit down."

That snaps me a little bit back to reality, though the animal lust still swirls angrily inside me. *What am I doing? I can't keep propositioning my bodyguard! And she's a woman. Am I even into women?*

I watch her as she moves through the room in her tight pleather dress and pink body stocking. She's checking every point of egress to make sure I'm safe, and I'm checking out her ass like the most lawsuit prone employer to ever walk the planet.

Then again, I'm not really her employer. That's Nathan. That's my stupid brother-in-law who's gotten me into this mess. The asshole who's caused nothing but misery for me ever since he took over our pack.

My anger does nothing to ease the screaming tension in me, the clawing need, the pure, aching *want* that only seems to get worse the further away Xiao is from me. I have a brief, vivid hallucination of her holding me down, grinding her bare pussy on my thigh while we writhe naked together in my bed.

"Please," I whimper again, to no one in particular. I hike my skirt up high, hear a seam of the dress tear, and jerk my panties aside. The two fingers I plunge into my pussy do nothing but make me feel more empty, more of that unbearable *want.*

"It will wear off soon," Xiao says, locking all the doors and closing the curtains over the windows. "You'll just have to wait it out."

She doesn't look at me. She looks everywhere but at me,

and how can I expect anything different? How would I react if someone started fingering herself right in front of me. *I'd like to find out,* the chemical hold over my nervous system says.

"I'm going to die," I sob, even though I know it's not true.

"You're not going to die." She finally faces me and her eyes dart briefly to my hand between my thighs. *Yes. Look. Watch me do this filthy thing shamelessly in front of you.* Knowing that she's watching only increases the already unbearable level of desire in me and I moan.

"Please," I beg her.

"Please what?" she asks, tossing her hands up. "What do you want me to do about it?"

"I want... I..." My words falter on a long, pathetic whine as a nearing orgasm once again eludes me. "I don't know what I want."

Her jaw tightens. Her gaze drops between my legs again. I see her chest hitch, rising and falling more rapidly now. Her hands fist at her sides. "You won't want it later. Whatever you think you need? You'll end up regretting it."

"I don't care!" I shout. Sweat trickles down the back of my neck. "I want... I want..."

Her control snaps just as I realize she's struggling to maintain it. She hasn't been drugged. She knows exactly what she's doing as she strides across the room to me.

She leans over me, and I whisper, "Yes."

That's all it takes. She jerks me to the floor and falls on top of me, her mouth covering mine as her hand gropes down my body. I sink my fingers into her hard biceps and hold on, chanting, "Yes, yes, yes," with increasingly strangled breaths.

"Is this what you want?" she purrs beside my ear, her voice surprisingly gentle in contrast to the force with which she rams two fingers inside me. It's so much better, so much more effective than my own hand and I moan as those fingers curl up and press hard on my g-spot. Still, it's not enough. Her mouth finds my throat, her teeth graze over it and she asks again, "Is this what you want?"

And I realize... it's what *she* wants, too.

Her loss of restraint, her sudden change in demeanor, the relentless pump of her fingers inside me, none of that comes from an aphrodisiac.

She's giving into temptation that she's fought for a long time.

"My dress..." I say, tugging down a strap to free one of my breasts. Her mouth is on me in an instant, tongue swirling around my nipple. She lifts her head, and a long string of saliva stretches from her bottom lip to my skin. The sight alone makes me moan. She sits back on her knees, and I curl up to stay with her, but she pushes me flat and uses her free hand to rip my dress right down the middle, laying me completely bare except for the sopping scrap of lace panties twisted askew and plastered to my skin. Then, she falls on me again, her hand still working inside me as she laves her tongue over my nipple, between my breasts, scooting down over my belly. As she draws closer and closer to exactly where I need her to be, I moan loudly.

"Keep your mouth shut," she orders, and a renewed thrill races through me that has nothing to do with the aphrodisiac. "Or I'll shut it for you," she adds in warning.

"Yes, ma'am," I whimper.

She pushes my thighs wide apart and nuzzles her face against my mound, inhaling deeply in the damp brown curls there. "Fuck, I've wanted this for the longest time," she whispers to herself.

Her tongue finds my clit like wet electricity; I arch up from the floor and shout with relief. She raises her head and I reach for her, try to push her back down.

"I said be quiet," she snaps, and with a firm twist of her hand, the panties rip down both sides. She pulls them free and before I have time to object, she wads them up and forces them into my open, gasping mouth.

The taste of myself on the fabric and the way I gag as her fingers push too far back in my throat only make me want to get louder.

She goes back to work with her lips and tongue, sucking and teasing my clit while I writhe and make muffled pleas through the makeshift gag. It's a hellish loop: closer, closer, almost there, and nothing. Nothing but the suspense of need on the edge of unbearable pleasure, and she keeps going, hammering her fingers against that sensitive spot inside me, using the point of her tongue to flick my exposed clit while she holds its delicate hood captive between her lips. I hump against her face, embrace how out of control, how utterly feral the passion between us is in the moment.

Then, something changes. I feel it, all of those denied orgasms coiled deep in my pelvis, ready to spring free.

"I think," I mumble through the gag, cutting myself off with a high, desperate whine. "I think... this is..."

It.

My climax rages through me, seizing every muscle, freezing the breath in my lungs. My body bows up from the floor. My thighs tremble and spasm, my legs flail, drumming against her back. I buck and scream and the panties in my mouth do nothing to silence me as every orgasm I've been cruelly denied bursts, one after another, through my tortured body.

When the last of them takes me over, I howl, loud and long.

Xiao carefully slides her fingers from me and sits back on her heels. Her face is smeared with my juices, dripping, actually, but she doesn't wipe it clean.

Her hands tremble when she pulls the panty gag from my mouth.

"I'm..." She closes her eyes and looks away. "I'm sorry."

I push my sweat-soaked hair back from my forehead. The voice that comes out of me is barely a whisper; my throat sticks shut, and I cough a little as I try to say, "Don't be."

"Come on." She takes my hand to help me stand, then just scoops me up in her shockingly strong arms and takes me to my bed. I flop spread eagle and panting across the duvet and wait as she goes into the bathroom. I hear the water run and she returns with a glass for me.

She doesn't apologize again, and I'm grateful, sipping my water and watching her as she collects up my ruined dress and panties. I couldn't bear it if she apologized. Now that the effects of the aphrodisiac have worn off, I'm shocked at how I behaved with her.

I'm the one who should apologize.

All I can really do is embarrassingly offer, "Should I... you know. For you?"

She laughs ruefully. "No. Go to sleep."

Maybe the effect of the werewolf cum hasn't faded because a renewed flush of heat suffuses my body and I say, "It wouldn't be any trouble," in a timid, low tone.

Because I want to return the favor. I want whatever just happened to keep happening.

"Go to sleep," she repeats. "We have to rendezvous with the magician in the morning."

"Do we have a plan?" I ask with a yawn.

"Don't worry about it," she assures me, snagging the extra blanket folded neatly over the end of my bed. She flops down on the couch, pleather dress and all, and huddles under the blanket. "Go to sleep."

CHAPTER 16

TARA

The morning light brings a lot of awkwardness with it. I do my best to pretend that the events of the night before were just an uncomfortable sex dream, but every time I glance at Xiao, I think about how her hands felt on me. In me. How her mouth—

"Are you done?" she asks, nodding toward the plate I'm not touching because I'm too busy staring off into space.

"Hmm? Oh. Yeah. Just let me drain this coffee," I say, swallowing from my fifth cup.

"You drink more coffee than anyone I've ever seen," she muses, wiping her mouth.

We're eating our breakfast in a cheerful yellow room decorated with oil paintings of pastoral scenes. It's exactly the type of posh that my mother would love; the amount of wainscoting in our otherwise contemporary home was truly jarring.

I smile over the rim of my mug. "Our metabolism is different from yours. Trust me, this is still going to keep me barely awake."

"Well, after last night—" she cuts herself off and tosses

her napkin down. "Getting in late, staying out dancing. Drinking."

"Drinking werewolf cum," I blurt, and a sharp, shocked laugh bursts from her. And then I laugh, and then both of us are laughing, and it suddenly seems so absurd in hindsight.

"What were you so lost in thought about?" she asks. "Are you worried about meeting up with Jonah again?"

I shake my head and swallow a sip of coffee. It's still too hot to properly chug. "No. No, I was actually thinking about my mom. How tacky our house was. She was trying to cram too many styles into a single building."

"Oh." Xiao studies me a moment. "I thought you might be nervous about seeing him, after what he did to you."

"That was an accident." I realize I never explained to her how the whole thing went down. "I mixed up my drink with someone else's."

There's no need to explain the circumstances, though I am concerned that he might have spiked the drinks of those women I'd seen leaving. Then again, they seemed pretty psyched about whatever went down before I got there.

Disgust twists Xiao's features. "Humans are drinking werewolf... stuff?"

The fact that she can't say the word is oddly endearing. The bad-ass bodyguard is too prudish to say the word "cum," but had no trouble eating me out last night.

The entire encounter flashes through my mind on triple speed and I blink the images away. There was nothing polite or restrained about her when she dragged me to the floor and had her way with me.

The uncomfortableness that briefly dissipated returns. She clears her throat and adds, "Whatever the reason, I'm sorry that happened to you. No one deserves to lose their agency like that."

I wave my hand. I've never really had agency; my childhood was scheduled, my marriage arranged, my entire life decided for me by someone else for the good of the pack. "It's fine."

"It's not," she states firmly. "And what I did wasn't okay."

"What you did was totally okay!" I won't pretend like I didn't like it. *I liked it so much, I can't stop thinking about it,* I want to shout at her. *I want you to clear this fucking breakfast table and rip my clothes off on it.*

"You were under the influence of the potion. I shouldn't have taken advantage."

"You didn't take advantage. You helped me out. You took care of me when I was miserable." It hurts to think that what turned out to be one of the best nights of my life was awful for her. "Don't feel guilty about it. I don't."

"Why should you?" She scoffs. "The person who should feel guilty is the magician, and I'm sure he doesn't."

The grandfather clock in the corner warns us of the impending hour.

"Speaking of him," I say, dropping my own napkin and ruefully abandoning my cup, "I'm not sure what's happening today."

"We're meeting him in the park." Xiao stands and pats her side; the gun is there once again. "Follow my lead."

"I don't think you can... open carry." That's the term for it, isn't it? I don't know much about guns, aside from things in the rare television show or movie I was allowed to watch. "Isn't that going to get you in trouble?"

"Greater London has a long relationship with law enforcement here," she says, striding for the door. "Like I said, follow my lead. Whatever I do or say, you go along with it."

That's not much of a plan, but it's probably all I can pull off, anyway.

Following Xiao's lead just like she instructed me to, I go with her to the park. I'm not sure how to recognize the magician out of context; he's certainly not going to be strolling around Hyde Park shirtless in the early morning. Unless he's there running or something. Xiao scans the park with narrowed eyes, then points to a figure in the distance.

"That's him," she says, taking something from one of the many pockets of her uniform. I catch a glimpse of metal as she tucks it into her sleeve. Is it a knife? Is she going to murder him right here in broad daylight?

Jonah stands alone near a bench, a wool beanie pulled low over his shaggy blond hair. I'm struck all over again by the disappointing mundanity of what a human magician really is like. I'd been imagining someone mystical, with long robes and gnarled fingers that would comb through his scraggly white beard.

But nope. Just a dipshit in an Adidas track suit.

He lifts a hand and jogs toward us, and Xiao picks up our pace, though not enough to be suspicious. We're all just three friends who are just happening to meet up by chance.

I play along, raising my hand in a wave, too, and calling, "Hey!" like I'm thrilled to see him.

"Hey!" he responds just as enthusiastically as he slows his steps upon arrival. Lower, more serious, he says, "Let's get this over with quick or else this looks like a drug deal."

"Maybe you shouldn't have dressed like a drug dealer," Xiao says wryly, and gives him a friendly punch in the shoulder.

He fakes a laugh and a smile, and I hear a distinct click.

"What the fuck—" he shakes his arm and I see the handcuff around his wrist.

Xiao reaches down, but not for her gun. She takes out another pair of handcuffs and shows them to him. "You see what those are made of?"

Terror fills Jonah's eyes, and they dart to me in panic.

My first guess was that the other set of cuffs were made of wood, but on second glance, they're too highly polished, with veins of milky white running through the stone surface. The chain between them is thicker, iron instead of steel.

They're black moonstone.

One touch, and I would shift into my werewolf form.

"You can stay cuffed to me and do everything we tell you to do, or I can cuff you to her. With those." Xiao dangles them perilously close to me. "It's your choice."

"Gosh, you're really giving me a hard fucking decision to make," Jonah seethes. "Put those away."

My heart beats like I'm climbing a mountain. If those cuffs touch me, I'll turn into a raging beast right here in the middle of London. There's a woman pushing a stroller. A man on a bench reading a book and eating a sausage roll. There are people all around. I wouldn't just kill Jonah. I would kill Xiao, too, and probably the toddler running around on the grass.

Please, please put them the fuck away, I echo Jonah's words silently. Xiao said to follow her lead, so I keep silent and make my face a blank mask. But until she puts them back in the pocket on the outside of her thigh and snaps it up, I don't feel safe.

"Where are we going?" Jonah asks casually, and he links his fingers with Xiao's, swinging their arms a little. We still look like three friends having a very normal morning meet-up.

"Canada," Xiao says flatly.

"Home sweet home." Jonah's voice drips with sarcasm. "But I'm afraid I don't have my passport on me."

"Don't worry about that," I say, trying to sound like I'm not as surprised as he is. "Greater London is well-connected."

"So are magicians, baby," he warns with a smile that isn't friendly at all. "And we can be just as scary as any werewolf."

"Then why are you so afraid of us?" I counter.

He drops his head and shakes it like I've just said the dumbest thing he's ever heard. "You think I'm afraid of *you*?"

My mouth drops open at what he's implied. He's not afraid of me. He's afraid of *Xiao.* He's afraid of the thralls.

How afraid of them should the pack be?

Human magicians might have a lot of power, but they're still human. The syringe of sedative Xiao injects Jonah with the moment the jet is in the sky works fast, leaving him snoring in his seat. She zip-ties his ankles to the seat supports, anyway.

"I wish you wouldn't have done that," I say quietly, my stomach still roiling with fear at the thought of those black moonstone cuffs in her pocket. What are those for? Why would the thralls make those, if not to keep us in bondage in our animal forms?

She frowns and rises. "If the sedative wears off, we don't

want him loose in here. And I can't use the cuffs because—"

I know that we can't use the handcuffs because they might raise suspicion with the thralls staffing the jet. Xiao assured me that service thralls—our drivers, pilots, housekeeping staff—won't be able to tell the difference between a regular human and a magical one on sight, but they'll know a prisoner if they see him restrained. The zip ties aren't visible under the legs of his track pants.

But that's not what I'm talking about. "I meant drugging him."

"It had to be done. One word—"

"I know," I interrupt her again. "I know why you did it. I wish you didn't have to. I don't like the idea of drugging people. Removing their agency, remember?"

She looks away, but not before I see the shame that tightens her jaw.

"Like black moonstone would remove my agency," I say, quieter.

Her shoulders sag.

"If you had done that to me," I go on, "it would have been exactly the same as if Jonah had dosed me on purpose last night."

"I know." She still doesn't look at me. "I never would have done it."

"Then why do you have them?" I demand.

She swallows. "They're part of the regulation defense kit."

"Because you'd rather defend yourself against a werewolf than a werewolf in their human form?" That doesn't make any sense. "Come on."

Her expression hardens as she turns to face me. "I don't

know what they're for. But I do know I wouldn't use them. And I sure as hell wouldn't use them on you."

Maybe she wouldn't. And maybe there really is a reason the thralls issue those cuffs in the first place; I can't imagine one, but my imagination has lived a sheltered life. But I'm not so naive that I accept that our enemies, who've laid in wait for millennia to carry out their attack, have created those cuffs to protect us.

Their existence just proves that the thralls can't be trusted. They might prove that I can't trust Xiao.

CHAPTER 17

BAILEY

"I think I saw a polar bear on the other side of the lake this morning."

Nathan's tone alarms me. He doesn't sound like he's joking.

After my sleep-walking accident, the forest around us seems more alive. I know Nathan can sense it, too; any time he's gone outside, he's taken the black moonstone with him. He hasn't used it to change yet, and I'm not sure we can take down the apex predator of the arctic, even in our true forms. But he's arming himself with our greatest weapon just to go get firewood.

"It's not a polar bear," I say quietly, though I know he doesn't want to hear it again.

"Bailey..." He sighs and takes a moment to choose his words carefully. We both know he's running out of patience. "I know what you think you saw—"

I cut him off. "Please. Don't do that again. I know what I saw. And we both know there's something out there. And that it's not a bear."

He looks away.

"Please," I try again. "I know you're not superstitious but you're acting like a human."

"Yes, I suppose fearing polar bears is something I have in common with humans. How silly of me," he grumbles, turning to the small table that has become the center of our entire lives these days.

"I mean the fact that you're stubbornly refusing to see something that's right in front of you." I get to my feet and give myself a second, waiting for the dizziness that's become routine to pass. "We're here because of a magic spell predicated entirely on the lore of our kind, but you won't entertain the possibility that there could be something out there connected to that?"

"I entertain the much higher probability that whatever it is out there is something naturally occurring." He stops himself. This is the first time he's admitted that he feels the change in the forest, too.

"You know there's something there." I refuse to frame it as a question, to give him that way out. "We used to bathe outside, make our meals there, leave the cabin for more than just a quick sprint to the outhouse. Suddenly, and for no reason we seem to want to talk about, we're staying inside. It feels like we're being watched out there."

"It feels like we're being hunted," he corrects me, uneasy. He collects up our dinner dishes and dumps them into the empty washtub, then goes to the hearth to collect the steaming kettle. "I'll do the washing up."

"Yeah, that's what I was really concerned about," I mutter, flopping down on the mattress. We finally moved the rickety, rusted bedframe outside and rearranged the space a little, but it's still practically a shoebox and I'm losing my mind.

As if sensing my thoughts—something he's been doing more and more these days—Nathan says gently, "We won't be here much longer."

I make a noise of half-hearted agreement but say nothing.

"It's almost the full moon," he says, as if we don't mention that to each other at least once a day. The full moon has become some kind of unofficial deadline for us, like we've decided it's the end of our sentence or something. Since we have no idea if that's going to be true, I don't take the comfort in it that I once did.

Especially since Nathan decided we're not going to transform.

I'm bitter about that, though I understand. While we trust Xiao, the hearts she brought us are from thrall stock. We don't know if the thralls are planning a full moon attack. Nathan took the organs far into the woods and hurled them over the bog for the carrion birds to find, so they wouldn't go to waste, but I'm still disappointed to miss out on yet another transformation.

"We could use the moonstone to change," he says, and I sit up in surprise. He pours the kettle over the dishes, then adds some cold water to adjust the temperature, going about the chore like he hasn't just promised me something I've been longing for ever since my first and only transformation. "Not on the night of the actual full moon, since we don't know if the thralls have something planned. But maybe tonight?"

My heart leaps. "Are you serious?"

He shrugs his broad shoulders. "I'm serious. I could use the exercise. And in our wolf forms, we should be able to outrun the polar bear."

"Which doesn't exist." I don't know why I feel the need to dig at him, especially since he's being kind.

He looks over his shoulder and gives me a warning glance.

Dusk is fading fast outside the cabin's only window.

"You really mean it?" I ask. "Tonight?'

He turns to me, temporarily abandoning his chore. "I know you've missed it. I've missed it. And I've missed doing it with my mate beside me."

Butterflies awaken in my heart. "Really?"

"Yes. I waited for a very long time to take a mate. And now that I have you, I want to be with you as we were made. It's not natural for werewolves to go without changing for so long." He goes back to the dishes. "I learned that when I invoked the Right of Accord."

The butterflies go still. "You sound like you regret it."

He shakes his head but doesn't look at me. "How could I possibly? Magical curse or no magical curse, look what I gained from it."

The butterflies whip up to a frenzy.

I spring to my feet and go to the door, where the plastic bag of moonstone bracelets hangs on a nail like car keys. "Let's go. Right now."

"Right now?" he asks. "I'm washing the—"

"Oh, do you think the dishes have big plans tonight and they need to look their best?" I tease, taking down the bag. "Come on. What are we waiting for?"

He dries his hands and follows me outside.

I can see my breath in front of my face as I hurry to undress. I've got my shirt and bra off by the time Nathan closes the door behind him. "How do we do this?"

"Put on the bracelets," he says. "One touch was all it took for me to change at Wyrding House."

"Does it feel different than changing the real way?" I chew my bottom lip nervously.

"It feels the same. But sped up. You might be disoriented for a moment." He steps out of his jeans, and I kick mine, and my panties, aside. He holds out the bag and says, "Ladies first."

With a roll of my eyes, I reach inside, my fingers closing around one of the strings of beads. When I withdraw my hand, it's covered in fur.

He's right, the change does happen quickly. So quickly, I momentarily lose my center of balance. I stagger back, remembering to keep my fist closed around the bracelet until my head clears and I can wriggle the beads over my claws and onto my wrist.

Nathan grins at me. Though I can't speak to him, I know he can interpret my quizzical glance. "You're so fucking beautiful."

What's beautiful is the world around us. My senses are sharper, my body more attuned to the throb of energy that pulsates from every blade of grass. There are more stars overhead than anything I can see with my usual eyes. It's not just because we're far from the city lights; whole galaxies swirl above me in the gray-blue twilight.

Maybe the most beautiful sight is my mate, who shifts into his bulky muscles and silvery coat in an instant. The primal connection between us shimmers in the air. It's not the binding, but our *bond*, etched into our auras by fate.

I drop to all fours—well, all *threes*. Though we don't look like wolves when we've transformed, we do have the ability to run like them. Closer to the ground, all the smells are so much more vivid. I spot a glittering green trail and know instinctively that a fat bullfrog is at the end of it.

I'm not about to eat a bullfrog, even in my werewolf form.

Nathan crouches beside me, scanning the area, probably seeking out the predator he's so certain has been lurking around. To my satisfaction, there's no trace at all of any animal besides the frog. Not even a lingering scent trail of bear exists anywhere around us.

But the feeling of being watched? That's there, and it's keener than before. The hairs stand up on my back. I shake the feeling off and jog toward the woods, and Nathan follows me. He feels it, too. The edge of the clearing somehow promises safety. We trot into the shadows of the trees and the evergreen scents sting my nostrils in the best possible way. If I could giggle in this shape, I would; instead, I yip happily and roll on the carpet of fallen pine needles before springing up and sprinting off again. Nathan is right on my heels, nipping playfully at my feet before tackling me and rolling us both down a short incline.

I've never transformed without him. Without my mate. I don't know how it feels any other way, but I know it would be incomplete. I lean up to bite at his throat and he releases me, sitting back crisscross applesauce and lifting his canine head to the sky to let out a long, happy howl. I join him, standing fully upright, my muzzle open to the night sky. It's not the full moon, but it's full enough through my wolf eyes; the dark sliver of shadow is barely perceptible, even to the eyes of a creature attuned to the moon.

A creature that belongs to the moon.

How have we gotten so far from it? The trappings of humanity have tainted our existence. Desire for comfort led to desire for luxury; desire for luxury to desire for riches. And the thralls had been more than happy to provide us that life.

When I return to power, things will change.

The voice doesn't come from my own mind. It comes from something invading my mind.

I sniff the scent coming to me on the wind. Nathan picks it up, too. We barely glance at each other before we're in motion, moving toward the bog.

Toward the forest beyond it.

CHAPTER 18
BAILEY

Nathan and I stand at the edge of the clearing. The muskegs are treacherous, hiding beneath what should be solid ground. But in our werewolf form, they're powerfully foul-smelling; we should be able to avoid them.

One scent rises above the murky traps as we follow the trail from my dreams, something fresh, like sweetgrass and lemon. It grows stronger the further we go, the closer we get to where I know we're going.

It's the place from my dream. I know it will be there.

We reach the edge of the towering pines and I no longer need a scent to guide me. I know the way. The same heavy feeling of desire falls over me, tingling up from the ground into my clawed hand and feet, settling low in my belly, parching my throat. Nathan's breath huffs beside me. He feels it, too. The urgency. The desperation.

By the time we reach the standing stones and the altar inside, we're frantic for each other. He lifts me up, rising to stand over me. We've never done it like this before. Never in these bodies. The newness excites me, prickles my skin all over as I lay back and reach for him. His cock is less human, longer, throbbing red and already dripping in anticipation of our mating. I'm ready, too, and frantic to join with him here, in this place that seems like it's been made for our kind, for exactly this purpose.

He climbs onto the stone with me, his deadly sharp claws beside my head as he lowers himself. I rise up to meet him, open to him, take him in. The shimmering fluid already coating him shocks me into higher need, higher pleasure, and I sink my claws into his back, trying to pull him deeper. He's holding back, a high whine of distress issuing from his panting mouth beside my ear.

I wrap my legs around him and arch up, forcing him the rest of the way inside, and immediately realize what his hesitation was for. The base of his cock is thicker, pushing me open wider than I've ever been stretched, and it continues to grow. He's locked deep inside me, and he can't withdraw, only thrust against me in short, sharp movements.

As out of control as he'd seemed during the mating ceremony, he was holding back then. I've never felt so full, nor so trapped; there's no way we can pull apart now, and he's filling me with burst after burst of that torturous fluid produced only in werewolf form. I'm desperate, howling for release right along with him. And I'm full, so full of him, of his jerking, twitching erection, of the cum sealed up inside me by the thick, swollen base of him. The walls of my cunt become as sensitive as the very tip of my clit. The rush of sensation speeds through me until every millimeter of my skin, every nerve is a pleasure receptor meant only to speed me to my release.

I come hard, and when I do, I don't stop.

Neither does he. We twist and writhe together, prisoners of pleasure so keen that all sense of time abandons me. His palm slaps the rock beneath me, and he whines frantically as if he's desperate to pull out and end it. Maybe he doesn't want to. But if I had a human voice, I would be screaming, begging him to make it stop. To let me stop coming. To save me from the waves of agonizing pleasure I'm drowning in.

Nothing exists now but a warm, red-tinged blackness that pulses in time with the throb of him inside me. I've never experienced anything but this never-ending orgasm. I'll never experience anything else. I'm lost to it; I'll remain lost to it. It's in the air around me, filling my lungs. It's in the stone beneath me, seeping into my skin. All I can do is cling to my mate, whose howls rip the silent forest apart. He drops his head and sinks his teeth into my shoulder, and I taste my blood as he tastes it. I feel his endless release as he feels mine. We're not just united in body, but in our very being.

I open my eyes to the moon. Its light swirls, spiraling down, bathing Nathan and I in a silver cloak of primal sensation. We're joined together and joined with the celestial body that rules us. We're mating with it as we're mating with each other, the brilliant white orb strobing in my vision in time with the searing hot bursts inside me.

I want more, need more, and I reach out for the silvery tendrils of light that surround us.

They become wholly tactile, ropes of light that bind my wrists and force them down to the stone. More whip tight around Nathan's back, holding him. Our ankles bind together, and that binding grows taut, stretching us both until he remains inside me but can't move. And all the while, every muscle in my body quivers and clenches, trapped in that perfect release that has now become torment.

Flashes of silver around the clearing force me to focus, to try to rise above the searing hot climax that won't end.

Wolves.

White wolves ring the clearing, their eyes flashing silver. The same wolves I saw in my dream, the same that watched me in this place.

It wasn't a dream.

He emerges from the shadows, that half-changed beast with a man's face. His long white hair covers his nude body like a cloak. He walks around us in a slow circle, and while I want to growl at him, no sound will come out of my muzzle.

The half-wolf lifts his hand in a gesture that looks familiar and strange all at once, and four of the white wolves come closer. They shimmer and reform as hybrid creatures like himself, impossible to tell apart from each other as their delicate features are all so similar.

"You won't be needing these, anymore," the leader says, and reaches one long claw out to the bracelet at my wrist. He slices through the elastic, sending the moonstone beads scattering off on the forest floor, and I'm back in my human guise in a disorienting flash. Pain rips through me as I change around Nathan's werewolf member; that bulge keeping us tied is far, far too big now that I'm half the size I was. But that lasts only a split second, as he suddenly reverts, as well, and his deflating cock slips from me on the tide of cum he left inside me.

His first words are a snarled, "Let us go!"

The effect of the pleasure-heightening aphrodisiac haven't worn off, though the feeling is less intense and fading fast. The four half-transformed creatures around us raise their hands high, catching that tangible moonlight that still swirls over us and binds us. They sigh in unison and begin to softly glow.

"When we're finished with you," their leader promises. It doesn't sound like a threat, but it feels dangerous.

"Who the fuck are you?" Nathan demands, and his back suddenly arches. I feel him grow hard against me again, and with a slight shift, he enters my battered cunt.

"We are what you once were," the leader says. "What you could be again."

The four sigh again, their eyes closed in ecstasy. The spectral ropes binding us rock gently, forcing Nathan to thrust. The werewolf cum slicked inside me and over me works its wicked magic and I moan, tossing my head back.

The female figures moan, too.

"It wasn't a dream," I whimper, my eyes locking with the leader's.

A slow smile bends his mouth. "It wasn't, my beloved. We called to you, and you came to us. Offered yourself to us, as you've offered him."

"No one offered anything!" Nathan snaps, but it's lost to a groan of ecstasy that's shared by the male figures.

"In our time, we shared ourselves with the moon. With each other." The leader sounds disappointed. "We lived beneath her and gave her what she asked of us. Don't you want to give her what she asks?"

I can't answer; my body shakes, nails digging into my palm as I scream my release to the sky. And the moon does seem to glow brighter, somehow.

The figures around us glow, too, the light growing in intensity as it takes them over. Nathan shudders against me, into me, but the bindings around us keep rocking us together. He curses and struggles, but the shimmering strands might as well be iron chains. The two male creatures jerk, thick ropes of cum splattering onto the ground again and again. The light releases us, and Nathan sags against me. We're still powerless, but now it's exhaustion that robs us of our escape.

But then the panic sets in. I roll to the ground and scoop up a handful of dirt and pine needles, then another, scrambling until my fingers encounter one of the scattered beads. The sudden transformation makes me stagger almost off my feet, but even my moment of stumbling is faster than the reactions of the half-wolves in the clearing. The rest of the white wolves ringing the space, though, are on me in an instant. Though I'm fighting no-handed while I hold the moonstone tight, I manage to use my forearm to fling one animal aside; it yelps as it slams into one of the standing stones and crumples to the ground. I lunge and rake my teeth across the muzzle of another, and it backs away, pawing at the bloody slashes. One wolf catches my arm in its jaws, but it doesn't bite down to maim. It shakes me, hard, and the black moonstone bead rolls from my grasp. I fall to my knees, arm twisted in the wolf's mouth, my skin no longer tough enough to withstand the pressure of the bite.

I can't lose my other hand, and I am no match for a wolf in this form.

"Enough!"

Though Nathan shouts the word, it's a simple, calm nod from the leader that causes the animal to release me. I scrabble backward, tucking my wounded arm tight to my chest.

Nathan kneels beside me, face contorted in concern. "Let me see. Let me see."

I don't want to look at what's become of my only remaining hand, but Nathan lifts it up, flexes each finger, smoothes his palm down my wrist. "It's just a nip." The relief in his voice speaks for both of us. "Not even a bad one. You'll be fine."

Of course, infection could set in, and I could get gangrene and lose the whole arm, but we have enough problems at the moment that I don't need to add a hypothetical one. As if only just remembering where we are and what's happening, Nathan pulls me with him to sit with my back against the stone altar, placing himself between me and the wolves.

"We don't want to hurt you," the leader says placidly. "But we will protect ourselves."

"Protect yourselves? You attacked us!" Nathan bites back.

"You entered our circle and performed our sacred rite of your own accord," the leader says. He gestures to the four hybrid creatures, who bow to us and shimmer into wolf form before moving to rejoin the rest of their pack.

"We didn't know that was what we were doing," I said, glaring at him over Nathan's shoulder.

The leader raises one white eyebrow. "Oh, didn't you? Even after you performed the rite with me just a few nights ago?"

"I—" I look guiltily to Nathan, but the guilt immediately transforms to rage toward the leader. "I thought I was dreaming!"

"What you thought and what happened weren't in agreement. There is little I can do about that, now." The leader shrugs elegantly.

Cold fire sweeps through me. I'm shaking, I'm so furious. I move to lunge at the leader, but Nathan doesn't budge, which is probably for the best. We're no match for all of these...whatever they are.

"You lured me here," I accuse him. "I thought I was dreaming."

I *was* dreaming... I had two hands...

"You were delirious," he admits with what seems to be actual regret. "I didn't see it at the time, and for that, I'm sorry."

"You left her outside the cabin," Nathan says, brow scrunched as he pieces things together.

"I returned her," the leader affirms.

"You left her to die!" Nathan shouts. "If I hadn't woken up—"

"Who do you think woke you?" The leader comes closer, and Nathan presses me harder against the stone. But the wolf-man doesn't touch either of us.

"We mean you no harm. Perhaps we no longer know how to communicate properly with our brethren, but I assure you, we have done nothing but protect you since you've arrived here." The leader's eyes flick toward me. "You especially know this to be true."

It's somehow both upsetting and validating at the same time. I nudge Nathan with my elbow and give him an I-told-you-so glare.

"Come," the leader says. "We have food and water and shelter nearby. We can speak more there, where you can warm yourselves."

He doesn't wait for an answer, but turns and moves toward the trees. Nathan hesitates, then finally stands and offers me his hand. We follow the wolves into the forest.

CHAPTER 19

BAILEY

"I apologize again for the way we welcomed you," the leader says, sitting cross-legged beside us. "It has been a long time since we've seen any of our kin."

We're inside a partially buried shelter with a conical roof of crudely stripped branches heaped with peat. It's something like—but not exactly—the shelters we learned our Viking ancestors built. It brings to mind the view of the ancient dwellings beneath the council buildings. All around the perimeter of the central fire pit, wolves lounge on heaping beds of grass. Some half-transformed ones sit upon them, too; one of them brings a blanket of rabbit pelts roughly stitched together and wraps it around our shoulders.

"Welcome?" Nathan scoffs.

"Your ways have changed from ours." The leader spreads his hands. "In the past, entering the circle and performing the sacred rite was an invitation. We did not realize we weren't wanted."

"What are you?" I blurt, and quickly revise. "*Who* are you?"

The wolf-man studies me for a long moment. Then, as if he's only just decided which version of a tale to tell us, he says, "Once, they called me Màni. Before I brought my kin here."

The name is familiar. I don't know how I know it, and that frustrates me more than the strange way he talks. There's no accent to his speech, but a faint ringing lasts just a breath after his words, as if we're not truly hearing him.

"What's wrong with your voice?" What's wrong with *my* voice, and why won't it stop coming out with such rude questions.

"You hear me as all earthly creatures hear me. In the tongue you understand." He tilts his head, silvery eyes flashing. "Have you forgotten me?"

"Màni," Nathan says, slowly enunciating the syllables. "The moon."

Màni shakes his head, a barely perceptible movement. His stillness is unnerving, especially after his comment about earthly creatures. "Of the moon, but not the moon herself. That was one thing your ancestors had wrong. There were others. More egregious."

Nathan turns to me, "The Viking god of the moon."

That's where I've heard the name. It comes to me in murky memories of boring history classes that had mentioned him only in passing.

"I was, once," Màni says with a casual shrug, as if everyone has been a god at one time or another and simply stopped. "Now, I am protector to your kin."

"Our kin," I repeat, my gaze darting around the room full of quadrupedal wolves and half-transformed wolf-people. I don't see much similarity between them and us.

His voice falls to a low, confidential tone. "Those who did not follow the dark magics south, as your kind did."

Nathan and I both sit silent. I have no doubt his thoughts are similar to mine.

"They have stayed here, and I with them, for a while now." Màni smiles to himself. "More than a while, I suppose, in the minds of earthly creatures."

"Nearly a millennium," Nathan supplies for him. "The migration south began almost a thousand years ago."

The god nods. "Since your ancestors took to the sea, and eventually found their way here. These are the ones who went no further."

"None of the clans stayed here," Nathan says, as if the words will make it true and all of this will vanish. "No one could survive."

"No human could survive," I whisper.

Màni fixes his silver eyes on me and I'm keenly aware that it wasn't a dream, I did have sex with him. With a god.

I wonder how Nathan feels about that. If he's angry or hurt. At the moment, he seems to be consumed, as I am, by having our history turned upside down.

"Humans survived here beside us for centuries," Màni says. "The first who knew this land."

"Natives," Nathan clarifies.

"The ones who were here when we arrived, yes." Màni nods excitedly. "They are still here, though not as many as before those across the water became the scourge of the land. You know of this?"

"Regrettably, it's still happening across the continent," Nathan says.

Màni takes a breath. I spring forward excitedly, without thinking about my movement at all. My hand falls on his chest, and he catches my wrist to stop me tumbling further forward.

"You're breathing," I whisper in wonder.

"You're bleeding." Nathan pulls me back and tucks the blanket around my shoulders. He lifts my hand and examines my arm.

Màni snaps his fingers. "Healer."

A wolf lying nearby changes into that half-and-half form and comes to my side with a satchel. She starts removing items, but I can't get past this discovery about Màni. "You're a god. And you're breathing."

"That began just a few centuries ago. I hardly noticed it." He pauses thoughtfully. "It was the heartbeat that disturbed me."

"So, you're a god who's turning mortal?" Nathan sounds like he doesn't believe him. Perhaps I'm imagining it. Or perhaps Nathan is...

Jealous?

Would Nathan be jealous of a god?

That seems entirely plausible.

"I don't know what I am becoming," Màni admits. "I know that I was called here by your ancestors when they found this land, and that I have stayed. I've picked up some of their traits." He touches one of his ears. "And they have picked up some of mine. We have followed our own ways, as you have followed yours."

"You stayed here without thralls, and our kind left with them," Nathan tries to understand.

But Màni shakes his head. "They took your kind. Stole you away. The humans here didn't want them to stay. The thralls could not survive without their magic. They could not survive without you."

"We thought we controlled the thralls," I whisper, then hiss sharply as the healer dabs some kind of unguent on my wounds.

"So skilled were their manipulations, you never saw the

truth; they needed you to survive. You did not need them." Màni looks sorrowfully toward the circle of sky visible through the smoke above. "You needed only this. But they gave you comfort. And after you took comfort, you wanted luxury."

"And we needed them to provide it." Our butler. Our drivers. The establishments at which we dined, the designers who made our clothes.

"You wanted them to provide it," he corrects me. "Look around you. Do you see need? Do you see us shivering in the cold? Do you see eyes hollow from hunger? Is there a lack of comfort, of warmth?"

I shake my head.

"Do you see the chains of want?" he went on. "Or the fear that we may lose what we have?"

"What I fear that I may lose is here with me," Nathan says sharply, gesturing to my stomach.

"I sensed it. The child is powerful," Màni says.

A cold chill goes up my back. "Powerful, how?"

"I feel him as I feel the moon," Màni says, without offering further explanation.

"And what does that mean?" Nathan asks, but I'm stuck on one word.

Him. *Him.* My baby seems more real now. A simple word has given him an identity beyond, "it."

Màni tilts his head, eyes narrowing. "I could not describe it to you. Not accurately. Earthly creatures can never know what it is to feel the power of another god."

"A god?" My throat tightens. Our gods have destinies. Some of them horrible. I don't want my child added to the pantheon with Lycaon. With Fenrir.

"Our baby is a god?" Nathan asks, his jaw tight.

"No. He has the power of a god. Something the thralls

have harnessed. They know the old stories." As if a dark cloud passed through the shelter, everything dims. Màni's back straightens; his furious presence fills the space. "How do they know our stories?"

I cower behind Nathan. The healer's touch is no longer gentle; I know that if I try to run, she'll hold me fast.

"The thralls teach us the stories," Nathan says, unable to keep a note of unease out of his voice, though I hear that he's trying. "They've always had them."

"They have not!" Màni's voice shakes crumbs of dirt loose from the earthen ceiling. As if remembering himself, he draws inward, his face troubled. The fire is able to push the darkness back again. He flicks a gaze to the healer, whose grip slackens.

I find my voice somehow, though it is timid. "For as long as either of us have been alive, the thralls have taught us our legends and history. We don't know who gave them the knowledge, but it wasn't us."

"It's probably not anyone still alive," Nathan adds. He puts his arm around me protectively.

"They stole it." Màni's whole being sags sorrowfully. "I knew they weren't to be trusted."

"You were correct. It only took us several centuries to realize that," Nathan says bitterly.

But we realize it now. And we need help. And we're sitting in front of a god.

"We want to steal it back," I blurt, rising to my knees. "We want to stop the thralls. They're trying to destroy all of us."

"They aren't trying to destroy us." Màni blinks at us like we're confused. "They don't know about us. Unless you tell them."

Every pair of eyes in the shelter turn to us.

"We never would," Nathan swears, though I know he would say anything to keep them from getting rid of us as witnesses.

"The thralls are as much our enemy now as they would be yours," I add. "And they're trying to get to my baby. They set a trap with a spell centuries ago. We don't understand why, and we're trying to figure that out now. If you can think of anything—"

"I can think of everything." The god blinked his unnerving eyes at me.

I have to be specific, I realize. "We need help."

"You believe we will help you?" The predatory way he tilts his head unnerves me.

"We believe you *can*," Nathan says.

Does he? Nathan is so difficult to read at the best of times. I have no idea what's going on inside his head nearly twenty-four hours a day. And since we don't have the smoothest relationship history, I can't trust my own interpretation. But he seems sincere.

But I have no problem believing that Nathan would bald-faced lie directly to a god.

"We don't know your world," Màni begins cautiously.

"We do." Nathan's resolve manifests into a tightening of his arm around me. "We don't need someone to understand our world. We need knowledge that you have, that the thralls have kept from us."

Màni nods thoughtfully. There's barely a heartbeat of silence before he says, "Yes. I will do this for you."

My jaw drops. "You don't need time to think about it? Like, to make conditions or have us sign anything?"

Nathan nudges me.

Màni regards me through bemused eyes. "You confuse

me for Loki. When I say I will help, I mean I will help, regardless of repayment."

"But what if we asked you to do something really terrible?" Why is my mouth still talking when I know I should shut up? "Not that we would."

"I told you; I will help you. How you exploit that help is a matter of your own conscience."

Nathan's shoulders slump with relief. "We're indebted to you."

Màni still seems unable to understand. "There is no need to talk of repayment. You are both in danger. She is the mother of my next-born child. If I protect you, I protect my child."

"Excuse me?" Something is clearly getting lost in translation.

The god gestures to my belly. "You came to me. We performed the rite. I poured the essence of my godly power into your womb."

"Gross!" I shriek.

Nathan snarls and jerks forward but remembers himself before committing violence against the god. "That baby is mine. Conceived weeks ago."

"And the one that grows beside it now, that you will raise and who will call your son his brother, is mine," Màni explains patiently. As if it's totally normal to knock up a pregnant person twice.

"You're telling me…" I rise to my feet, anger making my vision go black and red. "That I am carrying a baby with the power of a god, and a baby who is the son of a god?"

"Yes, that is how a mortal creature can understand it."

That wasn't *exactly* a "yes."

"You brought her here." Nathan rises to stand beside me, and I fight the urge to physically hold him back as his voice becomes tighter. "You lured her through dangerous terrain in the middle of the night, while she was sick with a fever. Then you raped her and threw her in the grass in front of the cabin when you were finished with her. She could have died—"

"She did not die."

"She could have died!" Nathan roars, and the other inhabitants of the peat house take notice. He swallows, a dry, audible sound. It only makes him hoarser. "Now, you expect her to carry and raise your child, along with that of her true mate?"

"I know she will raise my child. It is her destiny. It is the destiny of our entire species." He pauses, gaze flicking to the night sky through the smoke hole. Then he motions for two fully transformed wolves to come to our sides.

"That is all I need from you," Màni says, gesturing to the door. "The full moon will be upon us at the next twilight. We will watch you, and we will protect you," he swears.

But as we leave the shelter, I can't help but interpret the first part of his vow as a threat.

CHAPTER 20
TARA

We race the full moon back to Toronto and waste no time leaving the airfield for the ceremonial grounds. When he woke up near the end of the flight, Jonah groggily suggested that the key to keeping the full moon ceremony from happening might be found there.

I'm still not certain it's a wise move to bring a human magician into our sacred space, but there isn't time to come up with a better option.

"We need to stop somewhere first," Xiao tells me. "It's only for a second, and you have to trust me. Stay here, I'll be in and out."

"That's the kind of shit drug dealers say," Jonah says from the backseat. He's handcuffed, but we should have gagged him, too.

"I trust you," I tell Xiao, though it's not trust so much as a fear that she might use a tranquilizer dart on me if it makes things more convenient for her.

We get off the highway two exits before the route to the ceremonial grounds. Xiao's "second" is a lot longer than everyone else's second. She zooms through farmland, onto unpaved roads, skidding around dangerous curves for what feels like a full half hour before arriving at a dilapidated one-room schoolhouse surrounded by tall grass.

"Stay in the car," she instructs me again.

"Better in here than in there." I can't believe she's actually going inside.

But she doesn't go inside. She darts around to the rear of the building. She's only gone a minute before she jogs back with three odd, square parcels wrapped in black nylon fabric.

She opens the door and jerks Jonah out of the backseat while he protests and barely manages to stay on his feet.

Xiao flips the safety off the gun at her hip. "If you move, I'll kill you."

"No, you won't. You need me."

He has her there.

The corner of her mouth twitches. "You're right. But I don't need your kneecaps."

He doesn't have a retort for that.

"What are these?" I ask, catching the parcel Xiao tosses me.

"Thrall security forces spec ops pack. We're all going to have to suit up. There are too many cameras on the grounds." She unbuttons Jonah's pants and jerks them down as he yelps in indignation. "We don't want to get caught snooping around."

Inside the pack, there's a stretchy black suit made from thin, strong material, as well as gloves, goggles and a utility belt bearing more gadgets than I would have time to learn about.

I nod toward Jonah, who watches me expectantly.

"Turn him around," I tell Xiao, and wait until she complies to strip down and suit up. The garment is skintight, but not uncomfortably so. The belt fits low on my hips, and as I fasten the buckle, I hope I won't accidentally set off a bomb or tear gas or something in one of the compartments.

"Won't there already be thralls getting things ready for tonight?" I ask. They would be able to sense a human the moment we arrived.

"They'll be at the harvest, won't they?" Jonah asks, a mocking note in his tone.

"Shut up." Xiao mutters. There's a zipper noise and Jonah gives a little yelp.

"I've never heard of the harvesting." I feel around the lumpy material at the back of my neck. It's a hood. I pull it up and over my hair, and the material cinches to an oval around my face.

"Really? You never wondered how they get the hearts you all eat?" He laughs and directs his next words to Xiao. "You really have them snowed, don't you?"

"Tara, come here and hold this gun to the magician's elbow," Xiao said, clicking the handcuffs free.

"Oh, very creative," he says, stretching his arm out so I can comply. It also helps Xiao to remove his shirt, though the sleeve is tricky with the barrel of the gun in the way. I expect him to grab Xiao at any moment, but he's a surprisingly compliant prisoner, now that we've drugged him. I suppose it hasn't worn off, entirely.

Once he's suited, cuffed, and back in the car, I lean against the trunk and wait.

"Are you going to watch me?" Xiao asks, and not in a flirty way.

"Are you going to tell me what harvesting is?" I counter.

She lets out a long sigh. "It is what it sounds like."

"They sacrifice humans." It was something we never spoke of in our homes, though we all knew the hearts had to come from somewhere.

From someone.

I turn back to the car, absently messing with buckles and snaps on the belt. Xiao calls out, alarmed, "Be careful!"

Uh oh. "Are there grenades in this?" Oh god, did I pull a pin or something?

"The pouch on your left hip." She grimaces and starts to empty the many, many pockets of her pants. "There's a pair of these in there."

She holds up the black moonstone cuffs.

A chill runs up my spine. I'm a werewolf. I love being a werewolf. But I don't love the idea of suddenly changing without warning.

That's why the thralls have them. The realization takes my breath away. They have the ability to make us into an army of beasts for themselves, if they so choose.

I give Xiao a nod and open the car door. I half-fall, half-sit in my seat.

"Somebody's putting things together," comes sing-songing from the back.

I look at Jonah in the rearview mirror, and he meets my gaze with a smile.

I'm not in a smiling mood. "How do they choose who gets harvested?"

"I'm not a thrall. You'd have to ask—"

"Stop it. You're not cute and you're not charming. Certainly not charming enough to retain your life when we're done with you. Maybe consider that when you're deciding whether or not to cooperate," I snap.

He blinks slowly.

"If there are humans being held captive, I want to get them out," I say, holding his gaze firmly. "I want this to end tonight."

He grins. "I can come up with something."

"Good." I drum my fingertips on the dashboard. "Because I have no clue what we're doing."

———

It's sundown when we finally reach the ceremonial grounds. Or, at least, when we pull off the road and back the car into a tight spot between some trees. Night vision goggles pushed up on our heads, we follow Xiao into the forest, far enough that the road disappears from our view.

She stops and keeps her voice low. "I have a plan."

"Good, because so do I," Jonah whispers.

She glares at him. "They can't do the ceremony without the Hierophant and his acolytes. If we take them out—"

"Kill the Hierophant?" I gasp, louder than I intend to speak.

"Look, leave the ceremony part to me, okay?" Jonah says. "I can stop it from happening, really easy."

"With your magic?" Xiao asks.

He nods. "Trust me. I can keep a party from happening. You guys just focus on killing the Hierophant."

"I never agreed to—" I begin, but Xiao cuts in over me.

"You want us to let you go off by yourself?" she asks, incredulous that he would even make the demand.

"Yes, I do. I want you to give me space to do the thing you kidnapped me to do, so your girlfriend here doesn't make good on her threat to dispose of me." He huffs and casts a look between us, but a weird force in the air between Xiao and I prevent us from looking at each other.

Ah. Shame. *That* was the force.

She doesn't ask what he's talking about. She just uncuffs him. "Fine. You slip away on us, and I'm flying back to England to murder every patron at your club. Understand?"

She hit him where it hurt. Even he didn't have a strong enough poker face to hide it.

"We'll meet up back on the road," Jonah decides for us. "And don't make a move on the Hierophant until I give you the signal."

"What's the signal?" I ask.

He gives me a lopsided grin. "Oh, you'll know it when you see it."

He trots off in the general direction of the ceremonial grounds, and I wonder how he even knows where he's going. Then I realize: he can feel the magic.

My stomach churns. All the magic the thralls command comes from werewolves. We're standing in a vault of treasures stolen from us.

Still, killing the Hierophant is a risky move. As Xiao starts off in a different direction, I halt her. "Wait. We have to talk."

"This isn't exactly the time for a long conversation," she says absently, and moves again.

"I mean about our plan." I won't go another step until she listens. "We cannot kill the Hierophant."

She stops, her back straightening, but doesn't turn to me.

"Right now, the Hierophant is the only person with the power to let me rule the pack. And he's the only one who really knows what's going on with the spell over my sister and her baby," I go on. "It would be foolish to throw away a resource we need."

When she faces me, she's someone I don't recognize. She's angry. Furious.

Murderous.

"Fine," she says curtly. "What do we do? Leave him in charge?"

"No." I shake my head. "We take him captive."

"The thralls will riot."

"The thralls won't know. At least, not right away." I sigh in frustration. "Look, we take him back to Aconitum Hall. Lock him in the safe room. Tell him that there's been an attack by the St. Laurent pack and that he's in danger."

"And if he won't come with us?" Xiao's hands tighten to fists at her side.

"Then knock him out and later we'll say it's for his own good." We're running out of time to argue. "This is how we're doing this, Xiao. You don't get a say in it."

Her jaw tightens. Her nod of acquiescence is obedient in gesture only. She'll do what I've commanded, but she doesn't agree with me.

"You go to him," I add. "I'll rescue the sacrifices."

Her eyes go wide.

"There were other prisoners below the council chambers when my sister was there," I explain. I don't like to think about Clare in that cell. "Not just werewolves. Humans. Not thralls, just humans. That's where they keep them before the harvest, right? So, they can't escape?"

The pressed tight line of Xiao's mouth gives me my answer.

"We aren't at war with humans. We're at war with the thralls and the packs that are trying to murder my sister. There's no reason not to exercise mercy! I can gain access to the council chamber. I'm the acting ruler right now. You deal with the Hierophant; I'll release the prisoners." I push the urgent, dictatorial tone from my voice. "You want them to go free, don't you?"

She doesn't answer beyond, "Be careful."

Then she sprints off into the trees and out of sight.

CHAPTER 21

TARA

The length of time I have to plan is approximately as far as the council chamber building is from my starting position in the forest. It isn't long. I decide since I'm in charge of the pack, I can probably demand access to the building. I just have to think up a reason I would need access.

By the time I'm jogging across the manicured lawn and onto the path to the guarded front doors, I think I know what I'm going to do. I have to get past the first set of thralls outside. After that...

I have no idea.

You're good at improvisation, I lie to myself. It's too late to turn back; the thralls have spotted me and moved together in a human shield before the entrance.

"Urgent business on behalf of His Majesty, King Nathan," I call, out of breath.

The thrall guards don't move, but eye me skeptically.

"I am the Lady Tara, sister to Her Majesty, the Queen, and regent ruler of this pack. You *will* stand aside," I try again.

One of them reaches for her radio and my heart stops. The other nudges her shoulder.

"That's Lady Tara," he confirms.

The first guard drops her hand, and I have to force myself not to gasp loudly with relief.

"But we don't have any orders about a regent ruler," the second guard says, his ginger eyebrows drawing together in his pasty, Cro-Magnon face.

Before the first guard can rethink her decision and call me in, I ask, "Does the Hierophant tell grunts about confidential court business?"

I raise my eyebrows and move my gaze deliberately between them, my pulse an audible throb in my skull.

Finally, the first guard steps aside. "Apologies, Your Highness."

"Your Majesty," the second guard corrects her.

"Your Majesty," the female guard repeats. Her hazel eyes narrow. "With utmost respect...why are you wearing a spec ops suit?"

"Because—" The adrenaline coursing through me seizes my brain on a brilliant lie. Unfortunately, it might mean I'm throwing Jonah to the metaphorical wolves.

Oh well. I'm sure there are other human magicians.

"The King's private security forces have received word of an imminent attack from the St. Laurent pack. Tonight. Here, at the ceremonial grounds. Why else would the king send me here, as his stand-in, if it weren't an emergency?"

They both instinctively reach for the weapons at their hips.

"Stand down." That's a military saying, isn't it? It must be, because they comply. I continue. "There's a prisoner I must speak with. He has information that might help us, but there isn't much time."

The guards share a glance.

"What are you waiting for?" I hear a slightly hysterical rise in the pitch of my words. "Open the doors, the lives of the pack depend on it."

"There are no St. Laurent prisoners in the dungeon, Your Majesty," the second guard says slowly. "There aren't any werewolves in the dungeon, at all."

My control over the situation is slipping away. I have to correct this. "I didn't say it was a werewolf prisoner."

It's a gamble. There are humans in the dungeon. At least, I hope there are still humans in the dungeon and not at some gory sacrifice.

Did you really think that the hearts came from nowhere? From no one? I've been such a fool, for so many years.

The moment has come to set things right.

"Do you have any credentials, *Your Majesty?*" the second guard asks.

I didn't want to have to use them, but I reach slowly for the pouch at my belt. "I do. Let me get them."

"Slowly," the first guard warns, her hand going to the radio pinned at her shoulder.

She doesn't get a chance to use it. The change happens instantly when my fingers close around the cuffs. One furious swipe from my free hand knocks the first thrall's head from her shoulders.

The second guard opens his mouth but doesn't manage to make a sound before I crush his neck in my fist, his spine splintering through his pulped flesh.

I killed them.

I gag, my snout making the sound louder and harsher. I shake my disgust off. I don't have time to remember the stench of blood or the weeping of the pack as they watched my sister condemned to die. I don't have time to think of the taste of my own blood in my mouth after one of Josh's "warnings." I just fired the first shot in a war against the thralls and at the moment, I'm an army of one.

A snarling, fanged army of one.

Still gripping the thrall by the neck, I kick in the doors. The security measures don't do shit against a werewolf who's gone feral with panic. The thralls architects and security experts never intended to protect themselves against us.

There are two thrall guards in the lobby. When the mangled body of their co-worker slides across the floor and stops at their feet, they don't try to radio anyone. They don't draw their weapons. They freeze.

I drop the cuff and there's a vertigo-inducing blink as I return to my usual height and size, but the moment my voice is back, I use it. "Don't move!"

I'm not sure they were planning to.

"I am the Lady Tara, sister to Her Majesty, Queen Bailey, and current ruling regent of this pack." I hope my attempts to appear regal aren't entirely shattered by the fact that I'm wearing a spec ops suit with transformation blown-out sleeves and pant legs and sneakers that are very much sandals now. "We are under immediate threat of attack from the St. Laurent pack. Your friends outside attacked me when I arrived; our enemies have clearly gotten to our thralls. Since I have no way of assuring that you can be trusted—"

"We aren't in league with the St. Laurent pack!" The thrall who breaks first is so young; it wouldn't be difficult to believe him if he said this is his first full moon.

The second guard follows the first's statement with a vehement nod. He's older, with a white mustache that's brighter than his teeth against his sunburned face. He's not as nervous as the other guy. "Your Majesty, where do we report?"

I can get them to leave? I hope my face doesn't give away my surprise, but I never thought of just ordering people to leave. I point to the younger man. "Bring the other dead one inside. Both parts."

The young man's skin goes sickly sallow, but he moves fast to do my bidding.

"You," I say, motioning to the older one. "Give me your radio. Mine was destroyed in the fight."

He complies swiftly, and even clips it to my shoulder for me. I slide the earpiece over my ear and nod my thanks. I ask him for his name, which doesn't register to my fight-mode brain. I clap him on the back. "I'll remember that you helped me."

I stoop and use the ragged end of my sleeve to protect my skin while I pick up the moonstone cuffs and tuck them back into my belt. The dungeon. I just need to remember how to get to the—

"Your Majesty? Where should we report?" the older thrall asks again.

"Stay here," I say, heading off confidently in what I hope is the right direction. "Cover the doors. No one enters."

I know there must be a secondary way out that I can sneak the human prisoners. But I have to find them, first.

Unbelievably, once I'm deeper into the building, "detention" is engraved in little directory signs on the walls. It's absurd and surreal: *Conference Rooms B - G. Catering Office. Supply. Detention.*

In case one needs to pick up paperclips on the way back from the totally normal-to-have-at-work dungeon, I guess.

The door down to the detention facility is disturbingly

regular, just wood with a narrow rectangle window, the glass crisscrossed through with wire. And this is where I run into the biggest problem yet.

It has a biometric lock.

I should have brought the dead guy with me. It's definitely too late for that, now. Fuck. How am I going to get past this?

Maybe it's time to give up. Go back and find Xiao. This was a bad idea.

Jonah was right, though. Maybe he's manipulating me, but he was right when he said that the only real way to prevent the pack from turning at the full moon is to stop the harvest.

Think. Think. I reach up and run a hand through my hair.

Something squishy falls and hits my shoulder, and I instinctively catch it in my palm.

It's the ginger guard's blue, barely damaged eyeball.

I want to drop it and scream and wipe my fingers all over my tattered suit while making all manner of horrified noises. I refrain. Instead, I take a few deep breaths, push down my queasy stomach, and hope the guy I killed has clearance. I hold the eye up to the scanner and mentally cross my fingers.

The relief I feel when the light on the scanner goes green and the door lock audibly clicks pulls a sharp, involuntary laugh from my throat. I check behind me, afraid I'll have alerted someone to my presence, but it's a full moon night. The place is empty.

And then, it's very much not. The halls go dark, illuminated suddenly by pulsing red light and a shrill, high alarm. Marching footsteps echo from down the hall and in the stairwell beyond the door. Dashing to the end of the hallway, I find the nearest office and try the handle. Luckily, it's open; I jump inside and slide to the floor with my back against the door to wait in the darkness for the thralls to find me.

Will Bailey let them execute you the way she executed Tara? I taunt myself, knowing this situation is so, so much different. Maybe they won't wait for an execution if they find me here. Maybe they'll just kill me.

"Response red. All personnel to the ceremonial grounds," a voice orders over the intercoms. "Repeat, all personnel to the ceremonial grounds. Response red."

There are shouts and more pounding boots in the carpeted hallway. Then, nothing. Just the pulsing red light and repetitive announcement. I wonder what a "response red" is; I assume it has something to do with what Xiao and Jonah are up to out there.

Slowly, I ease out of my hiding place. It seems safe. I dash back to the scanner, aware that I'm still cradling the eyeball in my hand.

The King and Queen owe me so, so big for this.

I open the door and pause, trying to figure out what to do with the damn eye. I might need it again. It's not like I can put it in a pocket.

I'm going to have to hold it the *whole time.*

Trying not to think about the moist weight in my hand, I take the stairs down, deep into the earth. The industrial cinderblock walls give way to ancient, clammy stones and I'm there, in the single row of cells that was recently packed with prisoners. Werewolves I knew my whole life. Werewolves I loved.

My sister sat in one of these cells, the night before our other sister murdered her.

The cells are still packed, but not with werewolf

traitors. They're human, and their fear is an unbearable, sweaty stench.

"What the *fuck* is going on?" A woman reaches between the bars and snatches at me. "Let us out of here!"

"I'm going to let you out," I say, raising my voice so everyone in the cells can hear me. That only draws more attention. There must be forty of them, crammed into four cells. No room to lay down, no water, no toilet. They're desperate and panicked and they all start begging me at once, drowning out my voice.

When I can't get them to stop and listen, I do what I have to do. I run to the deserted guard's desk beside the exit door and start flipping switches.

The third cell buzzes open just as I have the thought that these people might want to get revenge on their captors.

I flip all the switches and run away, kicking off my ruined shoe to prop the door open before I dash up the stairs to do the same with the one at the top. I hear the prisoners pouring out behind me. I'm not sure if I'm leading them or being chased, but I barrel in the direction of an exit sign. There's a fire door, so I won't have to take them out the front.

And there aren't scanners on fire doors.

The moment I hit the open night air, I throw the eye on the ground and wipe my hand vigorously on the thigh of my suit. It's going to take so much sanitizer before I can feel good about touching food ever again.

The air outside is thick with smoke. It rises in an orange column from the other side of the council building, and I freeze, a sense of overwhelming dread gripping me.

Xiao.

She can take care of herself. Just like I need to take care

of the prisoners. They're frightened animals fleeing a predator.

"That way!" I scream hoarsely, waving my arms to direct them. "Through the woods! To the road!"

I can't tell if they're listening to me or just fleeing in the direction they exited from. A man barrels past me and I grab his arm.

"Did everyone get out?" I ask as he draws his fist back to punch me.

My words thankfully register, and he restrains himself, nodding frantically. "I'm the last one."

I give him a shove and yell, "Go!" as I run in the opposite direction. I take the concrete path around the building and stop in my tracks.

The ceremonial grounds are on fire.

I stumble and fall to my knees in the grass. The standing stones, brought across the sea by our ancestors, stand as charred shadows obscured by the leaping flames. The building groans in the impossible blaze as thrall firefighters futilely try to battle the roaring destruction.

A figure darts across the grass, headed straight for me.

"We gotta go, come on, come on, come on!" Jonah barely stops as he runs by, scooping me up with his hands under my armpits and dragging me to my feet.

"What did you do?" I gasp, looking over my shoulder at everything my pack holds sacred burning up.

"You wanted my help stopping the ceremony," Jonah says gruffly. "They're definitely not going to be having it now."

"I let the human prisoners go," I confess.

His jaw goes tight. "I guess it was overkill then."

We hurry into the woods, then back up to the car.

"Where's Xiao?" I want her to be there immediately, so

I know she's okay. So I don't have this sick worry in my stomach. I need to know that the last conversation I had with her isn't really the last.

"Get in, we're picking her up." Jonah gestures to the car. When I won't get near it, he holds up the keys. "Seriously, do you think she would have just handed these over?"

He could have taken them. What if he did? What if he killed Xiao and—

I don't have time to second guess. "If you're lying, if you're trying anything, I'm going to kill a third person tonight."

He shrugs and tosses the keys to me. "Here."

I hurry around the car and jump into the driver's seat.

"She'll meet us in front of the gate," he says, buckling his seatbelt and grabbing the bar above the door as I accelerate.

Xiao waits for us in the road at the end of the long drive to the ceremonial grounds. The fire is visible above the trees now.

The Hierophant is in front of Xiao, her gun between them. His hands are tied. I take a deep breath and put the vehicle in park.

I'm the regent. It's time to act like a queen.

I get out of the car slowly, aware of how beat up I look, shoeless, tattered, and covered in blood. Xiao's eyes go wide, but I don't react.

"What is the meaning of this... this... coup?" The Hierophant spits the last word like a bad taste from his mouth.

"We're under attack from the St. Laurent pack," I tell him, enjoying the confusion and anger that cross his face. He knows exactly who is under attack, and from whom.

I open the back door of the car. "We're taking you to Aconitum Hall. For your own safety, of course."

Xiao pushes him in and climbs in beside him, the barrel of her gun pressed firmly into his side, and I get into the driver's seat.

We peel away into the night, my pack's sacred home burning behind us.

CHAPTER 22
BAILEY

Our little cabin in the clearing seems surreal the next day. The feeling that we're being watched doesn't go away, but it isn't as unnerving as it was before. Nathan and I aren't as afraid to go outdoors.

We do seem to be terrified of talking to each other.

The moment I woke that morning, my first thought was of a second baby inside me. How is it possible that I conceived a baby with a god? When I'm already pregnant? As the day went on, I started to wonder why the thought of it didn't scare me or make me furiously angry. I tried to be angry all through breakfast. It didn't work.

Sitting on a stump beside the fire, I slip my hand under my shirt to touch the bare skin of my stomach. Màni said he felt power. I don't feel powerful at all.

I'm lonely, though. Nathan has barely spoken to me since we got back. He's not cruel or outwardly angry. He's just reserved and formal, like he was when we were first mated. I don't like it.

He's scraping the remains of our breakfast into the fire

pit when I finally reach my breaking point. I put my hand on his arm. "Hey. Can you talk to me?"

He frowns. "I've been talking to you."

"You've been asking me questions and commenting on the weather," I argue. "*Talk* to me."

He tosses the pan into the grass and paces away a few steps, then turns back and says simply, "I don't know what there is to say."

"You could tell me how you're feeling. And then *I* could tell *you* how *I'm* feeling," I suggest.

"What for?" He's not being rude just to be mean. He seems to be genuinely unfamiliar with the concept of talking about something that's bothering him.

"Well... so we know what we're both going through." If he won't say anything, I'll go first. It's not like he has anything better to do than listen. "I just found out I'm double pregnant. I didn't even know that was possible."

"I didn't, either," he says flatly. "But I didn't realize the gods were real, and that they walked the Earth." Quieter, he adds, "I didn't realize a lot of things, it seems."

Does he mean he didn't realize I would ever cheat on him? "Are you angry with me?"

A stricken expression crosses his face. "No. No, of course not."

"I thought... because what I did with him—"

I stop myself. I was under some kind of spell when that happened. And Nathan had cheated on me tons of times when he *wasn't* being magically influenced by a god.

Now, *I'm* angry.

"You know what?" I snap, sitting up straighter. "I don't care if you're mad about that. Because it wasn't my fault. I thought I was dreaming. I had my hand back and everything. How was I supposed to know—"

"You couldn't have," he agrees, coming to my side and laying a hand on my shoulder. "And that's why I'm angry, and none of it is directed at you."

My mood swings wildly to sadness and shame. "I'm sorry. I don't know why I was accusing you of... I don't know what I was accusing you of." I rub my cheek, trying to massage away some of the tension in my jaw.

Nathan drops to one knee beside me and holds my gaze. "Bailey, what he did to you was unconscionable. He took advantage of you when you had no idea what was happening. I know he's a god, and that his ways are different from ours. But I can't find it in myself to see what he did to you as anything other than rape."

I drop my head. "I know. I should feel that way, myself. I've been trying to, actually. But he *is* a god. And he doesn't seem to understand anything about us. We're all werewolves, but he's... like a different species."

"He's a god," Nathan agrees. "But when I look at him, all I see is a man who raped my hallucinating mate and threw her in the freezing grass to die."

I have no doubt that the wolves watched over me that night, but Nathan won't want to hear that, and I don't want to say it. I want him to have his anger, perhaps selfishly; his protectiveness and possessiveness are as close to love as I believe I'll ever get from him.

"And then what they did to us last night. That weird ritual—" he stops himself, face turning sharply to the sky. "Do you hear that?"

I do. The low thrum of a plane's engine.

"It's Xiao," I say confidently.

"How can you possibly know that?" Nathan asks.

How can I know that? But I do. Maybe I can remember the sound the plane made before. Maybe it's that mother's intuition I've always heard of. Or, it's the power of the god-baby in me. All I can do is shrug.

"Go into the cabin," he says, never taking his eyes from the sky.

I know it's Xiao, but I feel his anxiety, so I do what he says, and I watch from the window as the plane lands on the water. It's the right plane. Nathan lifts his arm to signal Xiao as the pontoons cut a silvery wake through the dark water, and I see a flicker of movement in the trees crowding the shoreline at the edge of our clearing. As I watch, ribbons of white wind through the black trunks.

It's only then that I realize the danger.

We talked to Màni about the thralls. I know what he thinks of them. A thrall is about to step onto the dock, too far from Nathan for him to help her, and he was outmatched, anyway.

I sprint outside just as Xiao's boots hit the wood, but it's too late. Flashes of white shoot from the trees, wolves and werewolves alike running to cut off her access to the land.

"Stop!" Nathan shouts, though I'm not sure if it's to me or to the wolves.

Xiao grunts as she's carried off her feet, the sound bludgeoned out with the breath from her lungs as Màni slams her full-body onto her back on the dock.

"Màni, no!" I scream, my calves pumping as I outrun Nathan and reach the wolves clustered at the edge of the water. They surround me, holding me back with their silvery stares. Even the half-changed werewolves crouch defensively and growl up at me.

All I care is that Màni's raised, clawed hand doesn't descend; I have no doubt he can knock her head off with a single swipe. He looks to me, puzzled, his foot on Xiao's neck.

"Let her up, please!" I beg. She's still struggling, so she's still alive. "She's not like them."

"She is one of them," he says, but lifts his foot off her windpipe.

"She's on our side. She's one of the most effective weapons we have." I glance down at the gap between two of the wolves surrounding me. They're not going to hurt me. They're just trying to scare me.

I push past them, even as they snarl and snap their jaws. Màni's chin lifts, almost as if he's admiring me.

I approach him slowly. "This thrall is called Xiao. She is working against the thralls with us. She protects us and brings us supplies so that we can survive out here."

He looks down at her like a person trying to decide whether to squish a bug or scoop it up with a magazine and set it outside.

I glance to the shore. Nathan stands outside the ring of wolves. I see his fear and indecision from where I stand. He must feel so powerless, the worst thing for Nathan to feel. He relishes control. Lately, he has none.

"Please," I say, and hesitantly lay my hand on the god's arm. "Please let her go."

He stares into my eyes for a long time. His are fathomless. Ancient. Looking into them, I see the stars, the planets, the universe unfolding throughout time.

After a disorienting second, he shrugs and starts back down the dock with a cheerful, "Okay."

I offer Xiao my hand. She's slower getting to her feet than I suspect she would be if anyone else had body-slammed her. She glares after Màni. "*Okay?*"

"Don't," I whisper urgently.

"Who the fuck is—" she begins, but I tug her arm hard. I shake my head and her furious expression returns to on-duty neutral. "Yes, Your Majesty."

We follow Màni to the shore, where he gestures to his wolves. They head directly for the fire while Nathan looks on, as if he's superfluous to all that's happened. I hate the powerlessness he must be feeling but there is no way to relieve it without coming across as patronizing.

Xiao keeps one eye on the strange creatures laying in the grass around the fire as she kneels before Nathan. "Your Majesty."

"I take it you're not bringing good news," he says wearily. "Rise."

Xiao stands. "No, it is not good news, Your Majesty. May we talk where there aren't... where we'll... I'm sorry, Your Majesties, who are these...people?"

She deserves to know, since they just tried to kill her. I'm just not sure how she'll take the explanation. I know that it's real and it still sounds so far-fetched in my mind. "Please just take my words as fact, no matter what your rational mind might tell you. It will save us time," I begin. "They came here from Iceland, with our ancestors. But when our pack moved south, they stayed behind. They've been living here, exactly as werewolves lived centuries ago, ever since."

Xiao nods slowly, but points out, "Your Majesty, your ancestors moved south because nothing could survive here."

"Thralls could not survive."

Xiao, Nathan, and I jump, all three of us making startled exclamations at the sudden, silent appearance of Màni beside us.

"This," I say, pressing my hand to my chest to try to still my racing heart, "is Màni. He's a god."

"The god of the moon," Xiao says, her voice faint with wonder.

"I accidently..." How should I put it? "Fucked. Him. A god. I had sex with—well, it wasn't really sex, it was like—"

"It was sex," Màni interjects.

Nathan's fist clenches at his side.

"It was a ceremony," I quickly correct myself. And the god. "I thought I was dreaming but... you know, the point is that now, somehow, this pack is involved and I'm pregnant with two babies and one of them is the son of a god."

Xiao just blinks at me.

Oh no. I've broken her.

"You've brought news," Nathan says, drawing Xiao out of her open-mouthed confusion a little. "What's happened?"

She takes a deep breath and collects herself before she tells us. "Your Majesties... to prevent the full moon ceremony, drastic measures were taken."

"How drastic?" Nathan snaps.

"The ceremonial grounds have been burned." Xiao delivers the news as a thrall guard giving a report. Flat, emotionless. Factual. "The Hierophant is currently hostage at Aconitum Hall. The Lady Tara freed the humans that were meant to be harvested."

"Fuck!" Nathan's shout rings off the water and startles birds from the trees. Some of the wolves in the grass raise their heads. Nathan turns away, one hand in his hair as he takes a few angry paces away. Turning back, he demands, "One of those things would have sufficed. Just one!"

"I take full responsibility, Your Majesty," Xiao begins.

I cut her off. "No, you don't. You said my sister released those humans. Don't take responsibility for that."

"In that case, I won't take responsibility for the fire." Her eyes widen at her verbal slip-up. "I apologize—"

"We need to get back to Toronto. Now." Nathan stabs his finger toward the ground for emphasis. "Bailey, get your things—"

"You cannot take her away from here," Màni says. He's calm and quiet and motionless and terrifying. "I won't allow it."

"Won't allow it?" Nathan's face twists in fury. "She is my *mate*."

Please, don't push him, I beg Màni silently. No matter how Nathan has treated me in the past, I know that he won't let anyone take me from him. He might never love me. He might take up with another mistress again, for all I know, but I'm his mate. He'll never stop taking his duty to protect me seriously.

He would die, first. And Màni could make that happen.

I put my hand on the god's arm again. "My pack is in danger. They need me to return."

"Your pack is here." He nods toward his white wolves. "Nathan's too. You are with us now."

"It doesn't work that way." How do I explain to a god that we're turning down an honor he's offering? "People I care about are in trouble. If I stay here, I'm abandoning them. Surely, you understand that."

He says nothing.

Then Nathan reminds him, "You offered your help unquestioningly. Letting us go is helping."

"Ah." Màni nods his understanding, but adds, "How will we help if you are in Toronto, and we are here?"

"I—"

"I'll have to go with you," he says simply, and walks toward the dock.

"Wait, wait," I say, hurrying after him as the wolves rise to follow.

Behind me, I hear Xiao say, in a panicked voice, "I can't fit all these people on that plane!"

"My pack will remain here," Màni calls without looking back. "I will go. They are not in danger here, but my son's people are."

"Your..." Xiao's professionalism is stunned away. "What is even going on?"

I wish I knew.

CHAPTER 23
BAILEY

There is so much that Màni is unfamiliar with.

Not the flying; he takes that in stride. He's seen search and rescue planes before, he explains. He knows about ATVs because they've crossed the bog for the same reason. He's familiar with, but has never used, snowmobiles.

The car ride from the airport to Aconitum Hall baffles him. He spends much of the drive putting the window up and down, marveling at the buildings and other vehicles we pass.

"And that?" he asks excitedly, pointing at a Tim Horton's.

"Restaurant. You can go there to get food." I hurry to rephrase it. "Humans can go there, with currency, to purchase food."

"You said that happens at a store," he says doubtfully, as if I'm trying to trick him.

"A store has the raw ingredients," I explain. "A restaurant has the food all prepared. But werewolves tend to go to werewolf-owned businesses."

"And this 'Tim Horton,'" he says, sounding the name out slowly. "He is not a werewolf?"

"No." They do have good coffee, though. Some of my friends and I snuck into one on a school outing and indulged in forbidden human coffee and a donut.

It's possible that you've been living in a cult, I think, and push it firmly away.

"You've gotten good at reading, fast," I compliment Màni. "You couldn't read at all when we got on the plane, and now look at you."

"I could read. Just not this language." He rolls the window up. "I learn things quickly because I am a god."

"As you keep reminding us," Nathan says. He's riding in the front with Xiao. I've kept one ear on their conversation as Xiao filled him in on what's happened while we've been away. My sister has been busy, kidnapping magicians and the Hierophant, blowing up the ceremonial grounds, letting a bunch of humans loose to tell all the other humans about werewolves in the city.

All right, so I can't blame my sister for the kidnappings or the explosion, but she did go along with them. And while I expected Nathan to rage-out at every new development as he listens to the story, he never does.

"Has any announcement been made?" Nathan asks after Xiao finishes recounting the events of the night at the ceremonial grounds.

"I don't believe so." Xiao puts on her turn signal and guides the car around a corner. "The Lady Tara was waiting for Your Majesties to return."

"That's the first thing we'll need to handle when we arrive." Nathan drums his fingers on the armrest on the door. "Bailey, be dressed and ready within fifteen minutes after we get home."

"Please," I add for him.

To my surprise, he gives a short grunt of laughter. "Be dressed and ready, *please.*"

Traffic is light and we pull through the gate at Aconitum Hall minutes later.

"This is where your pack lives?" Màni asks, peering up at the gothic castle's spires through the sunroof.

"It's where the king and queen live," I tell him. "And my sister and people who are important to the court."

"All members of the pack are important," he responds with a small frown of confusion. "Why do you keep separate from them?"

From the front seat, Nathan answers, "Because our ways have changed. We've adapted to blend in against the world of the humans."

"Camouflage," Xiao adds, then says, "I'm sorry, Your Majesty."

Nathan waves a hand. "I think we're long past this type of formality."

We can't just walk Màni through the front doors. We don't know who might be inside, apart from my sister. If human law enforcement has shown up with questions about the prisoners or the fire, how do we explain a half-wolf, half-human, snow white god? There could be members of the council inside, too, and as far as we know, our fellow werewolves are trying to kill my baby. Xiao drives us to the private royal entrance and pulls the car up as close to the door as possible.

As it turns out, that's pretty close; the car nearly scrapes the brick, and Màni and I are barely outside for a full step before we're through the door and into Aconitum Hall.

Home.

Before our exile, I thought I would never feel like the

royal residence was my true home. I didn't care if I ever returned. I wished we wouldn't have to, then. But being back is like being enfolded in the warmest, most loving embrace I've ever felt. Like...

Like being in Nathan's arms.

I glance at him in utter shock, and he frowns back, concerned. "Everything all right?"

"I'm fine," I say, nodding too fast. "Got a little dizzy."

That's the truth. The realization that Nathan does love me, even if he doesn't know it himself, rocks every needy emotional receptor in my brain. The sweetest, tightest fist closes around my heart and stomach, and I ache to touch him. I want to tell him that I've figured it out but that seems like a sure-fire way to make him completely shut down.

Or maybe I'm just imagining things.

"There," Màni says, gesturing to the open kitchen door. "You could easily house a dozen of your pack mates there."

"Our pack has changed," Nathan says tightly.

If Màni recognizes Nathan's disrespect, he doesn't react to it. "It can change again."

"We need to put him someplace no one is going to run into him," Xiao says in a deeply exasperated tone I've never heard before.

"The safe room?" I suggest. It's secure and within the residence, plus it has the bonus of being a place Nathan and I won't ever go again. Not after what happened to us to put us in there in the first place.

Xiao shakes her head. "The Hierophant is in there."

A shadow falls around us, cloaking the hall in darkness. It's Màni's rage, swelling into every millimeter of available space between all of us.

"We need him," I say softly. "Just for now."

The shadow recedes and the air lightens, but Màni says nothing.

With a grimace, Nathan orders, "Put him in my bedroom for now. Get him whatever he needs, food, water in a bowl—"

I nudge Nathan hard with my elbow.

"Just do what needs to be done to keep him happy and contained," he finishes. Then, to Màni, he says, "We wish to offer you hospitality."

"Yes, the bowl of water sounds particularly hospitable."

I look over my shoulder at Màni. Was that sarcasm?

He lifts a white brow. I face forward again.

"Where's Tara?" I ask Xiao, though how I expect her to know when we've both arrived at the same time, I have no clue.

Still, Xiao has an answer. "Probably in the conference room. Hannah has been here all night."

"And Ryan?" I ask. It's unlike my best friends to not rush to my aid.

"With the Council," Nathan answers confidently for her, adding, "They wouldn't sit idle after what's happened."

A flight of stairs and a locked door brings us into the living area of the residence. It's deserted. Not a thrall in sight guarding anything.

"It's empty," Nathan states the obvious.

"The Lady Tara will need to explain that," Xiao says, stopping beside the door to Nathan's study. "Shall I take your guest upstairs?"

"Yes, please," Nathan says, and continues on by himself.

I want to go after him, but it feels rude to turn my back on a god. I lift my chin to look up at Màni. "Thank you for being here to help us. We do appreciate it."

"Your mate is angry with me." His tone is curious, not condemning, and he observes Nathan like he's an exotic bird.

"He is, and I can explain why later, okay?" Something about Màni makes me want to protect his feelings, and not just because he's a powerful being. His odd mixture of innocence and phenomenal wisdom form a charisma trap. I want to be his friend and guide him through this totally new world, but I crave closeness to his god nature, too.

"Later," he repeats, and walks directly into the study. I watch through the door as he strides to the switch in the wall that opens the very dramatic secret door there.

He knew how to do it without being told.

One concern at a time. My current issue is that my husband, the king of a werewolf pack currently at war with its thralls, has marched off unprotected. I catch up with him, but I'm out of breath by the time I do.

"We should stay in pairs, at least," I wheeze. "For safety."

"I couldn't be near him another moment," Nathan mutters, still walking too fast.

"I know, I know." I feel like I'm trying to keep the peace at a slumber party. "But you have to stop this. We have a god helping us. A god! You're going to let your jealousy endanger that? And endanger you?"

"It's not jealousy!" he snaps.

"It sure seems like it is." I stop and put my hand and stump on my hips.

He turns and stalks back to me, until we're toe-to-toe and he towers over me. There's a storm in his eyes as he grinds out, "You are my mate. I have every right to be jealous—"

A vision of my palm connecting with his jaw makes my

hand twitch. I vent my frustration with words, instead. "What about me? Did I have a right to be jealous when someone was putting their hands all over *my* mate?"

"I never said you couldn't be jealous!" he shouts back.

"You are so..." Heat flares in my cheeks and I go lightheaded, I'm so angry. I take a step back and he stops crowding me, visibly swallowing a lump of remorse.

"Bailey, I am so sorry." He moves to take me into his arms, but at the moment, I've had enough. I hold up my hand and side-step him, heading for the conference room doors.

"We don't have time for this." And I don't want to talk about her, and I don't want to fight over my connection to a god in comparison to his gross affair. "In fact, I'd be fine if she never came up again!"

I threw the conference room doors open. Three very startled faces greeted me: Hannah, Tara...

Amber.

CHAPTER 24
BAILEY

I wish I still had my moonstone bracelet. I would put it on and lunge over the table before anyone could stop me from ripping the bitch's head off.

My ex-best friend and ex-sister shoot to their feet and curtseyed to me. The two closest people to me in the world show proper deference but Amber just stays in her chair, her expression neutral.

"It is customary to rise when a queen enters the room," I snap at her. Turning to Tara, I demand, "What the fuck do you think you're doing, having her here?"

Nathan enters the room just a few steps behind me. *That's* when she stands.

And she has the nerve to answer on my sister's behalf. "*She* thinks she's saving this pack. And I *am* a queen."

"Were. You *were* a queen," I correct her with a sneer.

"She is a queen," Tara says quietly.

Behind me, Nathan chuckles. "Manhattan?"

"But of course." Her lips, the dark shade of port wine, bend into a triumphant smirk. "It's good to see you, Nathan."

"If you take one step toward her, I'll kill her," I growl. I'm angry enough that I can.

Wisely, Nathan doesn't move a muscle.

"Can we not threaten to kill each other?" Hannah snaps. "First of all, hi, Bailey. Nice to see that you survived, *best friend.*"

I take a deep, calming breath. Begrudgingly.

"You both need to be debriefed on what's happened in the last twenty-four hours." Tara pushes a rolling chair out of her way and moves to one of the several white boards on easels spread through the room. When we left, there was only one board. Now, there are seven, and they're all crowded with increasingly cramped handwriting. They're also organized with headers like "Mythology" and "Pack Threat" and "Thrall Problem." She pauses and tells us, "Sit down, Your Majesties."

I place myself on the other side of the room from Amber and shoot Nathan a warning glare. He sits between Hannah and I and spreads his hands as if to say, *I'm doing what you want.*

But what I want is to not have to threaten anybody's life. I shouldn't even have to ask my mate not to be interested in someone else.

Even with a centuries-old binding spell on us, I can't make him want me.

I can't believe I let a long vacation in the woods trick me into thinking he loves me.

"Bailey?" Tara's voice jerks my attention back to where it belongs. She gives me a sisterly scowl and points to the board. "This is a rough outline of the plan. Red is what has been done, green is what we need to do."

"Start with how the ceremonial ground burned," Nathan says.

"I'll start from Wyrding House, if that's all right with Your Majesty?" She doesn't wait for his permission. "Xiao and I went to the magician's club. We deemed him useful and kidnapped him. He cooperated with us in the siege on the ceremonial ground."

"Where is he, now?" I ask.

"In the dungeon at the council building." She grabs a marker and draws an asterisk beside his name. "Not sure what we're going to do with him yet, but that's what the brainstorm is on board six."

"We'll deal with him." Nathan motions to the whiteboard in front of us. "Please, continue."

"We embarked on a three-pronged siege of the ceremonial grounds just after dusk last night. While Xiao took the Hierophant hostage 'for his protection'—" Tara makes air quotes with her fingers. "—I freed the human prisoners meant to be harvested. The magician burned down the ceremonial grounds."

"How did he manage that?" Nathan asks.

Tara shrugs. "He cast Magic Missile? I didn't ask him. After that, we brought the Hierophant here, and he's currently in the safe room."

"Xiao told us that part," I say, forcing myself not to spare even a flicker of a glance at Amber. "It doesn't explain what my husband's former mistress is doing in my home."

"We blamed the attack on the St. Laurent pack." Hannah opens a folder and produces a sheet of paper. "This is what Ryan is currently presenting to the council."

Nathan takes it and scans the words, his hand cupped idly over his mouth as he thinks. Then, he pushes the paper to me. Phrases like "results of our preliminary investigation" and "response team led by royal security forces" swim around my head as I note the conclusion:

"This unprecedented attack on our ceremonial grounds can only be interpreted as an act of war."

"Queen Amber is here on her husband's behalf to pledge Manhattan's support for our side in the war that Council will urge you to declare later tonight," Hannah explains.

"On your husband's behalf?" Nathan directs to Amber and chuckles fondly.

I eye the ballpoint pen beside Hannah's folder and briefly consider plunging it into my mate's eye.

I don't look at Amber when she speaks, but judging from the tone of her voice, she's considering the same violent option. She says coolly, "I'm here as a diplomatic emissary. Would you like Manhattan's help or not?"

"My apologies, *Your Majesty*," Nathan responds with a sarcastic lilt. "Please, let your husband the King know how grateful we are for your support."

"We were going to issue a statement as soon as we returned," I interrupt their little spat before I vomit on the table. "It must look strange to the pack that we haven't been seen or heard from in the wake of this."

"No one knows you're missing, still," Tara reassures us. "And we made it clear that you've been taken to a secure location for meetings with your advisors."

"Are my advisors aware of this?" Nathan asks.

Tara blinks. "What advisors?"

Nathan gives my sister a rare smile. "Exactly. I don't have advisors."

"Maybe you should get some," I snap.

He ignores me. "Which is why the excuse may cause some suspicion."

Tara taps the board beside an unfinished item. "Xiao

feels it's too dangerous for you to physically go to the council chambers."

"Ryan agrees," Hannah puts in.

"We're leaning toward an emergency pack meeting here, in the throne room." Tara tosses her marker onto the table and drops into a chair. My rage at Amber's presence has cooled enough that I finally see the dark circles around my sister's eyes, the unwashed state of her hair, her overall paleness.

"Have you slept?" I ask her, guilt gnawing at me. I've been on a camping getaway while she raced across the ocean and back.

"A little. On the plane." She shrugs. "This is my top priority at the moment."

Nathan isn't as concerned about her as I am. "Judging by the information you disclosed in front of her, I assume Queen Amber is aware of the thrall treachery?"

"I have a basic understanding of it," she confirms. "They put a spell on you?"

"I'm surprised she didn't already know that," I say with a cutting cheerfulness. "Since you involved her in so many other areas of pack business."

"Our relationship ended before we knew of the binding," Nathan replies. "At your request."

"I don't bear you any ill-will," Amber says, and I realize with horror that she's speaking to *me*.

That's it. I shoot to my feet, cutting off whatever bullshit she's about to spew next. "You have no right to, in the first place. You were fucking *my* mate!"

She blinks slowly. Calmly. Once again, I've lost my temper, and she appears to be the rational one while I'm shouting.

Shame burns through me. I'm standing in front of

what my mate wants. What he would prefer me to be. And I'm being the exact opposite of her.

I sit down and, fighting back tears, manage to keep my voice even as I ask Tara, "Do we believe the thralls suspect that they were our target?"

Tara and Hannah exchange glances.

"Answer," Nathan commands.

Tara looks down at the table, then meets our gazes. "There was a complication at the council chamber when I arrived to free the prisoners. I killed two guards."

"*You* killed them?" My sister doesn't even like to step on ants.

"The situation made it unavoidable," she says.

"How did you manage to kill them?" Nathan asks, eyeing her doubtfully. I don't blame him. She's short and slim and doesn't look like she could lift a five-pound weight with her skinny arms.

It had to be black moonstone.

My suspicion is confirmed when she says, "It's classified. I would be perfectly happy to explain it to Your Majesties in private."

They hadn't mentioned the black moonstone to Amber, then.

"What's the situation with the thralls in Manhattan?" Nathan asks Amber.

"It's not like I've had time to interview them about this new information," she begins. "And I obviously can't ask any of them, directly. Let me see what I can find out from our Hierophant in New York. He's not a fanatic like yours. He can be bought, for the right price."

I snorted. "I'm sure he can."

Nathan nudges my knee with his beneath the table. I dig my heel into his toes in answer. He doesn't react.

"Well. This has been insulting," Amber says, rising from her seat. "My car is waiting and it's a long drive. My husband's office will send you a formal decree of his support. I'll also send some of my personal security staff here; they're werewolves, not thralls. If I can help in any other way, do reach out. I know you both wish to be freed from this binding spell. I very much share that desire."

My nails cut into my palms.

Nathan rises, too. "I'll see you out."

I open my mouth to object but that's exactly what she wants. Another chance to prove that I'm not as sophisticated and self-assured as she is. That I'm not fit to be a queen.

"Tara, Hannah, we need to discuss what I should wear tonight," I say, hoping I come off as too distracted by practicalities to care about what my traitor mate is doing. Of course, the second the words leave my mouth, I criticize myself for sounding like a vapid, fashion-obsessed teenager. I add, "And we need to formalize arrangements for this announcement."

"Of course, Your Majesty," Hannah says, and Tara echoes her, but all three of us are looking at the door my husband and his mistress have left through.

I wait until I no longer hear their footsteps and say, "Excuse me." I don't look at my sister or best friend as I leave. I don't want to see pity or concern on their faces, because I know that they know exactly where I'm going.

I'm able to follow Amber and Nathan without being seen, through a combination of distance and them being distracted by the conversation they're having. They don't go through the royal residence. At least, I know they're not going to sneak up to his bedroom for the sex he claims they don't have. If it were sex, somehow that would be so much better than whatever weird relationship they have now. But Màni being hidden in the royal bedchamber would really be a mood killer for Nathan.

He'd have a difficult time not being the only god in the room.

I stop at the top of the stairs that lead down to the main hall, grateful for the echo off the checked marble tile below.

"You're endangering her," Amber is saying when I'm close enough to catch the words.

"You have no idea what's happened while we've been away," he replies angrily. "There are other parties involved in this now, ones who are invested in Bailey's safety and the safety of my heir."

"Are you implying that I'm not invested?" Amber demands.

"I'm implying that you have the most to gain from her death." Is Nathan making an accusation? Is that what I'm hearing? That he doesn't trust Amber?

Under normal circumstances, maybe this would make me happy. But hearing him state that as a fact, like it would just be a foregone conclusion that he would make things with her official if I died, even knowing she might be the cause? That robs me of any spiteful glee I might have had. And it wounds my heart.

To her credit, Amber calls him on it. "Would I? I didn't think you were the kind of man who would marry the person who assassinated his mate."

"You're twisting my words," he argues. "I was suggesting a motive, not guaranteeing your success."

"If you're so concerned that I'll hurt your child-bride, I'll send someone else here next time," she snaps.

He calls her bluff. "I would appreciate that."

I can't help myself. I have to see them; have to know

what their body language is toward each other. Even if it hurts me. I creep down a few steps, hoping I'm still in shadow. Nathan stands with his back to me, and Amber is too focused on him to notice me. At least, that's what I assume, because if she knows I'm there, she has a lot of nerve stepping as close to him as she does and laying her hands on his chest.

"This would have been so simple, Nathan," she says, all the anger in her voice and bearing fading into regret. "We could have been happy."

"But I wouldn't be a king. You wouldn't be a queen," he says, and gently moves her hands away. "That was always the goal. To rule."

"To rule together." There's a pleading in her tone that cuts me deeply. She still wants him. "If you had just waited until Greater London—"

"What's done is done." He steps back. "Your car is waiting."

"Nathan!" she calls after him, but he's already turned his back on her.

And he's heading straight for the staircase I'm standing on with no place to hide.

I didn't think this part through very well. I'm frozen in place as Amber hurries out the door. Nathan passes me, his face expressionless, and doesn't say a word.

CHAPTER 25

TARA

"I made a huge mistake," I say, staring guiltily at the door my sister just stormed out of.

"Oh, you think?" Hannah seethes.

"What was I supposed to do?" The Queen of Manhattan showed up within hours of the fire, looking for answers and offering the help of her pack. "If I sent her away, it would have been a diplomatic catastrophe."

"Causing a royal mating split up, that wouldn't be catastrophic." Hannah rolls her eyes.

"I'm doing the best that I can. I didn't ask for this!"

"I didn't ask for it either." Hannah spreads her hands and lets them fall. "I never wanted this proximity to the crown and all this danger, but Bailey is my friend. She deserves my loyalty."

"Like Clare deserved Bailey's?" I stand and take a deep breath. I've been trapped in the conference room all day. I'm exhausted and I never got a chance to really scour all the gore off me. Everything aches. "I'll see you at the announcement."

"Tara—" Hannah calls after me.

I ignore her. It's better than staying and talking it out and saying things I don't mean.

I stalk back through the residence, my skin tingling with apprehension. Xiao has only been gone a few hours and I know that she got back safely, otherwise my sister and the king wouldn't be here. Still, I have to see her with my own eyes to know that she's okay.

Aconitum Hall without guards and servants is terrifying at a time like this. It feels like every door I pass could open for an assassin waiting inside. Worse, there's no one to ask for directions; Xiao had convinced the head of thrall security that the building should be placed on lockdown and all of the passcodes and badges be deactivated. The empty corridors seem so much longer now.

I expect to find my way to the royal residence via sounds of shouting and things being thrown, but like the rest of Aconitum Hall, it's eerily quiet.

Maybe they killed each other, I think with an uncharitable snort of amusement. Then, I spot Xiao.

"Hey," I say, lifting my hand in a timid wave as I approach. She's standing outside the door to the king's study. "Are they in there?"

Xiao shakes her head. "To be honest, I'm not sure what's in there."

I lift my eyebrows in invitation for her to explain.

"It's not my place," she begins, then rolls her eyes and says, "Fuck it. They brought someone back with them."

"They brought someone back from..." They've been hiding in the woods. Who could they have possibly met there?

"I'm willing to risk the ire of the King and Queen to show you something. Will you have my back?" she asks.

The request startles me. Xiao has done nothing but faithfully serve without asking any favors in return. This must be important.

"I want to promise that I won't let anything happen to you, but I think we both know exactly how much power I have." I don't need to say Clare's name to make my point. "I'll do what I can."

She looks both ways up and down the hall.

"They're having an argument," I say with a shrug. "I assume."

She doesn't question me and opens the door to the study. Inside, a bookshelf is slightly out of place. Xiao slips her hand behind and pushes it aside, revealing a secret staircase.

"The king's bedroom is up there," Xiao explains.

Now, things feel a little more dangerous. The place where the king sleeps should be the most secure part of a palace. Entering it without permission must carry some kind of treason charge.

I don't believe Xiao will get me in death-sentence trouble, though. I follow her up the stairs, to exactly the type of room I'd expect someone like Nathan to have; checkerboard floor, taxidermized animals, antlers carved on everything and, ugh, red satin sheets on his giant bed. It's like someone mixed every Disney villain's lair together and threw the bucket against the walls.

A fire is burning in the massive fireplace. It illuminates a flicker of white at the edge of a high-backed chair in front of the hearth. I take a step forward and note that Xiao is going no further.

"You may come closer." The silky, deep voice is unfamiliar but compelling. A figure unfolds from the chair, rising like a pillar of ivory gilded by the firelight. He turns to face me, and I have a very difficult time taking in what I'm seeing. He's normal…ish. A face like a person, a body like a person, but with the silky-white coat of a wolf. A curtain of hair in the same pale shade falls all around him like a hooded cloak, broken by two white wolf ears atop his head.

"Are you…" I can't even think of what I should ask. "A furry?"

He looks down and strokes the hair on his arm. "I am furry, yes."

"This is Màni," Xiao says from the top of the stairs. "He's some kind of god."

I know the name well.

I fall to my knees and bow my head.

The god's feet move into my view as I stay crouched over, my heart racing. His palm falls on the back of my head.

I'm too familiar with the myths and lore of our pack to not utterly geek out, but it's not like I can just start babbling questions at a god. I don't know how I should address him. If I even should address him. Maybe I should stay quiet.

"Rise," he says, and I lift my gaze. He's naked, like we are in animal form, but partially mimicking our human-like appearance. It's disconcerting.

"You're supposed to have black hair," I blurt.

He tilts his head.

"It's just… it's in all the stories… you have black hair." *Stop criticizing the appearance of a god!* "I'm sorry, I've never met a god before."

He says nothing, seemingly content to just watch me.

"Um…why are you here?" I ask.

"Your sister and her mate brought me," he answers.

"No, no, I mean." My brain races over all the old stories. "Why would you be here, with us? We're wolves."

His eyes light with a strange silver glow. "You do know me."

"I know that you're supposed to run from wolves." I can't find the strength to stand, so I sit cross-legged on the floor, staring up at him. "In fact, you can't *stop* running, or—"

"Or I'll be devoured." His lips bend in an enigmatic smile.

"Exactly." The story of the two cosmic wolves chasing the moon and sun through the sky was a popular picture book for the young in our pack. I read it endlessly, tracing the illustrations with my finger in fascination, until I outgrew bedtime stories.

"Come. Sit with me." He gestures to the other chair, and I somehow find my feet and make my way to it. I don't want to stare at him, but I can't help it. He's here. A god. Sitting in my brother-in-law's ugly bedroom.

I clasp my hands together in my lap, my body practically vibrating with nervousness. Is there protocol when faced with a god?

"In the days when humans first walked the earth, they, too, were pursued by wolves," Màni begins. It's a conversation, not a sermon, which makes the experience surreal. He asks, "What did those humans do to avoid being devoured?"

I open my mouth, but it takes a moment for my answer to come out. "They tamed them."

He spreads his hands as if it's that simple.

It's not, by a longshot. "We're the descendants of Fenrir—"

"Are you?" He motions to a tattered, leather-bound

book on the ornamental table beside him. "According to the teachings of your thrall holy men, you're the descendants of Lycaon, as well. And Lupa. Now, the wolf who will devour me?"

"I—"

"You have been deceived." He picks up the no doubt priceless book and tosses it casually into the fire.

"He's been doing that for a while," Xiao says.

"I read them, first," he explains. "I only burn the ones that contain lies. So far, they all have. Lies, written about you by your servants, who then feed them to you as if they were the milk of truth and you the suckling babes at Lupa's teats."

"I don't understand." Anything. Literally anything, at this moment. I've never been more confused.

"I did not wish to flee across the night sky for all eternity. So, I tamed the progeny of those cosmic beasts, as Lupa tamed the dangerous creatures that would hunt her." He frowns. "Your thralls tell you the beginning of our tales. They don't tell you the end."

"With all respect, your..." I pause. "Do I call you 'Your Majesty'?"

His frown deepens. "You know my name."

"I mean... to be polite." Of course, a god isn't bound by earthly ideas of social propriety. "What I was going to say was, they do tell us the end. They tell us about Ragnarök."

"They tell you visions of a future they know nothing of." He examines the glossy claws at the ends of his fingers as if he's inspecting a manicure.

"So, Ragnarök isn't going to happen?" Not that I've been looking forward to it. It's all just stories to me. Or was.

"Your thralls are certainly hoping it will." He shakes his head. "None of the gods are interested in their war, anymore. It seems the humans you've grown so attached to wish to force the issue."

"Is that why you're here? To deal with the thralls, the way you dealt with us?" Meanwhile, my brain screams, *It's all real! Everything you've read! All of it is real!*

His response cuts through the wonder and fear in my brain. "I would not tame them. Some animals cannot be tamed. They must be put down."

I look to Xiao. She stands stone-faced and doesn't react.

Màni tilts his head. "I'm sorry, are those the wrong words? I've only just learned to speak your language."

"No, they're the right words. It's just not something we want to do," I say gently. Like I can dissuade a god from destroying anything.

"Because they keep you comfortable." He nods in understanding.

"No, because culling is barbaric." I stop myself. "Not that you're barbaric. We just... we don't like killing."

"You kill to change. You devour hearts. And I smell death in this place." He lifts his head and sniffs to demonstrate.

"Are you sure it's not the taxidermy?" I quip. *Why are you cracking jokes in front of a god?*

He studies me for a long moment. "You're compassionate."

"I try to be." It's been difficult to find compassion for my sister, for her mate, for my own mate, banished.

"It is a noble quality but one that can disguise the truth as cruelty." He reaches one clawed hand toward me. "You are tired."

"I had a rough night." I don't know why, but I extend my hand to his. The moment our fingers touch, my earlier exhaustion leaves my body on a wave of warm peace. My eyelids grow heavy.

"It's you," he says peering into my eyes. In his, I see the endless, swirling universe.

"Me?"

"You are the death I smell in this place. You've taken a life. Two lives." Then he nods. "You've done well, though it pains you."

I jerk my hand back. "Are you reading my mind?"

"Yes." He seems confused as to why I would object to that.

"I..." I push myself up from the chair slowly. "I'm gonna go talk to my sister."

He waves a hand in dismissal and leans down. There's a stack of books knee-high on the other side of his chair.

I really hope there are extant copies that aren't in this house.

As I pass Xiao, I motion for her to follow me. I wait until we're down the stairs and in the hallway before I whisper, "You were absolutely right to show him to me."

"Is he really a god?" she asks. But it's not what she's asking. She wants to know if the thralls are truly in danger.

"He's a god," I confirm. "And we have to get you as far away as we can, as fast as we can."

But how does one outrun a god?

CHAPTER 26
TARA

I find Bailey and Hannah in the walk-in wardrobe in the Queen's bedroom.

"There you are," Bailey says in a fake chipper tone. "I was wondering where you were."

"I was in the King's bedroom. Meeting Màni." It tumbles out of me. I wouldn't have been able to lie, anyway.

Bailey says, her face going pale, "How did you—"

"Xiao showed me. And I can't believe that wasn't the very first thing you said when you got here." Who just fails to mention the presence of a god in their home?

"I was going to tell you. I just couldn't because of who was in the room." Bailey turns back to the rack of gowns she and Hannah are picking through. "Speaking of things we should tell each other."

"I think 'heads up, there's a murderous god in the house' is a little bigger than 'heads up, your unfaithful mate's ex is here.'" How can she not see that?

"As I said, I couldn't tell you at the moment. And then you were gone." Bailey pulls a blood-red gown with slashed, puff sleeves and a voluminous brocade skirt off the bar. She holds it up and says, "What about this, with a white underdress?"

"Yeah, if you're going for a Red Riding Hood look," Hannah responds.

"Hey, are you not even a little bit interested in the fact that there's a god here?" I demand. Is there a gas leak in Aconitum Hall? Is that why they're acting like it's so normal?

Hannah shrugs. "Bailey said he was here, but I haven't met him. I can't really get my head around it, so I'm choosing to ignore the whole thing. We have too many problems at the moment. I can either focus on dresses right now or I can focus on the idea that a literal god is under this same roof, lose my mind, and be no help to anyone."

Fair, I suppose, considering my reaction to him.

"For the record, I didn't invite Amber here," I begin. "And I didn't know when you were arriving."

"I told her," Hannah says, so at least she has my back there.

"You still let her just barge in. While we're going through this major security issue." Bailey tosses the dress down on the padded bench that already bears several other options. "This is a maybe, I don't care what you think, Hannah."

Frustrated, I turn away and start rifling through gowns without looking at them. Is Bailey really going to act like a spoiled brat over this?

"I didn't *let* Amber do anything," I mutter, not caring if Bailey wants to hear me or not. She can tune me out, for all I care. "She arrived in the city and I received her. I didn't tell her any of what was going on with you or the king. I don't think she's even aware that you're pregnant."

"I wish she was. I wish she knew that I was having his baby and she will never—" The tears that cut off my sister's voice hurt my heart.

Who the hell is Nathan Frost to treat Bailey this way? He's the king, big whoop. She's the queen, his mate. She's providing him an heir.

Maybe she won't answer me, but I ask anyway. "Is he with her right now?"

When I look over, Bailey is shaking her head. "No. She left. And he's in a mood now."

Hopefully, not a head-chopping-off mood.

"Look, we're all exhausted," Hannah begins. "We're all at our emotional breaking points. I haven't seen my baby in over twenty-four hours."

"Where is she?" Bailey asks, her eyes widening with alarm.

"She's with Ryan's parents," Hannah reassures her. "But what I'm saying is, we're all so miserable, we're not looking at the positives. We have measurable success. The full moon ceremony was thwarted. The thralls couldn't attack us or gain power from us. We've cut off the Hierophant's access to his minions and we've built the perfect cover for why he needs to be 'protected.' He was the missing piece. He *will* know what's up with the binding spell. So maybe we all just take a breath, stop worrying about the things we can't control, and celebrate our victories."

"Like having a god on our side," Bailey adds, examining a dark green Anne Boleyn number. She slips it back onto the rack. "And a reason to finally take our revenge on the St. Laurent pack."

"Exactly. There's nothing we need to do now except

damage control within the pack." Hannah gasps. "I think this is the one."

The gown she's chosen is gray tule over silver silk. A sea of crystal rhinestones weigh down the hem, the placement becoming sparser as they rise up the skirt. The dress almost glows.

Bailey goes very still.

"What's wrong with it?" Hannah asks. "It looks glowy. It's perfect."

"It's what I wore the night Nathan and I met," Bailey says softly.

My stomach churns. The night the entire pack met to swear fealty to King Nathaniel Frost was the night everything changed for our family. The king set his sights on Bailey immediately and pursued her relentlessly. For what? To draw out his enemies? It worked, but did he ever truly want her as a mate?

He's been using her this entire time.

What would it be like, I wonder to myself, to be in her shoes. She didn't even know if she wanted to be a member of the pack. She went so far as to unearth an obscure rule to put off transforming for as long as possible.

Through no real choice of her own, she's queen now.

Her expression turns to stone. "I think it's the perfect dress, actually."

"You should go home, Hannah," I say gently. "Get a little baby time in before the announcement tonight."

She shakes her head. "Uh-uh. I'm not leaving until I get to meet a god in person."

"Hannah—" Bailey begins.

I cut her off. "I think it's a good idea. Hannah has been working on this with us for a long time. She interviewed the Hierophant this morning about the binding spell."

"Are we any closer to figuring out how to break it?" Bailey asks.

Hannah shakes her head. "No. But maybe Màni can help fill in the gaps. I promise, I'm not going to do anything weird and embarrass you in front of your god friend."

Despite her overall gloom, Bailey laughs. Then she looks down at her hand, a gesture I recognize as shame. "You've both been so good to us. I don't deserve it."

"Your husband doesn't deserve it," I say before I can stop myself. "Apologies, Your Majesty."

"Don't do that," Bailey says softly. "I don't even know how much longer I'll be the queen."

"What would make you say something like that?" My heart pounds in alarm. Were Nathan and Amber plotting something? Did I make a huge mistake seeing her at all?

It seemed like a necessary evil at the time.

Bailey shrugs and lifts her tear-stained face. "I don't know. Insecurity? It just feels like he would replace me in a heartbeat, if he could."

Neither Hannah nor I can reassure her.

"Let's just go and see Màni," Bailey says, forcing her sadness away with a wholly unconvincing smile.

"Brace yourself, though," I warn Hannah.

"How? How am I going to brace myself to meet a god?" she asks, following Bailey out of the closet.

"First of all, prepare for nudity," I say with a laugh as we walk down the stairs. "And try not to stare because it is... impressive."

"You're leaving out the ears," Bailey says. "And the claws. And his tail. Honestly, all of that threw me more than... that situation."

I note she won't look at us directly. But my sister isn't a prude. She's hiding something.

"Hang on," I say as she reaches the door to the hallway.

"Hmm?" Her voice is tight and too high.

"You're not telling us something." Hannah notices, too, so I'm not imagining things.

"What? Just because I said his ears are weird?" Bailey responds defensively.

"Because you blushed and got flustered when I mentioned his dick," Hannah says.

"Well, I don't like talking about somebody's dick if they're not my mate," Bailey argues.

I laugh. "So, we can talk about the king's—"

"No!" Bailey shakes her head. "Stop putting things like that in my mouth."

Hannah and I can't contain our laughter. Bailey, however, looks mortified.

"We're just teasing you," I say, not bothering to pretend I can be serious anymore. The lack of sleep is slowly destroying me. "Come on, he's an actual god. He's hot. It's okay to think that. It's not like we're saying you're going to bang someone who isn't your mate."

Her eyes dart to the floor.

"Wait..." Hannah says slowly.

Bailey explodes in a flurry of frantic hand motions and breathless confession. "It wasn't like a plan, okay? I didn't even know he was real. And I thought I was dreaming!"

"Are you telling me..." I don't know how to finish the sentence; it sounds so outlandish.

"Fine. I fucked a god." She throws her arms up and her hand smacks her thigh as it falls. "Are you happy?"

"I don't know, are *you* happy?" Hannah asks. "Because in my opinion, getting railed by a god would probably make me happy."

"If you had a choice in it and you weren't just

submitting to a weird mating ritual because you thought it was a horny dream," Bailey grumbles. "And I might as well tell you now. I'm pregnant again."

"You mean 'still,'" Hannah says.

"No, I mean *again*. Whatever weird ritual Màni and his pack performed got me pregnant with a second baby." She jabs at her stomach with two fingers. "I'm carrying twins conceived at different times with two different fathers."

"And one is a demigod?" My brain races over all the lore I know. "Hang on. He did this before."

Hannah and Bailey both look at me in a mixture of confusion and horror.

"It's only in one poem that I recall." Why can't I think of the title? I suppose it doesn't matter; it's not like my sister needs a bibliography. "But there was a story about Màni and a human woman."

"So, what, he's racking up demigods with every species?" Bailey shouts.

I hold up my hands. "I'm just the messenger."

"I'll kill him," she seethes.

"You know, maybe I don't need to meet him right this second," Hannah says, backing away from the door.

"Oh, we're going to see him." Bailey storms ahead of us, and when we don't immediately move, she pulls the queen card. "That's an order."

"Yes, Your Majesty." I shoot Hannah a roll of my eyes and we follow my sister as she marches toward the king's study.

Unfortunately, the only naked person we find when we reach the top of the stairs to his bedroom is him.

"Hey!" He yelps, diving behind one of the chairs in front of the fire.

Bailey is enraged beyond apologizing for the intrusion. "Where is he?"

I glance around, sure I'm going to see Queen Amber hiding somewhere.

He frowns at Bailey. "I thought he was with you."

She gestures at the two of us. "Do you see him with me?"

"I'm going to go downstairs and let you put some pants on, Your Majesty," I say with a brief curtsey to Nathan.

I'm in such a hurry to get out of there, I collide with Xiao on the stairs. She's out of breath, wide-eyed. "I need the king!"

Hannah is right behind me. She flattens herself to the wall as Xiao charges up the spiral stairs.

"Your Majesties, I need you to come with me!" Xiao calls out in a panic I've never heard in her voice before. It seems impossible that she's even capable of being this scared.

"Is it Màni?" Bailey asks, following Xiao back down. The king is close behind, clad in a robe, thank goodness.

"I never saw him leave the room, I swear," Xiao says, as we all run to keep up with her.

I know where she's leading us the moment we reach the hall and she turns for the parlor. The safe room. The Hierophant.

The door to the safe room is usually hidden behind the bar in the parlor. It hangs open now. Xiao stops at the threshold and stands aside.

"I didn't know he could get in." It's almost like she's begging for leniency without saying the actual words.

Hannah hesitates. The king doesn't. Neither does Bailey, so I don't, either.

The coppery tang of blood assaults my nostrils as we

enter the seating area. There, on the couch where I was treated for shock in the wake of my sister's coronation attack, is Màni. The fur on his hands and arms is stained red. Gore streaks his shining white hair and smears across his mouth.

On the floor at his feet is the Hierophant. With his throat torn out.

CHAPTER 27
BAILEY

"What did you do?" Nathan whispers beside me, his eyes fixed on the corpse of our former Hierophant.

"What did you do?" I echo. My throat chokes up. My baby. Nathan's baby. We were counting on the Hierophant's knowledge to break the binding spell. It was the only way to protect our child.

Màni knows that. I told him that we needed the Hierophant alive.

I lunge at Màni, screaming, "What did you do?"

He catches me easily, his bloody hand closing around my forearm. With my hand free, I can slap at him, so I do.

"We needed him! We needed him!" I shriek as Nathan runs to pry me off the god.

Màni opens his arms and pulls me into a tight embrace. I shudder at the smell and feel of the Hierophant's blood on him.

"I had to," the god whispers to me, stroking my hair as if to soothe me.

And it does, in a strange way, soothe me. I fall against him, sobbing.

"The binding spell," Nathan says, his voice thick with emotion. "We needed his knowledge to remove the spell on us. To protect our baby."

"You don't." Màni's voice rumbles through his chest and I feel it in my skull. His touch is like a magic calming potion. "I tasted the lies in him. He would not have helped you."

"Maybe not willingly. But I was going to torture him," I hear Tara say.

I can't imagine her actually torturing anyone. I assume she meant she would have Xiao torture him.

"That violence won't be necessary, now. I've absorbed what little knowledge he had. But I could not allow him to live. Nor can his acolytes be allowed to live. Not after what I read."

I push him back so I can look at him. In an instant, Nathan grabs me and hauls me to my feet, careful not to drag me across the Hierophant's mangled body.

"What you read?" Nathan bellows.

"Yes. I read several books on the history of your pack and the things that you've been told to believe and now, I've freed you." Màni blinks at Nathan in confusion.

"We didn't need to be freed!" Nathan pushes me toward Tara. "Take her to her rooms."

I twist out of Nathan's grasp. "I'm staying right here."

Nathan jabs his finger in the air in Màni's direction. "He's dangerous, Bailey! Look at what he's done!"

"I've freed you," Màni repeats, looking to me as if I can somehow step in and make Nathan understand. But I don't understand. He's *freed* us?

I shake my head. "You've just created a lot more problems."

"I know how to lift the spell now," Màni protests.

"That's what you wanted. A way to break the binding and protect our children."

"*My* child!" Nathan roars.

"Your Majesty," Xiao says quietly. For a moment, I think Nathan will turn his rage on her, but she's a master of gentle authority and miraculously, his shoulders relax a little, his fists unclench.

"And what I want," Màni goes on, "is to see those who have wronged me and my pack punished."

"How did he get in here?" Nathan asks, turning away from Màni in disgust.

Xiao shakes her head, defeated. "I don't know. The door was locked."

"Do you believe a lock will stop a god?" Màni asks.

"We're going to need some damage control here," Hannah says, all practicality while her face is cycling through shades of green.

Tara nods in agreement, her hand over her mouth. "We're going to have to explain where the Hierophant has gone."

Nathan dives his fingers through his hair and paces, and none of us, not even Màni, says a word. Finally, in a hoarse rasp, Nathan says, "It was a thrall."

"Your Majesty?" Hannah flicks her gaze toward Xiao.

Nathan notices and scowls impatiently. "Not her. Not one of ours. What do you take me for?"

A man who will do anything to attain his own goals and save his own ass. It's not a nice thing to think about my husband but maybe he should be nicer.

"The acolytes," Nathan says slowly, thinking aloud. "We'll frame the acolytes. That should satisfy some of this psychopath's thirst for vengeance and put another roadblock in the path of their power."

"You were relying on the thralls for help," Xiao reminds us. "If you lose their support, you lose your protection from your fellow werewolves."

Tara tries hard not to look at the dead body on the floor, but I can see she's losing the battle. "There will already be an increased threat from werewolves once we announce the war with the St. Laurent pack. No one in this pack would dare take action against you. Not during the war. They've seen how you deal with treason."

The tone of her final sentence sends a chill of alarm through me. Nathan is already furious. Now, my sister, whose mate is still exiled for treason, is seemingly challenging him.

"They have." His tone is pure ice. "And they should be aware that I will not hesitate to mete out even harsher sentences next time."

There aren't any harsher sentences than Lycaon's banquet. I remember Amber arguing with him that once he went to that extreme, there would be no further to go.

Hannah's voice cuts through the tension like a knife amputating a gangrenous limb. Or werewolf teeth amputating my hand. "What do we do with the body, in the meantime?"

"Queen Amber's security forces are on their way," Nathan says, and I hate hearing him say her name. "Xiao, seal the room, destroy the security footage, and you'll discover this mysterious death at the same time they do."

"And we'll be able to hold off on framing the acolytes," I suggest. "If the death is discovered later, we don't have to produce a suspect. The investigation will just be starting."

Nathan nods, and I think I see something like pride on his otherwise stoney face.

"When those forces arrive, how do we explain...?" Tara

tries to point discreetly at Màni, who studies her and mimics the gesture.

"We can't. He'll have to stay hidden." Nathan fixes a glare at Màni. "Do you understand that when we say you need to be hidden—"

"No one else saw me." The god gives the body on the floor a nudge with his bare toes. "Except for him. And he is unlikely to tell anyone."

"He's right." I hate to say it, but Màni did follow our agreement. He stayed hidden.

"There are werewolves from another pack coming to this house today," Nathan explains as if Màni is a child. "There will be too many eyes here. You will complicate things further for us if you are seen."

"I've simplified things for you," Màni says, looking to all of us for understanding. "You no longer need to worry about his involvement, and I know how to undo this binding between the two of you. You could call off your war—"

"The war with St. Laurent was inevitable." The others look at me with surprise. I'm surprised, myself.

It isn't that I want to go to war. The thought of bloody battles and chaos spread over two provinces doesn't appeal to me. But the St. Laurent pack tried to kill me. Whether it was in an attempt to thwart the thralls doesn't matter. I've lost so much. I want my revenge.

"There is no way to call off anything," Nathan says, more subdued than he's been since we entered this room. He's reassuring me, I think.

"The ceremonial grounds have been destroyed. Someone has to answer for that," Tara reminds us.

"We have someone who can answer for that. In our dungeons, right now," Xiao tells Tara.

Something passes between the two of them that I can't read. But I know Xiao is suggesting we put the blame on Jonah.

Nathan understands, too. "It's not a terrible idea."

"He helped us," I protest.

"He also burned up the ceremonial grounds," Xiao argues. "You'd be executing him for something he did."

"And we'd have kidnapped a man and murdered him." Tara's eyes go wide with disbelief. "You can't all be okay with this."

"Why aren't you?" Xiao's question is too knowing. Too pointed.

Something went on in London.

But that's not my concern at the moment. "The St. Laurent pack has committed offenses that fully justify this war."

"There doesn't have to be a war," Xiao says, folding her arms across her chest.

"This is not a conversation!" Nathan shouts. "They attempted to murder my mate! I will cut down every werewolf on this earth to protect her. The St. Laurent pack will serve as an example, that those who cross me will pay with their blood. That goes for everyone in this room! Do you all understand?"

"Yes, Your Majesty," Hannah, Tara, and Xiao answer in a scattered chorus of shocked mutters.

"If that's all, everyone leave this room," he goes on. "Do not make footprints. Do not touch anything. Tara, take Màni back to my bedroom, where he will stay until he is instructed to leave." The last is directed firmly at Màni, and I flinch to hear Nathan speak that way to the god.

That's something we might need to talk about before he gets himself killed.

"Màni, you should probably clean yourself off, too. Just so you don't get blood everywhere," I say, much kinder than Nathan would have.

The god stands and claps his hands together decisively. "Of course. Direct me to the nearest stream."

I throw a pleading look at Tara. She motions him to her, unwilling to get any closer to the Hierophant's body. As Màni moves to her side, she slips her arm through his to guide him out of the safe room. "Come on. I'm going to teach you all about showers."

"I'll get some bleach and clean up the obvious footprints," Hannah suggests.

"Bleach will leave a scent behind," Xiao says. "Better to use a sponge with plain water, until we can make fresh footprints when we re-discover the body later."

Her practical knowledge of murder scene staging unnerves me.

I give the Hierophant's body one last look as we leave. I thought we needed him to break the binding, but if a god says he can do the job, I have to trust him. Nathan doesn't, and maybe he won't until the spell is truly broken. At least, we agree on one thing.

Màni is far more dangerous and powerful than we originally thought.

CHAPTER 28
BAILEY

"Thank you for letting me intrude on your space," Nathan says as he smoothes down his tie. I've been covertly watching him in the mirror while Hannah dresses me. She closes the final hook-and-eye at the top of the gown while I pull a glove over my stump. She has to help me with the other one.

"It's fine," I respond. "I don't know why we can't keep him somewhere else, though."

"The chances of anyone entering a king's bedroom without express permission is low." Nathan turns and gives me a quick look over. I take in a breath that catches involuntarily in my lungs. Will he notice the gown I'm wearing? The significance of it? Is the night we met of any importance to him at all, at least, enough to remember what I looked like?

My memory of that night is practically a camera roll. I can so clearly see him, his handsome face without the long scar on his cheek yet, his silver eyes that burned cold fire as they met mine.

The way I wanted him, instantly, so badly that I dreamed of him.

His brows draw together, and I think for a moment he's trying to place the image before him. But he turns away, saying only, "You look lovely."

"Thanks," I squeak out. "You clean up pretty good, yourself."

He runs a hand over his freshly shaved jaw. "I look ten years younger, at least."

"You always look younger than your age." I'm secretly happy that he got rid of the beard for exactly that reason. I want us to look like we belong together.

It doesn't matter what you look like, the ruthlessly practical part of my brain reminds me. *You're mates. You do belong together.*

How much of that is the binding spell, I wonder? And what happens when it *is* broken?

That persistent worry is never far from my mind. I'm carrying his child. Would he leave us both?

All three of us?

Nathan and I haven't discussed Màni's baby. That gives me some worry. Will Nathan accept it as his own? Or will he ask me to send it off somewhere?

An unfamiliar ringtone comes from Nathan's phone and he silences it quickly. "Excuse me, I need to take this."

When he leaves, Hannah blows out a long exhale.

"What's that about?" I ask.

"He makes me nervous." She fluffs my skirt out a bit more, frowning as the tule catches on the silk underskirt.

I start to say that he's my mate and she shouldn't be nervous, but I wasn't able to protect my own sister. The mate of a council member would certainly be disposable in Nathan's eyes.

"I'm sorry," I say softly.

"Don't apologize for him." She steps back and takes aim at my hair. It's not the same tousled updo as the night of the fealty ceremony, but a more sophisticated, sleek twist. "Which crown?"

I go to the locked, glass-front cabinet at the end of the room and enter the code into the touchpad. The lights come up as the cabinet swings open, revealing the crowns and tiaras that come with my title.

Every single one of them belonged to my mate's mistress before I ever touched them. As the former queen of the Toronto pack, she's owned everything of mine first. My rooms, my title, my husband.

I press a hand to my stomach. I have one thing she will never have.

I select a wildly sparkly piece of platinum and diamonds that sweeps into a sharp central peak. "This will look the best with the dress."

"And the hair," Hannah agrees. "Sit."

I obediently take a seat on one of the leather-covered benches so she can settle the surprisingly heavy tiara on my head and secure it with pins.

"They found the body, by the way," Hannah tells me, glancing cautiously toward the door. "In case you hadn't heard."

I didn't, but not because I think Nathan tried to keep it from me. "It happened while I was in the shower, didn't it?"

Hannah nods, bobby pins held between her tightly clenched lips.

"I take like two seconds to bathe myself and I miss everything," I grumble.

Her response of, "Two hours," is muffled by her grip on

the pins. She slides them into place and gives the tiara a little tug. It's not moving even in a hurricane. "If you took shorter showers, you wouldn't miss as much."

"Forty-five minutes." That's the only concession I'll make for such a spurious accusation. At most, I was in there for an hour and a half.

"You got to see the show the first time," Hannah reminds me.

"That's true. And I didn't really want an encore." I do want to know how the aftermath was handled. If the Manhattan security force believe our lie.

"I feel better knowing there are werewolves in the house, not thralls," I muse aloud.

Hannah nods her agreement. "That's fucked me up this whole time. We had thralls in our homes. While we slept. While they were playing the long game to get rid of us."

"And then I became the final piece on the board." I sigh and rub my temples. My hair is on too tight. I look up at her with a grim expression. "I'm sorry. I should never have claimed the Right—"

"You couldn't have known," Hannah says firmly. "We found the Right of Accord buried in some ancient text. How could you have known it was a time bomb?"

I nod glumly.

"Plus, hello, there are way more efficient ways of getting rid of us. All they had to do was reveal our existence to the... humans..."

I feel my eyes widening in horror as hers do, too.

Tara set all of those humans free.

"Don't worry about that." I'm reassuring myself as much as I'm reassuring Hannah. "There are powerful people in the city who are fully aware of our existence. If any of the freed sacrifices try to tell anyone, they won't be believed."

"Do these powerful people know about the sacrifice element, though?" Hannah asks, chewing her lip nervously. "That might change their opinion."

Nathan enters and tosses his phone onto one of the unoccupied seats, and my conversation with Hannah comes to an abrupt end. I should bring the subject up with Nathan but surely, he's already considered the possible consequences of discovery due to my sister's actions.

Maybe he's considering consequences for *them*.

"Thank you, Hannah," I say, rising and clasping my hand over my forearm at my waist. Something about a crown just makes one stand like a queen. Which is good, because I can use help appearing regal. Much of the time, I feel like I'm playing dress-up.

"Your Majesty," Hannah says, giving me a curtsey that's not for me so much as for appearances in front of her King. She does the same for him before leaving us.

I know she won't linger near the door; she'll want to get away from Nathan as quickly as possible.

"You scared them," I say softly.

He takes his jacket from its hanger and makes a disinterested noise. "They should be scared. They've gotten too comfortable."

"They've done nothing but help us," I argue.

"And their help is appreciated. But not their criticisms." He puts on the jacket and eyes himself in the full-length mirror. "I don't want you out of my sight for a moment after this announcement is made. In fact, once pack members start arriving. You're never to be away from my side."

I roll my eyes. "I'll need to use the bathroom at some point."

"You know I meant it as a figure of speech, Bailey," he says wearily.

He's so tired. I ache to touch him, to massage the tension from his shoulders. If we were still at our cabin in the woods, I could have. I felt like his equal then. That he was my mate and partner. But in Aconitum Hall, he's the King.

"But you will be with me at all times." It's an order. A proclamation.

I love Nathan, my mate. I despise Nathan, my king.

"I don't have time to brief you on my statement. Would you like to read it?" he offers.

I shake my head. "It's not going to matter. You won't listen to anything I or anyone else has to say about the content."

Wisely, he doesn't take the argument bait.

"Who was on the phone?" I ask.

"Security. They're getting the lay of the land, so to speak, and had some questions."

I study him for any sign of deception. Was that answer too easy, too detailed, too much like an alibi? Or is he telling the truth?

In the woods, I never felt this much doubt with him. We were the only two people who existed. We didn't have roles to play, then.

The realization that I'll never have that again, never be with that version of Nathan that I've fallen even harder for than before, brings tears to my eyes. I swipe them away carefully with my thumb.

He sees. Of course, he does. He notices everything.

Except, maybe, how he appears to other people. What effect he has on them. How he should fucking treat them.

"I need to go look over my statement again. Memorize it as best as I can so I have to fill in fewer gaps from the dais." He takes me by the shoulders, his big hands eliciting a thrill through my entire body the moment they touch my skin. With a kiss to my forehead, he says, "You look beautiful. I would very much like to come to your room tonight."

Heat suffuses my face. "You already said I'm not going to be out of your sight. Do you really have a choice? Were you going to cuddle up to Màni?"

Nathan smiles at that, and it feels like praise to my lovesick brain. He gently bumps the side of his fist under my chin and says, "You'll do wonderfully this evening, my queen."

Then he leaves me alone, wondering what the hell it is I'm going to do wonderfully other than stand next to him being an heir factory.

I notice his phone lying on the cube. "You forgot your—"

I stop myself. Because I don't trust him.

I give him a moment to return, in case he heard me. When he doesn't, I pick up the phone and slide my finger across the screen to wake it. It's unlocked. Probably because he thinks no one would dare snoop.

And I know that I shouldn't. But that doesn't stop me from tapping the phone icon and checking his recent calls.

The name I see shouldn't surprise me. It was what I was looking for when I picked up the phone in the first place.

He was talking to Amber.

CHAPTER 29
BAILEY

We wait at the door behind the dais, listening in silence as the pack enters and finds their seats. I assume Nathan's steely quiet is due to the weight of the announcement he's about to make and the concentration required to remember all the fine points without reading them off a sheet.

He probably doesn't notice that I'm not talking to him because I'm not *talking* to him.

There's time for that argument later. And there will be an argument. His betrayal this time, at least, doesn't sting the way it did in the past. I view that as an achievement on my part; I've been come resistant to his callous indifference.

I glance down at my dress and wonder how much longer it will be before the pack tailors have to whip up a whole new wardrobe for me. Strangely, Nathan's rejections make me look forward to the babies arriving. Not just because they'll secure my place as Nathan's mate and the queen of the pack, but because I'll have something to distract me.

That's probably not a healthy reason to look forward to

the birth of a child—*children*, I remind myself—but it's where I am.

I glance over at Nathan, at his grim stare locked on the closed door, the visible tightness in his jaw. He's about to officially declare war. A war we knew was coming, but which seems to have arrived out of the blue.

And it strikes me that I'm at war, too. I am a queen at war.

Bad things happen to kings and queens who lose wars.

Nathan glances down at me from the corner of his eye. "You're trembling."

He's not concerned. He's critical.

"I'll get it under control," I say, my back teeth clenched.

"We can't show a flicker of weakness," he lectures me, as if I don't understand the stakes here. "Remember, no matter what—"

"I won't react to anything you say. I'll stand beside you, chin up, united front," I promise, and I hope he can hear the anger behind my compliance. "Of course, it would have helped if you'd let me, your queen, be involved in any portion of drafting this statement."

Before he can reply, the door opens and Xiao motions to us. "Your Majesties. It appears everyone is assembled."

I take a deep breath. Nathan does the same. Then he lifts his elbow and I slip my arm through his.

We step out to face our pack.

The last time the throne room was so full was the day of my coronation. I briefly freeze, dragged forward by Nathan's grip more than my own motion. While our pack's numbers were lessened by the attack at the coronation and the resulting executions, so too was the perception of us as rulers. There are too many pack members left who lost someone, too many restrained only by the threat of brutal recrimination. I wonder how many of the people waiting are secretly plotting against us. How many are dangerous animals held back by flimsy leashes?

There is no major domo to announce us. The absence of thralls is obvious to everyone gathered, and they look around the room at the Manhattan security forces. Are they afraid we've assembled the pack for slaughter? People don't trust Nathan. He's never given them a reason to.

We don't sit on the thrones. Instead, Nathan leads me to the edge of the dais, where he releases my arm and moves slightly forward.

I know my place. It's a step behind him.

"Thank you all for your prompt attention to the matters we address tonight," Nathan begins. The already tense silence becomes a tinnitus-inducing absence of all noise, a collectively held breath. "Your attendance tonight and compliance with this morning's decrees reassure me that this pack, fractured though it may have been before, has come together in strength at a time when courage and sacrifice are needed."

He didn't tell me about any decree.

I don't have to wonder about it for very long, as he continues, "I know that the loss of household thralls is not only inconvenient for your lifestyles, but also emotionally difficult, as many of you have treated long-serving thralls as members of your own families."

I almost snort at that and thankfully catch the involuntary reaction on time. I've never known any family in the pack to treat their thralls as anything more than robot servants.

Nathan continues, "You complied with this decree swiftly. Without hesitation or questioning. And now, in the secrecy and safety of this gathering, I can tell you the reason for this change. It is with deepest regret and sorrow that I inform you that our most noble and revered Hierophant... has been murdered."

I appreciate the theatricality of Nathan's pause at the end of his sentence, and the time he gives the shocked pack to accept the news. There's a horrified, stunned moment that breaks to whispers. He lets them continue for a beat before quieting them again simply by resuming his speech.

"Though the assailant was not captured, we know whoever they were, they were thralls sent by the St. Laurent pack."

More shock, more excitement. I scan the faces before us, a sea of terror and outrage, and it's nice that this time, those emotions aren't directed at us.

"We know this," he goes on, raising his voice to calm the crowd once more, "because it was a pair of St. Laurent collaborators who burned our sacred grounds. These attacks, like the ones against your King and Queen weeks ago, were unprovoked and meticulously planned. Your household thralls are safe and unharmed, but they are currently detained. They will each be interviewed extensively so that we may root out those sympathetic to or working with our enemies.

"At this time, Aconitum Hall, the ceremonial grounds, and the Council building are all guarded by security forces on loan to us from the Manhattan pack. The King and Queen of Manhattan have also pledged an alliance with Toronto and Greater London against St. Laurent and their allies, should any other packs be foolish enough to come to their aid.

"We will allow the thralls of the Toronto pack to perform the funerary rights of our spiritual leader and trust them to do so with reverence and dignity. The thralls are not our enemy," he lies firmly. "Any retribution meted against them without approval of the crown will be viewed as vigilantism and punished accordingly."

Nathan turns to me and extends his hand. I take it obediently and move to stand beside him, perplexed.

"I understand as much as any of you that the safety of your families, your children, are of utmost concern at this time." The tender expression on his face, the way he squeezes my hand, is almost believable. It probably is, to anyone watching. The stern, handsome king, besotted with his young, beautiful wife. "Queen Bailey and I await the arrival of twin heirs."

This time, the moment of shock is broken with applause and cheers instead of whispered fears. And while Nathan lets them go on a little longer than he did the earlier reactions, he somberly redirects everyone. "Of course, this is a cause for celebration. Not just our own, but for the entire pack. But it comes at a time when the danger for all of us is great. The Manhattan pack has graciously loaned us an ample number of their security forces, but certainly not enough to safeguard each household. That is why, in the coming months, many of you will be asked to bring your families here, to Aconitum Hall, to live under the protection of the court."

All of these people are going to live in our house? Of course, I know Aconitum Hall isn't actually *our* house, and I know there are countless rooms in the public areas of the castle, but we're going to feed and house all these people? How?

If anyone else has the same question, they don't get to wonder about it for long. Nathan plows ahead, stating, "You will, of course, retain your properties. But in times of war, a king must have his court close at hand. This news will not come as a surprise to those of you on the council, who proposed this plan. This will not be a permanent change. It is only until we can be assured of the safety of every werewolf in this pack."

He looks to me again. This time, I *can* believe the tenderness in his expression, and that fact chills the pit of my stomach. Before I can wonder at what he plans to say next, he announces, "And, due to the increased threat, the King and Queen of Manhattan will shelter Queen Bailey for the duration of the war."

I know my shock is plain on my face, regardless of what I promised him. But I don't care about promises to him right now.

I won't care, ever again.

CHAPTER 30
BAILEY

"Bailey, wait!"

I tear at my gown as I stalk through the residence, pulling so hard on the fabric that the zipper rips free. I tear off the front of the stiff bodice, gasping for air, and throw it on the floor as I increase my pace, not running but certainly not walking.

Nathan follows behind me, bellowing my name, annoyed at me. At me! As if I'm the one who's done *him* wrong.

I kick off my shoes and pick one up, turning with it clenched in my fist. As he gets closer, I raise it over my head in a threat. "Don't come near me!"

"As your king and your mate, I command you to put the fucking shoe down!" he shouts.

I throw it at him and, unfortunately, miss by far enough that he doesn't even react to it. That just makes me more furious. "As your queen and your mate, I command you to go fuck yourself, asshole!"

I turn and stalk away, my stomach a jumble of anger

and fear and flat out wondering what will happen to me if I go too far.

"Stop!"

The tone of his voice tells me that I have, in fact, gone too far. So does the expression on Nathan's face as he approaches me. I don't remember him ever being so angry with me. I try to keep my spine straight, but I shrink from him as he looms over me. His hand closes around my truncated forearm but... his hold isn't rough. The movement is jarring, but the intensity of force doesn't match his overall demeanor.

There's a guard at the end of the hall, one of the Manhattan security force.

It's for show, then. So he doesn't lose face in front of his girlfriend's employees.

I pull back and he tightens his grasp, dragging me the rest of the way to my chambers as I slap at his arm and curse at him.

Once we're inside, he slams the door and presses me against it, lifting my handless arm and examining it with concern. "Did I hurt you?"

"Yes!" No. But I want him to feel guilty. "I hope it was worth it to put on that little show for your mistress's spies!"

"It wasn't for her. It was for you." He steps away and runs a hand through his hair. "You're about to go to a very dangerous court, Bailey—"

"I'm not going anywhere!"

"—and I won't be there to protect you. We are at war, and you are an asset. Do you want to go to a new court a valuable weapon that can be used against me, or do you want to go as the inconsequential mate of an uncaring, cruel king? Because I know which one will get you killed!"

He slams his hand down on the top of a chair back and takes a moment to slightly calm himself.

I use the opportunity to ask, "If I'm in such danger, why are you sending me, at all?"

"Because you're in more danger here. Amber can protect you better than I can." He says it like a man spitting out poison. Softer, defeated, he repeats himself. "She can protect you better than I can."

All my rage-endorphins fall away, and I sink with them, sliding down the door with my skirt poofing out around my lap. "Why does it have to be her?"

He won't meet my eyes. "The Manhattan pack are allies. And she is the only one I can trust to protect you, on a personal level."

"Because she loves you." Hot tears rush to my eyes. I let them fall.

"Yes." He comes to stand over me, looking down from his great height as if he's trying to figure out a solution. I'm the problem. I'm the obstacle that he's trying to overcome.

"How do you know she won't kill me?" Is that why he pantomimed violence in the hall?

"Because she feels sorry for you."

The words sting so deeply, I can't breathe. I push myself to my feet and stagger past him, tired to the depths of my soul. "I can see why. You're just using me. You've always been just using me."

"Yes, I've been using you," he snaps, his voice shockingly raw to my ears. "And I wish I hadn't, now that I've fallen in love with you!"

Everything around me goes cold, and a high-pitched whine pricks my ears. I might faint. *I stood up too quickly. I'm hearing things.* "You don't mean that."

He shakes his head slowly. Like what he's just admitted

is the most shameful thing in the world. "I do. I love you. And I'm so terrified to lose you."

"You're not—"

He cuts me off. "Since the moment we arrived here, everything has been wrong. I never would have wanted this."

"You never would have wanted to love your mate?" That's all I ever wanted. I thought it was what I would have with Nathan.

"Not in my position. Not when loving you means I have something to lose." He hangs his head. "I thought you would match me in ambition, and you do. I admired you. I knew you could do this incredibly difficult job. But you're so young. I didn't think there would ever be a danger of falling in love with you."

"You said you never thought you could love anyone," I remind him.

He adds the important, "But I said that if I could, it would be you."

We stare at each other in silence, for far too long, and I can't take it anymore. "I thought you loved me. This morning, just as we arrived, I had a feeling... but then Amber was here—"

"Queen Amber."

My throat sticks shut. "Please, don't correct me about that now. Not in this conversation."

"It's only practicality, I assure you." His tone drips with cynicism. "You're going to her court. You'll be there on her terms. You need to get into the habit of addressing her properly. She won't care if you disrespect her, but she'll care if her subjects believe you're disrespecting her."

"I'm not going to disrespect someone in her own home,

when she's helping me." I can't help a childish, "Unlike some people in this room."

"You're angry that I didn't clear this with you ahead of time." He walks to me slowly, gaze cast downward. "I should have."

"You knew that there would be an argument and you wanted to avoid it," I accuse him, but I take a step forward to meet him.

"No. I think I wanted to have the argument so that you would leave here angry with me. Perhaps a part of me wanted us to fall out before you go, so that I won't miss you as much as I'm going to miss you." He cups my cheek and I can't help but lean into his touch. "I love you, Bailey."

"Maybe it's just the binding." Now that he's saying the things I've longed to hear, I want them to be false. "It's making you think you love me."

"The binding makes me want to fuck you," he says firmly. "I could have done that without marrying you. And I can certainly do that without falling in love. It turns out I can't be your mate without loving you, though."

This time, the chill that trembles my limbs isn't unpleasant. It's an icy cold that burns across my skin, awakens my senses, and scatters fractal impulses of giddiness through the pleasure centers of my brain. But tears still roll down my cheeks. "This isn't a trick?"

He winces, truly ashamed, unable to hide it from me. "I hate everything I've done to hurt you. I hate myself for making you doubt me. But yes, Bailey. I love you. And it isn't a trick."

A sob cracks my chest from within and I collapse into his arms. He crushes me tight against his chest and murmurs, "I'm so sorry."

I grip his shoulder, fingers digging into his jacket as if I can physically keep the future from dragging us apart. "Don't send me away."

His chest swells beneath my cheek and he exhales shakily. "I have to. St. Laurent has infiltrated our defenses before, and I can't guard you every moment of every day. Even when I am nearby, I haven't always been able to protect you. You're in more danger here than you will be under Manhattan's protection."

"Will I see you?" Will I want to? How can I possibly survive seeing Nathan there, knowing he has to be indifferent to me? That he'll have to speak with her and pretend she's the one he wants?

"Of course, you will. I had considered sending you to Mexico City's king or to stay with some friends of mine in the Olympia pack. Anything to get you as far away as possible. When I realized that I wouldn't be able to tell them about the thrall plot against us without risking your safety, Amber was the only option left," he says with a tired shrug.

"Queen Amber," I correct him.

A smile touches the corner of his lips. "But I was so relieved. Manhattan isn't so far that I can't still see you."

"And when you do, you'll have to pretend you don't care about seeing me," I point out.

"In public," he says firmly, wiping a tear from my chin with his thumb. "We're not like other couples, Bailey. Our every gesture will always be scrutinized. But don't doubt what's in my heart based on how I perform my role."

"I just wish we could go back to that cabin and stay there." I hiccup a sob, embarrassing myself. I don't want to seem childish, especially now that I know he planned to use our age gap as insurance against loving me.

To my surprise, he says, "I do, too."

Then he kisses me, softer and slower than any kiss we've shared before. My body comes to life. I rise on the balls of my feet to meet him, steadying myself with my arms around his neck. I dive my hand into his hair and hang on as his tongue slips between my lips. I open my mouth as if I can drink him in, slake my thirst for him with the increasing urgency between us. His arm locks tight around the small of my back, the other hand cradling my head. When he pulls away, we're both breathless.

"I love you," he murmurs, leaning his forehead against mine.

And I realize: it's a question.

I'm not sure I can bring myself to give him the answer. If I open my heart to him and this turns out to be some kind of political maneuver... if he's just using me again...

"You don't have to say it," he whispers. "But let me."

I close my eyes and nod, unable to find my voice. And he kisses me again and all I can think is how much I've wanted this from the very beginning. How much I doubted it could ever happen.

He's walking me backward in slow, careful steps, and I know where he plans for the evening to go. I put my hand against his chest and give him a gentle push to stop us moving.

"When do I have to leave?" I ask, my throat choked with tears.

He doesn't answer.

"Because if tonight is our last night—"

"It won't be," he promises fiercely.

"If tonight is our last night *for a while*," I revise. "I don't want it to be goodbye. I want it to be a new beginning."

"Whatever you want." He passes his thumb across my bottom lip. "Just ask."

The answer is so obvious to me in that moment. "Our mating ceremony wasn't about us becoming a couple. It was about you triumphing over Ashton. It was about our enemies. I want to do it over."

A sad smile tilts Nathan's mouth. "It's a nice thought. But the ceremonial grounds—"

"Here," I clarify. "We don't need the thralls. We don't need the Hierophant. Just me and you. A ceremony of our own." When he hesitates, I press my palm to his cheek and beg, "If you want to show me that you love me, make me your mate. Not your queen. Not your prize. Make me your mate."

He turns his face against my hand, kisses the pad below my thumb, and I know that I have him.

CHAPTER 31

BAILEY

My bedroom is dark. The light of the now-waning moon shows through a crack in the curtains, an echo of what I saw in the ceremonial chamber that night not so long ago, but which feels like an eternity away.

My arms are bound to a post at the corner of my bed. I lean against it and the wood is cold on my naked skin. My heart beats wildly at the base of my throat as I anticipate the arrival of my mate. This time, I know for certain that it will be Nathan who walks into this room.

Anticipation hammers through me at the sound of his footsteps on the stairs. My breathing speeds even faster. I look down, keep my eyes on my feet until his bare ones come into view. His body brushes against mine and he lowers his mouth to my ear.

"I don't have a whip at hand," he whispers. Something cold and smooth drags down my spine. "Will a belt do?"

My throat is tight, so I just nod. A shudder of familiar fear and desire transports me back to the moment I felt his presence in that chamber.

"Do you feel that?" I whisper.

"I do." He kisses my cheek, pressing his body tighter to mine. His cock is hard in the small of my back. His chest rises and falls as fast as mine does.

"It must be the binding spell."

"No," he corrects me softly. "No, it's more than that, now."

A tear of gratitude rolls down my cheek. This is what I've wanted with him, since the moment I caught his eyes on me in the throne room the night I pledged my fealty to him. Now, it's too overwhelming. Loving him hurt me. Having him return my love is excruciating.

Because now, I have more to lose.

The belt touches my back again and his lips rove over my ear. "Are you sure?"

"Yes." My voice is the barest trace in the silent room. I want this to be as close to a real ceremony, a true do-over, as possible. I wrap my arms around the bedpost and wait.

The first blow lands across my ass with a crack that makes me rise onto the balls of my feet and a pain that stuns me. Only a strangled gasp escapes me. The second strike pulls a shocked yelp from my throat and bulges my eyes. I squeeze my thighs together against the keen ache between them and tilt my hips to rock my mound against the post.

The leather whistles through the air, cutting into my already welted flesh, and this time, I scream. I wonder if it will bring the guards. But I can't help my sobs, any more than I can help the way my toes curl in the rug at every spike of pleasure left in the belt's throbbing wake. A fourth strike, a fifth, and I'm crying at the pain and so close to the edge that I know it will only take one touch to plunge me over.

The belt drops to the floor, and I gulp in breaths,

shivering and sweating. Yet, Nathan keeps me waiting. I can't see him. He doesn't speak.

Then, I feel fur at my back.

I didn't expect him to change tonight, but he's gotten black moonstone from somewhere. His muzzle brushes my throat, teeth poised to bite, and I tremble. I know what comes next, with him in this form. A pleasure so intense, the thought of it terrifies me, far more than the anticipation of the belt.

I think of the night we spent in the forest, both of us in our werewolf forms. My desperation for release overrides logic; I plead, "All of it. Give me all of it."

He hesitates, as if to ask if I'm sure. But it's only for a heartbeat. The only self-control his form will allow him snaps, and his claws scratch my hips as he lifts me fully off the ground and onto his enormous cock. Just like the night of our mating ceremony, there's nothing gentle about it, but that night, he showed restraint I wasn't aware of. I'd only taken some of his length then. Tonight, the thick base of him batters against my resisting cunt as he tries again and again to push fully into me and seal our bodies together. With every hard thrust, I mentally beg for this to be the one that forces that fist-sized bulge into me. It had been easier to take it in my werewolf form.

Just when I think it will be impossible, he rams hard against me, chuffing with exertion, and white-hot, tearing pain sears through my core to my limbs. I twist against the rope restraining me, try to wrap my arm tighter around the post in a feral attempt to escape, but it's far too late for that. Nathan's growl becomes a roar that rattles the windowpanes as he erupts inside me. The first hot spurt makes me explode with a scream of release. My body quivers, my legs kick as they dangle between us.

Panic seizes me. We're locked together, and he's flooding me, filling me up, every drop sealed inside to torment us both into a frenzy of pleasure. He howls, thrusting faster in short, jerky movements that bump the hard swell against my clit from the inside. The pressure and fullness in my most sensitive parts, coupled with the aphrodisiac fluid he continues to pump, tips one orgasm into the next, until every thrust is another climax, every beat of my pulse, his pulse, our breaths, all of it a trigger for releases that offer no relief. I burst apart again and again, with no time to put myself back together.

It's agony. It's bliss.

My vision flashes red and black, even when I close my eyes. I'm too weak to hold myself up anymore; I have to rely on the ropes and Nathan's clawed hands holding my thighs spread around him. But my legs kick and spasm and finally he swipes at the rope with one hand, sheering off the top of the bed post in the process. Still locked together, he tumbles us onto the bed, spooning up behind me, his frantic thrusts slamming the headboard against the wall. Something cracks and we tumble sideways as the mattress tilts. But it's all distant to me, lost as I am.

I scream until my throat is raw and I become vaguely aware of footsteps pounding up the stairs. A few guards flood into the room and Nathan snarls at them. I don't know if they leave but he doesn't stop, and I don't want him to. I want to find out how far this can go, how long it will last, if this kind of pleasure is fatal.

Nathan stiffens with an animalistic howl that turns into a human shout as he shifts form and folds his arms around me, pulling me in so tightly that I can barely breathe. If he did that in his wolf form, he would have crushed me.

"Fuck," he gasps, his hips still jerking against me.

Though he's changed from his wolf form, the effect of his cum hasn't worn off for either of us. He withdraws and rolls my limp body over, falling between my thighs and groaning, his face twisted in unbearable pleasure as he sinks into me again. Sweat drips from his hair onto my chest while I lay gasping and helpless beneath him on my destroyed bed.

"Are you okay?" he asks, slumping heavily on me, grinding his still-twitching cock into me.

I try to speak, but my throat is too dry, so I swallow and nod and wipe perspiration away from my eyes. Looping my arm around his neck, I pull his head to rest against my breast. He kisses the curve of my flesh, then nuzzles his stubbled cheek against it. When I run my fingers through his damp hair, they encounter something dry and sharp. Blinking in my confusion, I look up at him, then at the bed beside me, then lift my eyes to the enormous dent in the wall behind us. We're covered in plaster.

"We can't sleep in here," I manage to rasp. "The bed is broken."

He pulls out, shivering, and more of his cum gushes from my tired pussy.

"And wet," I add with a whimper.

It takes him a moment to get to his feet. First, he sits on the side of the bed, pinching the bridge of his nose and breathing deeply through what I can only assume is the mother of all head rushes. He gets up stiffly, the scar across his waist angry and pink.

"Does that hurt when you transform?" I ask, reaching out to touch him with a hand that isn't there. I pull back my arm as he shakes his head.

The bed is made, so the duvet has taken most of the plaster fallout and wood splinters. He pulls it aside and jerks the top sheet free, rolling me down the sloped mattress as I squeal in protest. Before I can bounce onto the floor, he catches me and cradles me to his chest, as impressively strong like this as he is in his werewolf form. Draping the sheet over me, he strides toward the stairs.

A murky memory of the security personnel busting in on us comes to the surface and I cringe as we move through the sitting room. Guards line the hall outside the door. They don't make eye contact with us, and Nathan seems completely unbothered by their presence as he walks naked, carrying me in his arms.

Let them pass *that* along to their boss.

We're halfway up the stairs to Nathan's bedroom when I remember that it's occupied. "Wait," I begin, but Nathan reaches the top step and curses.

Màni rises from the bed, which remains neatly made up. He's dragged the bearskin rug from the floor around his shoulders and appears to have been sleeping.

I didn't know gods slept.

"Everyone heard you fucking," he greets us cheerfully.

Nathan turns back to the stairs. "I believe the sofa in your office pulls out into a bed."

"You needn't leave," Màni assures us, moving in his bear-rug cloak to lay beside the fire. "I wouldn't presume to take your pallet."

"I'm tired," I whisper, entreating Nathan with my eyes to just let us sleep there.

With a heavy sigh, he moves to the bed and pulls the duvet back. He lays me gently on the sheets and kisses my forehead. "Let me get you some water."

As he goes, he clicks off the bedside lamp. The waning fire in the hearth provides only a dim glow, but Màni seems illuminated from within, surrounded by an aura of silver.

I sit up and wrap my arms around my knees. "Màni?"

He lifts his head.

"Did you... feed off our... you know?" I'm not quite sure how to phrase the question, but I think he gets the gist.

"It isn't feeding," he says, not exactly a denial. "More like... collecting."

"Well, stop 'collecting' from us," Nathan snaps as he returns. His scowl fades as he hands me the water and asks again, "You're all right?"

I beam up at him. "I'm better than all right. Come to bed."

He climbs in beside me and unfolds his arm so I can snuggle against his side and use his shoulder as my pillow. For the first time, it feels natural. Stable. Like he'll be there when I wake up.

We lay in silence, nothing but the crackling of the dying embers in the fireplace filling the stillness. Nathan strokes my hair idly with one hand and covers my shortened arm against his chest with the other.

"Is this the last night?" I whisper.

"For a while," he says, and my heart squeezes hard. "But not forever."

And even though I believe him, I don't want to sleep. I don't want it to end.

CHAPTER 32

TARA

"Your sister's shoes."

I look up as Xiao drops Bailey's expensive leather pumps on the kitchen counter. "Ew. I'm trying to eat."

"I also have a... fabric tube?" She drops the torn bodice of Bailey's gown atop the shoes. "It was all on the floor in the hallway."

"Mmm," I hum thoughtfully, taking another spoonful of my soup.

"Something tells me these weren't ripped off in a fit of passion," Xiao says with a snort.

I reach for the frayed bodice and a metal zipper pull tinks off the counter and rolls to the floor. "Not that kind of passion, anyway."

"The shoes were about ten feet apart. I assume one was used as a projectile." Xiao takes a seat across the island from me and leans her elbows on the counter. "Not that the King probably didn't deserve it."

"I can't believe he sprung that on her right there, in front of everyone." If Nathan is still alive in the morning, I'll be shocked.

"So, you don't think she had any advanced warning?" Xiao is clearly asking for confirmation of what she already suspects.

I give it to her with a shake of my head. "We would have heard about it. Believe me."

I take another bite of my soup, then realize guiltily that I'm eating in front of her without offering her anything. "Are you hungry?"

Xiao shakes her head. "I'm too nervous to be hungry."

"I can't imagine." Xiao is about to go to war. I'll be... well, locked up in Aconitum Hall, I assume, but never in danger. I'm not important enough, now that the King and Queen are back. "Have you been trained for war?"

Xiao shakes her head. "I've been taught to guard against security threats. We don't cover war in our training."

"Do you know what was is like?" There hasn't been a pack war in either of our lifetimes, but the thralls seem to know all sorts of things about us that we don't.

Her forehead creases. "They don't teach you about it in school?"

"They tell us who won, what the fight was about." Knowing what I know now, all of that was probably a lie. "Not how it was fought."

"Because you didn't fight them." She gives me a bitter half-smile. "They weren't really your wars."

"When the humans have a war, they make it everyone else's problem," I observe. "I assume our wars are more discreet."

"Espionage. Assassination. Hostages. That's why the King is sending your sister away." Her attention drifts to the middle distance, and she muses aloud, "I wonder if he'll send me with her."

"Or me." I take another bite, though I no longer taste it.

Xiao looks away, toward the door, and my heart sinks.

"You're thinking that you should go," I say without meaning to.

"No. I'm wondering whether or not I should explain that you're a hostage." She hangs her head, unable to meet my eyes.

It takes me a moment to process what she's saying. "Did you hear something? Did the King or Bailey tell you something?"

"You were never *not* a hostage," she explains. "You're still a hostage. You have been ever since the Queen called you back from your banishment."

"I..." How did that slip my mind? The king trusted me with the regency, but I was still kind of their prisoner. They never offered to let me go back to Josh. Not that I would have.

"You have family in exile," Xiao goes on, as if reading my thoughts. "But you're still here. If you asked to go back to them, do you think the King would let you?"

"Bailey let me take the news about Clare to our parents." *Let.* Like it was a privilege and not a nightmare. I don't have a lot of love for my parents—the cold formality of our childhood didn't engender closeness—but I hated to see them in pain. Whatever amount of love they were capable of showing us, they did at least love us in their way. Losing Claire devastated them the way the loss of a child devastates any parent.

"And your mate?" Xiao asks.

I shake my head. "I didn't see him. I didn't ask to, though." I don't know why, but I blurt out, "I didn't feel like getting hit. Or raped."

"Tara." Xiao's voice is a horrified whisper.

I wish I didn't say anything. "It's okay. Don't do the—"

"It's not okay. *You* don't do *that*." Now she's angry, but I know it's not at me.

And that's part of why I wish I didn't tell her. Or anyone. If I kept it to myself, I could have kept my anger to myself. It's what I'm entitled to.

"Don't tell me how to deal with my life, okay?" I snap.

"I'm sorry, Lady Tara."

The formality slaps me. I know that's not what she intends. It's protocol she's lived her entire life. But suddenly, I feel so... alone.

And I break down sobbing.

And Xiao puts her arms around me.

I'm not used to kindness. Emotion in our house growing up wasn't just discouraged. It was punished. Not with physical abuse or material deprivation, but pursed lips and lectures.

But Xiao is standing here with me in my pain. Not taking responsibility for it or taking it away from me. Holding me up under its impossible weight.

I loop my arms around her back and squeeze her tight. This moment can't end. If it does, I'm alone again.

"I'm sorry I upset you," she murmurs against the top of my head.

"You didn't. This situation did." I sniffle, consider the fact I might be getting snot on her, then decide she knew what she was getting into when she hugged a crying person. "I hate him."

"I know." The tone of her voice is an affirmation. "But he's the king of this pack. If I'm his hostage—"

"I didn't mean the king." Her arms shift and she lifts

my chin with two fingers to look in my eyes. "I hate your mate for hurting you."

"Can't it be both?" An unexpected laugh burbles up my throat.

She laughs, too, but quickly sobers. "Don't make jokes to avoid feeling. I'm here for you, Tara. In whatever capacity you need. If you need a friend, I can be your friend. If you need a protector, I will always protect you."

"I thought you said we couldn't be friends because then you wouldn't be able to protect me," I remind her.

"It turns out, the more I get to know you, the more fiercely I want to protect you." A smile touches the corners of her mouth. "It might make me bad at protecting you."

"You've never let me down so far." I release her and wipe tears from my eyes.

"I've been really..." She searches for the words while her gaze searches my face. "Ever since London, I've kept you at arm's length. That wasn't to hurt you."

"I know it." My face flames hot at the memory of what happened during that trip. "It was awkward. We don't have to talk about it again."

She shakes her head. "I don't regret that. I regret that it happened to you, but I don't feel awkward about it. What I've been more concerned about is the way I treated you after that. Threatening to use the black moonstone on you... after what you'd just went through..."

A knot of tension unravels in my chest over a conflict I didn't think we would address. "I was angry with you," I admit.

"You should have been. You should be. I wanted to scare him, and I didn't think about your feelings. And maybe that night, when you needed my help...I probably shouldn't have."

"I wasn't complaining." I don't know what possesses me in the moment, but I add, "It was the best sex I've ever had."

She blushes. Xiao *actually blushes* and smiles wider than I've ever seen, and she has *dimples.*

Making her smile like that is a high I instantly know I'll never quit chasing. "Did they teach you that at thrall school?"

"No, it was all field work," she admits, still unable to face me, still smiling.

Her hand is on the countertop and for some reason, I'm compelled to cover it with my own. She looks down at my hand atop hers and the smile fades. The mask of formality is creeping back on and I hate it. I never want to see it again.

"You don't have to keep me at arm's length," I say gently. "I'm not Lady Tara. I'm just a member of the pack whose sister was unlucky enough to catch the eye of the king. In any other circumstance, we might have been friends."

She slowly pulls her hand back. "Probably not. I never had friends. I was recognized as a child for being calm, thoughtful, quick to learn... all the things that get you fast-tracked into high clearance level security. And once they see that path for you, they teach you to view the pack differently."

I tilt my head. "Different how?"

"Reverently, almost." She considers a moment. "Like you're more than employers."

"Gods?" I suggest, my gaze drifting up to the ceiling. There is a god in this house with us, right at this moment. It's such a weird thought.

She shrugs. "More like... every one of you is king of the pack. And the King of the pack? He's the god."

"Ah." My stomach curdles to hear my brother-in-law described that way. "Well, confidentially, I don't think he's anything like a god."

"No, he's a total dick," Xiao says. The color immediately drains from her face.

I give a whoop of laughter.

"I shouldn't have said that." But she laughs a little.

"I like that you said it." I push the stool back and stand. "I like seeing you be yourself."

"Yeah?" she asks, taking a step toward me.

We're not that far apart but it's taking a while for us to drift together. And I'm not sure why we're moving in that direction. It seems almost dreamlike. I'm lost in the euphoria of seeing Xiao as herself. Not as a cohort or a bodyguard or any of the other things she's had to be to me.

"It makes me feel special," I go on softly. My bare toes hit the front of her boots. "Like I'm getting to see something no one else ever does."

She angles her head down; she's already taller than me, but in her boots, she towers over me. "You are. And you're showing it to me, too."

My eyes are drawn to her lips. I know what they feel like. How soft they are. How hot her mouth is...

"I don't know who I am," she whispers. "Unless I'm with you."

CHAPTER 33

TARA

There's a moment right before our lips touch that I think: *this can't be happening.* Then, as she cups my jaw and kisses me, I think, *this can't happen.*

There will be consequences. I know there will be. What, I'm not certain; I don't know what happens to thralls who cross this boundary with the werewolves they're meant to protect.

Xiao knows. And she's kissing me, anyway. Her lips are so soft against mine, her tongue vaguely minty. Excitement swells something inside my chest, lifting me onto the balls of my feet like a balloon. This isn't like when she helped me in London. Then, she was need. Now, she's necessity.

Her hand splays at the small of my back, the other dives into my hair. I can't escape her. I don't want to. I moan into her mouth, tilt my head back as her lips move down my throat.

I wonder if I should remind her that we can't do this. That the uncertain future makes this a bad idea. We should stop.

But I don't want to stop, and I don't want to say or do

anything that might shatter the moment. Something tenuous binds us in this small piece of stopped time and I don't want it to break.

She doesn't either. That's the only explanation for why she boosts me onto the island and stands between my legs, reaching for the bottom of my sweatshirt.

"Wait," I murmur as her hands encounter my hot skin. "Wait, there are guards everywhere."

"Where, then?" she asks with an impatient bite at my bottom lip.

I take her hand and head out of the kitchen. We won't go all the way back to my rooms. It's too far, too much time to think. All we need is a lock.

There's a small sitting room not far, one that never gets used. The furniture is covered with drop cloths; no one will suddenly come poking around. I pull her in with me.

As soon as we're safely locked in together, I pull off my shirt and her hands find my braless breasts. Her touch ignites a fire more urgent than what I felt from the aphrodisiac. I have to have her, or I'll die.

Her tight braid hangs over her shoulder. I find the elastic and tug it free, combing my fingers through the ink-dark strands. She shakes her head, then runs a hand through the tightly woven locks to loosen them.

I've never seen her with her hair down. It falls in a dark, crimped cascade over her shoulders like a princess out of a Pre-Raphaelite painting. If the princess wore tactical armor with reinforced leather plates.

"Please, take this off," I beg, indicating her uniform.

It would be easier for her to get undressed without my hands clumsily seeking out the skin she reveals, my mouth desperately roving over her neck and jaw, but she manages, sliding the top of her suit to her waist. She has a no-frills black bra underneath, and I reach behind her to pop the clasp.

"It's in front," she says, and when she unfastens it and her breasts spill free, I finally understand the appeal of that kind of bra. My toes curl at the sheer hotness of this woman, the lean, defined muscles of her arms, the tight, chiseled abs she's been hiding under her clothes.

I push my pajama pants down and stand totally naked in the big, silent, empty room. She's still got her boots on, but she gives up undressing at the sight of me. Before I know what's happening, she rips the drop cloth from a wing-backed chair and pushes me onto the seat, falling to her knees in front of me.

"Every time I see you, I think of this," she murmurs against my inner thigh. "The way you taste. The way you sound when you're coming. I hated that we had to be quiet before. I wanted to make you scream."

"If you make me scream right now, someone will hear," I warn her.

Her eyes shine mischievously in the dimness. "Do you care?"

I shake my head, but add, "You have more to lose."

"Am I going to lose you?" She fixes me with a shockingly vulnerable expression, asking far more than the question she's spoken aloud.

I don't trust my voice or my ability to form my own sentences. I can only shake my head.

It's enough for her. She jerks my hips to the edge of the chair and runs her tongue up between my labia. I grip the back of her head and hold on; it's too much stimulation, too fast, but it's also been far too long since we've touched.

I've been craving her this entire time without putting a name to my hunger.

I reach behind me with one hand to hold onto the back of the chair, lifting my hips to grind against her mouth. Her throaty moan reverberates through my pelvis. The first time, she did this out of duty. This time, she allows herself to want me. I feel that in every flick of her tongue over me, in the sucking kisses that draw my intimate flesh between her lips. I feel it in the urgency of her fingers digging into my thighs like she never wants to let me go.

I come fast and hard, crying out too loud in the quiet house. Someone's going to find us. I don't care.

Xiao lifts her head, panting, "Did you like that?" with a lop-sided smile that takes my breath away.

I nod silently and she laughs, climbing up my body to kiss me with my juices smeared across her mouth. *What is this?* I want to ask. Everything around us is uncertain now, but I need to know that this feeling is certain.

I want to know that when this is over, we won't go back to the strained silence, the suspicion. She lowers her head again, kisses my inner thigh.

"I can't get enough of you. I've wanted you... fuck, I've wanted you."

She could have had me at any time. The night of the attack on the ceremonial grounds, when I was so confused and hurt by her coldness, she could have had me. That day in the park when she threatened to use me as a weapon against Jonah, she could have had me. I don't care how pathetic that makes me seem. Xiao is the only person who treats me like I'm not a child, not a prisoner, not an afterthought.

Her mouth covers me again and I moan loud and long, gripping the arms of the chair and holding on while she takes me away again and again, until I can't stand another climax, another desperate climb. Sweat slicks my skin all over, her saliva and my own wetness coat my thighs. I push my hair back and feel the moisture at the roots, the weakness in my limbs, and I know I'll be sore tomorrow, just from the constant tensing and releasing of my muscles as I come over and over on her tongue.

"Please," I whimper, pulling at her hair. "Please, let me touch you."

She hesitates.

"What's wrong?" I ask, pushing her back more firmly and sitting up.

"It's..." she drops her head. "Look, I'm not saying I don't want you to. But I've never... with another person..."

"You've never had an orgasm with someone else?" I ask.

"It's too personal," she says flatly.

I laugh in disbelief. "Too personal? You just ate me out for like forty minutes but me returning the favor is too personal?"

"I've never let anybody," she admits. "I don't like to lose control."

I consider for a moment. "Don't lose control."

"How is that possible?" she asks doubtfully.

It seems simple enough to me. "Make me do it. Tell me what to do. What you like. Then, you're still in control." I lean down and kiss her. I can smell myself on her hair. "And I'll still get to make you come."

She shudders at the word, and I wait patiently, watching the war of indecision battle across her features. Finally, she looks up, the hardened warrior I'm so familiar with. "Get on the floor," she orders.

I scramble down, my limbs trembling. With a firm hand, she pushes me flat and, before I can ask a question or say another word, she straddles my face, her sopping pussy just centimeters from my lips.

"Beg me," she says, and I moan.

"Please, let me eat your pussy," I plead.

She lowers herself onto my mouth and gasps as my tongue curls out, dipping into her cunt. She's so fucking wet that I can fill my mouth with what I coax from her with each lap. Her knees pin my hair to the floor, but my hands are free, and I reach down to stroke myself, pumping my hips in rhythm to the pumping of my tongue inside her.

"My clit," she rasps. "Suck my fucking clit." My hips jerk under my hand. She tastes surprisingly like nothing at all. Sea water is the closest comparison my sex-drunk brain can conjure.

I want to drown in her.

Her cries as she rocks against my face are loud enough to penetrate the muffling effect of her strong thighs gripping my head. Her back arches, breasts bouncing with each rock of her hips as she rides my face, and I come hard a second time. When she screams her release, I'm shocked that we aren't inundated with armed guards crashing through the door.

Her legs are still shaking when she climbs off me. My hair pulls a little and I wince. I'm out of breath, my face is wet, and she lays beside me on the hard floor and kisses me.

"I promise, we can do slow and steady next time," she rasps in a throaty, sex-drunk voice.

"Are you always going to be so bossy?" I ask, and when she looks taken aback, I add, "I'm joking."

"Oh." She smiles, embarrassed. "Sorry, I'm not used to jokes."

"This isn't the first time we've met," I remind her wryly.

Timidly, she picks up my hand. I weave our fingers

together and bring hers to my mouth, kissing each knuckle. I've never wanted to do that to anyone before.

"What do we tell the King?" Xiao asks somberly. "This is a violation of my oath."

"Then we don't tell him," I decide firmly. What Nathan doesn't know won't kill him.

Unfortunately.

CHAPTER 34
BAILEY

I don't know what to pack for the Manhattan court.

Pushing aside gown after gown, I sit on the floor of my dressing room and cover my face with my hand. This is happening too soon, with no time to plan anything. I feel like I'm grabbing up my valuables before I flee.

"Bailey?" Tara's voice calls from my bedroom.

I wiped my wet eyes and clear the sadness from my throat. "In here."

She enters timidly, looking around at the mess I've made. "Are you okay?"

I nod and say, "No."

She eyes the trunks standing open, making the space half its size. "Hiding jewels in your corset, yet?"

I laugh despite the grim emotions I'm trying to avoid feeling. "I need more time."

"You need staff to pack all of this," she says firmly. "Hannah and I will make sure you get everything you need. Why don't you take a small bag with the essentials, just for now. The rest can get to New York later."

"Then it will feel even more like I'm abandoning my

entire life." But I know she's right. I look up at her helplessly. "I keep getting ordered out of my own house. First, it was to come live here. Then, oops, we have to go hide in the woods. Now, I'm going to Manhattan, to live by myself with people I don't know. And one of them wants my mate and I'm the only thing standing in her way, so that feels safe."

"The king would never let anything happen to you."

Maybe in the past, I would have thought Tara was saying it to make me feel better without really believing it. Now, though, it's a statement of fact.

"I know that," I admit. "But he's not going to be there every second of every day."

Sure, Nathan loves me. But that's not going to stop Amber from trying something to remove the obstacle of me.

On the other hand, Amber loves him. Maybe she loves him in a way that means she doesn't want to cause him misery. I just have to hope that's the case. Nathan trusts her, so I have to trust her. I don't have much of a choice, at this point.

"Come on. Let's get stuff you'll need this week. The rest can get there later." Tara gives me her hand and pulls me to my feet. "You're going to need a tailor to make you new clothes soon, anyway."

"I've thought about that," I say as I follow her out to my bedroom. "I'm pregnant with twins. It's going to show a lot faster than just one baby."

Tara stops and faces me, her expression deadly serious. "You shouldn't mention the twins to anyone in the Manhattan pack."

"I think they're going to find out when I have ultrasounds. Or deliver." I hope the war doesn't drag on that long. We gestate for six months. I won't be there for six months.

I'll probably be plotting my escape after six weeks.

"But for right now, when everything is this uncertain, telling people that you're pregnant with the child of a god might change the diplomatic situation." Tara frowns. "Do you know what's happening to Màni now?"

"I really don't." Despite his pledge to help us, all he's done is murder our Hierophant and burn up our stuff. "Nathan should probably send him back to his pack."

"My pack will join me here."

Tara and I both let out startled yelps. Màni stands beside my destroyed bed, looking it over with interest.

"How long have you been here?" I demand. I don't appreciate the way he moves soundlessly or keeps so unnervingly still.

"I heard my name, and I thought I would find out what you were saying about me," he explains.

"Where we're from, shameless eavesdropping isn't something people admit to," Tara says dryly.

"I'm not from here." He bends and picks up Nathan's belt from the floor. "Explain the whipping."

Tara turns wide eyes to me, then takes in the state of the bed for what appears to be the first time.

"In ancient Greece, the Luperci—a type of priesthood that wore the masks of wolves—would chase maidens through the street with leather thongs to celebrate Lupercalia," I explain. It's nice to be the one to rattle off the lore for a change, despite my sister being in the room and more equipped to do so. I hope she's impressed with my knowledge. "It's a fertility rite."

Màni sniffs dismissively. "This was taught to you by your thrall priests, no doubt."

"Isn't it accurate?" Tara asks nervously.

I feel bad for her; she's always prided herself on being brainy, but now we're slowly finding out that a lot of what she's learned might not be true. That has to be a shock to her identity.

"Nothing they've taught you is accurate." He gestures to himself. "Do you have altars to me? Do you teach the true origins of your kind?"

"I thought we did," Tara says softly.

"Màni ... are you saying we're your descendants?" If so, ick. I'm carrying his baby. No amount of great or once-removed is going to make that less disgusting if it turns out he's my grandfather generations back.

"You're my creations," he corrects me casually, probably unaware that he's completely rocked our entire belief system and worldview.

He's good at that.

"It's time I take some responsibility for you," he says decisively. "I should never have allowed those who left my hearth to live."

"Um..." Tara raises her hand like we're in school before asking, "You're not going to cull us, are you?"

Màni seems shocked by the question. *Good job, Tara. You can shock a god.* "No. I will merely bring you back under my protection and counsel."

If that means living in peat houses in a bog, I might not be okay with this.

Màni moves toward me slowly. The air around him fills with a buzzing aura of urgency and importance. I feel his emotions like a rush of adrenaline. Tara steps back and my feet urge me to do the same, but I'm not afraid of him. I stay right where I am.

He comes close enough to take my hand in his large,

clawed ones. "You carry the most important part of my plan with you. Call on me if ever you are in danger among those in Man Hat Hunt."

"Close," I say with a small smile. He pulls his hands away, leaving a small, pewter amulet in my palm. I hold it up. "Is this for protection?"

"No. It is to call on me." He gives me the puzzled expression he often exhibits when we don't instinctively understand his meaning or ways. "I will come to you."

"Wait... can you teleport or something?" Tara asks.

"I don't know that term. I can move through the world beside this one. I *am* a god." He arches a brow, admonishing us for forgetting.

"Well, I don't know that I'll call on you all that much," I begin hesitantly. I don't want to offend him, but there are practical reasons for not conjuring gods into existence in someone else's home. "We're trying to keep you a secret."

"Soon, all werewolves will know of me, if I'm to set the way of my creation right. Do not be reluctant to call upon me because of something as trivial as manners." There's a tenderness to him as he adds, "I can take care of myself, Bailey. You are the one who needs *my* protection."

Then, he goes back to the broken bed, the plaster crumbled on the sheets and asks, "Do you need protection from your mate?"

My face flames with embarrassment. "No. I asked him to..."

I don't finish the sentence. Tara looks like she wants to leave.

All Màni says is, "Hmm."

"I'm going to grab a bag and start packing up your toiletries," Tara says, making her escape to the bathroom.

"Your mate loves you very much." Màni turns back to

me. "I can feel it. I could feel it the night we met. The power in the circle was overwhelming." He narrows his eyes. "You didn't know?"

"Not until last night." I correct myself. "I had suspicions. But I was constantly second-guessing."

Màni regards me in a way that makes me want to crawl off and escape his pity.

"Lift your head." He orders.

I meet the strange fathoms of his gaze, nearly trembling under the stern kindness I find there. He comes to me and places his hands on my shoulders.

"You are not simply the queen of this pack. You are the chosen of Màni. You are the queen of all werewolves." He leans forward and presses his forehead against mine. "No more doubt."

I'm too stunned to speak. Maybe it's magic. Maybe it's my pregnancy hormones. But the feeling of love and power and simple support that washes over me is something I've been craving without realizing.

If a god can believe in me, I can believe in myself and my ability to survive this.

"And if anything happens to you in this court of Man Hat Hunt, there will be retribution on a scale they could not imagine," he promises.

Not that it will help me if I'm dead. But it's a nice thought, all the same.

CHAPTER 35
BAILEY

Nathan insists on having lunch together before I leave. He doesn't speak much, except to reiterate the details of my journey to New York.

"Xiao can come with you as far as the doors of the court's building." He's told me this several times, but since this is the last I'll be hearing of his voice for a while, I listen. I try to memorize the cadence of his speech.

I know he'll come to see me when he can. That doesn't calm the raging panic the binding spell screams through me at every thought or mention of our separation.

But I'm not sure it's entirely the binding spell causing this reaction. I feel like I've only just got Nathan and now he's being taken away from me.

"After that," he continues, "she'll need to return here. She'll provide security for me and for Lady Tara."

I glance down at my plate and push my fork through the pasta salad I was craving before, but now can't stomach. "Tara is my lady-in-waiting. Shouldn't she be going with me?"

"Lady Tara's husband and parents were closely allied with the St. Laurent pack. She's no longer your lady-in-waiting. She's my hostage." He clears his throat uncomfortably. "I'm not going to hurt her. She's merely an insurance policy."

"St. Laurent doesn't know that you won't hurt her. I understand." And I still hate it. But it was Tara's mate who did this to her. Not us.

"She'll still be involved in the war council, and in learning how to break the binding spell," Nathan assures me.

"Màni is planning to bring his pack here," I say quietly, fully aware that he can probably overhear us from wherever it is he's hiding in the house.

Nathan's eyebrows lift in surprise. "Well, I'll have a difficult time explaining that."

"You're not going to try to stop him?" What will happen when the wolves, accustomed to being outdoors and roaming freely, come to a city full of humans?

"I don't see how I can. He's a god. We'll just have to get him to agree to keep them under control." Nathan sighs, resigned. "I need to be more respectful of him."

"No!" I exclaim sarcastically and can't help laughing at him. "Whenever did you come to that conclusion?"

He lifts his hands in an *all right, all right* gesture. "I haven't been welcoming of the man who..." he pauses, clearly to correct his word choice. "Engaged in a sexual act with my wife while she was insensate."

It's not that I'm ungrateful for Nathan's defense of me. And if I heard about the experience happening to someone else, I might share the same interpretation of the events.

"I know it's difficult to understand, but I don't have

any ill-will toward him," I say. "I'm not traumatized. Maybe a little, by the idea of suddenly carrying twins that weren't conceived at the same time. If he were just another werewolf, I would probably feel different. But he's a god, and he's using me for a greater purpose."

Nathan's mouth quirks into a sad smile. "I just would have preferred that he choose someone else's mate to fulfill that greater purpose."

"It's probably just the binding making you feel super possessive," I toss off casually, reaching for my water glass.

Nathan shakes his head firmly. "No, Bailey. It's my love for you."

Hearing the word again fills my chest with a bubble of emotion that makes it difficult to swallow the drink I've taken. I think of Màni's admonishment, that I shouldn't doubt that Nathan loves me. And wouldn't a god know that?

"I need to know what happens to me if you're killed." Saying the word is so difficult. "I know you're not going to be fighting on some battlefield. But the whole city will become a battlefield. If I'm not safe here, neither are you. But will I still be safe in Manhattan if you're gone?"

"A—" He stops himself, but I already know from the vowel exactly whose name had come to his lips. "The Manhattan pack are our allies. They won't let any harm come to you, even if I'm gone."

Tears come to my eyes, and I try to fight them back. I try hard. But the thought of losing him is too much. Everything is too much, too real, and now it's all happening whether I want it to or not.

"Oh, my love." His voice is strained. That only makes it worse. I hang my head so he can't see my face, as if he won't realize why I'm doing it, and he pushes his chair back. "Come here."

I get to my feet and go to him, and he pulls me into his lap, cradling my head against his chest. He doesn't say anything. He lets me cry, stroking my hair and holding me tight.

I try to memorize the feeling of his arms around me, the smell of his cologne. Tonight, I'll be too far away for him to hold me like this.

"Call me tonight," I try to demand through my tears, but it comes out as a plea.

"Every night," he swears. "But you must keep it between us."

"Because I can't be seen as an asset. I understand that." I hate it, but I understand. "They can't trace my cellphone."

"No. But don't take my calls in front of others. No speakerphone. And delete everything from the log."

"I will."

He tucks two fingers under my chin to lift my face up, and he kisses me long and sweet and slow. I shift in his lap, then gently push him back.

"Look, it's not that I don't appreciate it, but we don't have time to..." I roll my eyes. "You know."

"Right. Better to not part in frustration." He smiles and sets me on my feet.

There's a knock at the dining room door. My stomach plummets.

Xiao enters and bows to us. "Your Majesties. The driver is here."

The Manhattan pack has sent a car. Xiao will ride with me. It's a long trip, but Nathan doesn't want me on a commercial flight. If something goes wrong with the babies and a human doctor examines me, we could risk exposure of our kind. A simple blood test would prove I'm not human.

"Thank you, Xiao," Nathan says. "Give us a moment?"

"Yes, Your Majesty." She bows again and leaves us.

"We have to say our goodbyes now," he says softly. "There will be members of the council downstairs to see you off. I don't want any weeping or sentiment in front of them."

"I understand." I wipe the tears from my cheeks.

Nathan stands and draws me into his arms again. "As soon as I know you're in Manhattan safely, I'll begin to plan my first visit there. We shouldn't be apart more than a few weeks."

That's too long. I don't say so because I know that he shares that opinion already. There's nothing that can be done, so there's no use dwelling on it.

"Just kiss me goodbye," I say, trying to smile through my tears.

He does, lifting me off my feet. I wrap my legs around him, frustration and our clothing be damned, anchoring myself to him with my legs. I dive my hand into his hair and hold his mouth to mine until we're both breathless.

With a low groan, he raises his head for a breath. "Remember this?" He palms my ass. "I took you this way our first time together."

Heat flares through me. "Of course, I remember. Even when I hated you, I could still remember every single detail. Not just that night. Every night."

He sets me on my feet with a sigh of regret. "I'm not proud of some of those nights. I'm not proud of how I've treated you at all."

"When this is all over, you can make it up to me." I

force myself to smile, to joke, because reality is too grim. "So, don't die."

His smile is small and sad. "I promise."

I stand there gazing up at him, until finally he says, "It's time to go."

I want one more kiss. One more goodbye. One more tender moment between us. But even that one more won't be enough, so there's no reason to chase the end. It's already here.

He holds my hand as we walk through the residence and down to the entry hall. At the first sight of council members, he drops my hand, almost a finger at a time, lingering as long as he can. We're the king and queen now. Stiff, formal, regal, while my heart collapses in on itself.

I'm too used to this routine.

Council members line the entryway, bowing as we pass. The two lines continue outside; Ryan opens the door for us to exit.

The handoff of the Queen of the Toronto Pack to the Manhattan Pack is more ceremony than I expected. Not only is there a car from Manhattan, but a balding white man in a nice suit and a big watch is there. He bows to the King and Nathan extends his hand for a shake. The man repeats this greeting with me, then turns back to Nathan. "Your Majesty, the Queen is in good hands," the man promises.

My heart hammers in my chest. I look to my left and see Tara there, beside Hannah. They both give me brave smiles.

I'm too numb and terrified to respond.

"Your Majesty."

I turn toward Xiao's calm voice. She stands beside the driver at the open car door.

Nathan places his hand on my shoulder. For someone

who said he didn't want a display of emotion, he certainly seems emotional as he leans down to kiss my forehead. He briefly presses his hand against my stomach before stepping back.

It's the first time it's occurred to me: Nathan isn't just sending his mate away. He's sending away his child.

His eyes shine with tears I know he won't shed. Before I turn to go, I sweep into a low curtsey before him.

Then I turn away and don't look back as I get into the car. I don't look at him once Xiao and I are closed inside. I don't look at him as we drive away.

I wonder if he looked at me.

***

We cross the border into the United States at dusk. As the sun sinks below the horizon, I feel more hopeless than ever. I'm in a strange land, under the protection of a strange pack. Once the sun sets, my last day with Nathan will be over.

"You'll see him again," Xiao says quietly.

"Do you think so?" I ask, as if she can give me a definitive answer.

"I'd like to think so." She leans forward and takes my hand, startling me with the intimacy of the gesture. "I will protect him with my life."

Just acknowledging that his life is in danger sends a spear of agony through my heart.

"And Lady Tara," Xiao adds. "If they die, it's because I'm already dead."

"That doesn't exactly make me feel better."

"The truth rarely does." She turns toward the window. "You're going to be all right here, Your Majesty.

You're tougher than you think. You're smarter than you think."

I hope she's right.

I know she's right.

Manhattan might prove to be dangerous, but I don't have to worry about being fed to the wolves.

I'm the queen of them.

ABOUT THE AUTHOR

Jenny Trout is a *USA Today* bestselling author, blogger, and funny person. Jenny writes award-winning erotic romance, including the internationally bestselling *The Boss* series (written as Abigail Barnette), as well as young adult and new adult novels.

As a blogger, Jenny's work has appeared on *The Huffington Post*, and has been featured on television and radio, including *HuffPost Live*, *Good Morning America*, *The Steve Harvey Show*, and National Public Radio's *Here & Now*.

She is a proud Michigander, mother of two, and wife to the only person alive capable of spending extended periods of time with her without wanting to kill her.